THE MAN FROM THE CREEKS

THE MAN FROM
THE CREEKS

a novel

Robert Kroetsch

VINTAGE CANADA
A Division of Random House of Canada

Grateful acknowledgement is made to Robert Service
for his poem "The Shooting of Dan McGrew" and
the current copyright holder. Used by permission.

Canadian Cataloguing in Publication Data

Kroetsch, Robert
The man from the creeks

ISBN 0-679-30982-9

I.Title.

PS8521.R7M36 1999   C813'.54   C98-932537-7
PR9199.3.K76M36 1999

Printed and bound in the United States of America

10 9 8 7 6 5 4 3 2 1

———◆◆◆———

"The newspapers were filled with
advice, information, stories of hardship and
good fortune; but not one [person] in ten,
or a hundred, knew what the journey
meant nor heeded the voice of warning."

— Tappan Adney, *The Klondike Stampede*

———◆◆◆———

Then I ducked my head, and the lights went out,
    and two guns blazed in the dark,
And a woman screamed, and the lights went up,
    and two men lay stiff and stark.
Pitched on his head, and pumped full of lead,
    was Dangerous Dan McGrew,
While the man from the creeks lay clutched to the
    breast of the lady that's known as Lou.

— Robert Service, "The Shooting of Dan McGrew"

1897

1

We were stowaways, my mother and I. We wanted to get to the Klondike. More exactly, we wanted to get rich on gold.

Up there in the lifeboat where we were hiding we could smell the loaves of fresh bread and the pans of baking-soda biscuits, set outside the galley door to cool in time for breakfast. But, worse yet, we could almost taste the freshly baked cinnamon rolls.

Back in Seattle we'd stowed away in something of a hurry. Somehow we got into a lifeboat directly above the steamer's galley. As a result, our diet of hardtack and equally hard cheese and stale water got to be less than exciting. Not that my mother's salary of five dollars a week would have bought us much else.

After eight days in that lifeboat we could smell fresh food right through the canvas and wood, and that in spite of the fire bucket at our feet that was our toilet.

The real trouble, though, was my birthday. That ninth

morning was the morning of my fourteenth birthday. October 24, 1897. That was three months and a week after the gold rush began.

My mother got it into her head that I deserved a birthday treat.

"Please don't risk it," I said. I was pleading, but I tried to sound logical.

"It's a bit late," she said, "to start telling me what I should risk."

Every stampeder on the *Delta Queen* was so preoccupied with getting to the Klondike goldfields that my mother really believed she could crawl down from our lifeboat, swipe some cinnamon rolls and carry them back up to me as a birthday present without getting caught. To clinch her argument she pointed out that the sun wasn't yet above the horizon.

"Okay," I said, trying to sound conspicuously resigned. "At least don't stop to look for birthday candles."

The *Queen* was three days late on a voyage that was scheduled to take five, and still Skagway was nowhere in sight. We were somewhere in the Inside Passage, south of Skagway, north of Juneau. We knew that much. The old tub was leaking like a sieve. It was running out of coal too, but that was not the immediate problem. The problem was our having to proceed at only half-speed or sink.

The Klondike gold strike had started up such a flutter of greed that people were willing to buy tickets on anything that promised to float in a northerly direction. My mother had hoped that a four-day food supply would take us the thousand miles to Skagway, and then luck would take us up over the Coastal Range and down the Yukon River. After that all we'd have to do was figure out how to carry home our bags of gold.

Instead of taking two cinnamon rolls, my mother picked up a pan of twelve that was intended, it turned out, for the captain's cabin.

She slid the pan under the coat she carried over her left arm. It was too chilly and too damp for anyone to be carrying a coat on one's arm instead of wearing it. But that wasn't the giveaway. The rolls were so fresh the smell caught the attention of one of the pastry cooks, a big, tough customer who was on his way back to the galley from the head. Most of the people on that boat, what with the water system out of commission half the time, didn't smell like cinnamon rolls fresh out of the oven.

"Up with the birds I see," the cook said.

Little did he know what he was saying. We were up with the gulls, directly over his head.

Passengers were supposed to be asleep at that hour on the old steamer. But a lot of them had developed the habit of standing at the rail and staring toward the horizon, cursing while they did it. And some didn't have cabins to begin with.

The cook was waiting for a response.

"Just who do you think you are, lady?"

"Don't lady me," my mother said. "The name is Lou."

Just like that. That was the name she gave herself, as if she'd picked it up with the pan that was warming her forearm.

That's what the poet called her, later, when he wrote his famous poem.

"The name is Lou," my mother repeated. She said it to the cook. Perhaps she was saying it to herself as well, there on the slick, narrow deck between the galley door and the icy waters of the Inside Passage. Listening in the lifeboat, I had a feeling she was saying it to me as well.

"The captain's breakfast," the cook said, "seems to be missing."

Lou was a shade weak and staggery. Three days out of Seattle we'd guessed we were in trouble and had gone on reduced rations. That strategy would get us to Skagway. What we'd do when we got there, Lou hadn't explained. I hardly had a chance to ask about our plans before we set sail. We were on the steamer, trying to look like sightseers, looking for a place to hide. Some guy in a uniform stopped us and asked what we were doing. Lou said that she and her son were there to see his father off to Skagway. When I whispered that I didn't have a father, she said, "Everyone has a father."

I could somehow *hear* the cook studying Lou and the rectangular coat over her left arm. That's when I raised an edge of the lifeboat's canvas cover just enough so I could see out.

The cook had sores around his mouth. I remember that. He leaned toward Lou. "Just where the hell did you come from?"

By that ninth morning he knew every face on the ship.

Lou didn't quite lie. She pointed straight up at the lifeboat directly over his white hat, the lifeboat illegally loaded with a few boxes of blasting powder that would fetch one fine price for the first mate when we got to Skagway.

The cook thought she was pointing at heaven. "You know the captain's orders?"

Lou couldn't resist a smart answer. "I didn't know this ship had a captain."

Delicately then, the cook reached and took Lou's coat off her left arm. He did not take the pan.

"Come along, Lou."

She had given herself that name. Somehow I almost felt like an orphan.

The cook wiped at his mouth with her coat. Apparently his mouth hurt when he talked. He spoke carefully. "You'll have to explain to the skipper. Captain Poole says any trouble of any sort and you're off his ship, no matter who you are or where we are."

"Except," Lou said, "that we're too much in a hurry to stop."

Lou and I, there in the lifeboat, had heard all kinds of conversations about hurrying up and going slow and the cost of feeding seventy irate and mutinous passengers on a trip that was already three days longer than scheduled.

Lou, gripping the pan now in her left hand, followed after the cook. She didn't have much choice.

There were maybe a dozen stampeders listening in by then, and not a one of them was amused.

The old *Delta Queen* was carrying twice the weight she was built to carry, and that included quite a few passengers who were paying handsomely for the privilege of sleeping under a stretched tarpaulin on the bow deck, next to the rear ends of many horses, a few pens full of hogs and twenty crates full of chickens.

Captain Poole was not a mean man. He, like the ship, had been called out of retirement, and while the disruption bothered him a little, the real trouble was he had lost his edge. He knew his engineers were doing their best to get that rust bucket of a ship from Seattle to Skagway according to the schedule the owners ran in *The Seattle Post-Intelligencer.* He didn't have the heart to become a bully. He could hardly bring himself to raise his voice.

By the time Lou stood face to face with the captain on the bow, there were two dozen passengers and a few crewmen gathered around.

"I'll have to see your ticket," Captain Poole said.

"I don't have a ticket." Lou was concentrating on keeping the pan. She and I were hungry.

Captain Poole shook his head. "Well now." But he wasn't looking at Lou. He was eyeing the stampeders gathered around him, and what he saw or sensed was making him uneasy.

Those men had paid thirty-five dollars a head just for standing room on the deck — with breathing extra, as someone said. As far as they could see, a petty thief was getting a free ride, and free meals to boot.

Those stampeders were greenhorns, with a vague idea of what gold dust might look like. All of them, in Chinook talk, were *cheechakos*. A little bit less than newcomers. But a ship had sailed into Seattle's harbour out of the north, just three months and a week earlier, a ship loaded with sixty-eight prospectors and two tonnes of placer gold. And that did it. After that the gold rush was on, and the devil himself couldn't stop thousands of people from throwing down their newspapers and rushing out to buy mining pans.

Thousands and then tens of thousands of ordinary folk became gold-hungry lunatics. Half of them couldn't find Dawson City or Bonanza Creek or Eldorado Creek on a map. They just dropped whatever they were doing, which for some of them was nothing, what with the depression into its fourth year, and headed for a port. Seattle and San Francisco got the fever first. Then Vancouver and Victoria. Then Chicago and Boston and New York. Then London and Sydney and Cape Town and Buenos Aires.

Those stampeders on the *Delta Queen,* setting out too late on a boat that was too slow, felt they were just on the verge of losing the race. They were ready to get raving mad at whatever came along — and my mother obliged. She became the thieving cause of their not getting to a place where all they had to do to pick up gold nuggets was bend down.

She made a mistake. Someone asked her, ironically and scornfully, if she proposed to share the stolen goods.

"Yes," she said. "With my son."

That was the straw that did it. Maybe she was hoping to get some sympathy.

Those hollering fools hadn't even laid eyes on me. But they acted as if they had. They were furious because they weren't getting to their misery fast enough. And now the one freeloader in their midst had turned into two, and there was no guessing what might happen next.

They were shouting at no one and everyone, as if the glaciers and mountains and islands around us cared a whole lot. Maybe they were shouting too because they had up and left their loved ones, their families, their kids and wives and whatever, and in eight days they'd had time to figure out just what they had got themselves into.

Maybe what made them maddest was Lou's saying she didn't have a penny to her name. She said as much when someone asked her to pony up or else. She reminded the whole lot how close to broke they all were. We were on the poor man's route to the Klondike, and poor meant just one uncertain jump ahead of flat broke.

Someone banged down a capstan bar on the wooden deck.

Someone said to the captain, "If you don't do something, we will."

Captain Poole hesitated. He was tired. He didn't want to tell anyone what to do or what not to do. He wanted to go back to his captain's cabin and pour himself a drink. Except that, like everyone else on the ship, he was out of booze. He hesitated, and then he reached and took the pan away from Lou. He gave the impression that, having made that gesture, he had settled the matter.

Lou reached and took the pan back.

That's when somebody said, "Guess she'll have to walk the gangplank."

It was a voice from down below me. I thought at first that the guy was joking. And maybe he was. Maybe he just thought he was being witty, pretending he was on a pirate ship or something.

I raised my head farther out of the lifeboat, trying to escape the smell of excrement, trying to recover the smell of cinnamon and honey.

"Walk the gangplank." The mob was trying the words in its mouth, and liking them. "Maybe she ought to. Just plain walk the goddamned gangplank."

I was in the forward lifeboat on the starboard side. I could see the gaping, blue, empty water between the steamer's bow and the nearest shore.

I saw two men take hold of a gangplank that was there on the bow deck. They slid it forward so it jutted out ten or twelve feet over the water. Maybe those stampeders still believed they were being funny.

The *Delta Queen* was so small that I could see, from up there in my hideaway, the creases in the skipper's face.

He was scared. Captain Poole had been on enough ships in his time to know when to get scared, and he was glancing around as if he might take a notion to walk the gangplank himself and leave the whole mess behind. He was facing may-be fifty men, all of them with their backs to me, and all of them stirring around as if they'd got their feet into molasses and didn't like it.

I couldn't see Lou anywhere. That's when I panicked. For a moment I thought she was gone.

"She better walk right now, or we'll find that kid of hers and have him tag along."

Then I saw Lou. She stepped up onto the end of the gangplank that was nearest me and nearest all those stampeders. There she stood, looking like she was going to turn around and walk, just to spite that mob. Defiance. Her face was pure defiance.

Her eyes were tired, I could see that. We hadn't been sleeping too well. But they had a kind of fire behind them. Her coiled hair, not much darker than her eyes right then, had skittered out from under her green felt hat. Her blouse was nothing but wrinkles. Her long green skirt made her look taller than she really was and not at all helpless.

She lifted her winter coat away from the cook, who was still carrying it on his left arm. For some absurd reason Lou was going to take her coat and the cinnamon rolls with her, as if there was a door instead of a chasm at the end of the gangplank.

"Go ahead," the ringleader said.

Someone in the crowd said, "Kee-rist, Mr Plow. Take it easy."

Mr Plow pointed toward the shore. "She can swim that far. It isn't four hundred yards. She can float that far just by hanging onto her coat and that stolen pan."

Lou, in a gesture that to me seemed unbearably slow, positioned the pan on her right hand. She threw the pan and its twelve cinnamon rolls into the face of the man named Mr Plow.

Two men took hold of the near end of the gangplank and

were about to lift it and send Lou slipping down into the Pacific waters. It wasn't as if they really intended to kill her. It seemed more that they thought they were in some kind of play, and Lou was only acting. So those two men wanted into the act.

That's when the stranger spoke up.

"That water will kill her," the stranger said, "before she can swim halfway to shore. You know that."

That's what I called him there at first, in my mind. The stranger. Because I could tell just by hearing his voice that he didn't quite fit in with that crowd. He was listening as well as talking.

"That'll be her problem," Mr Plow said. He was scratching warm honey and cinnamon off his face as if it was poison.

But the men raising the gangplank hesitated. They waited for an order. When it didn't come they let the slippery, wet gangplank back onto the deck.

The stranger stepped up beside Lou. He was a shade too gentle to be stepping up in front of a mob.

He was a man of average height. He had a wide chest, strong-looking arms. He was wearing a green mackinaw that was the same green as Lou's hat. His head of tousled hair was hatless, as if he'd rushed out of his cabin without having time to finish dressing.

His voice was a searching voice. In that sense he was a Klondiker. But of a strange kind. He seemed to think he could make peace simply by raising his right hand, or by being decent and polite.

"Boys," he said. "I'll pay this woman's fare."

We waited. A horse whinnied. Some of the pigs were either grunting with pleasure or complaining about the lack of feed.

Instead of reaching into his pockets, the stranger offered his two empty hands. He was the same height as Lou. He was wearing a look of resignation along with his concern.

"I'll pay it, Mr Plow. Right here. This minute."

Captain Poole was trying to get his voice into the conversation. He made sounds that only I seemed to hear. I was hoping he would speak up.

"It would be nice," Mr Plow said, "if we could pay our overdue bills by raising our empty hands." He had his composure back. Or most of it. He was tall and full of angles, under a black leather hat. His racoon coat didn't quite fit. He had an awkward elegance about him. He gave the impression that he might have by mistake got onto the wrong boat and didn't yet know it. Mr Plow continued, "It's going to take some tall talking to settle this account."

The stranger paused before speaking. Then he said, "I didn't get up here to talk."

The laughter that followed was the laughter of mockery and contempt.

"Promise to give us a sack of gold, Ben," someone suggested, in a voice rich with self-satisfied irony, "once we get to Dawson City."

People pushed and laughed and hollered some more, letting out something they'd been trying too long to swallow. At last, something was happening. They gave each other little shoves that were affectionate and angry at the same time.

"Promises," Mr Plow said. He recognized that he had an audience and the audience was on his side. "Promises won't save anybody's hide, Ben. Not even yours."

Ben didn't give up. He gestured out at the glaciers. "Put Lou ashore. Her and her son."

That too sounded like a scary prospect. But then, before anyone could agree or disagree, Ben added, "I'll go with them."

Every man in that crowd was stumped. Or, possibly, not one of them wanted to confess to having thought of getting off the steamer and turning back.

Someone shouted out too loud, "Great for you, Ben. But what's in it for us?"

"I said I'll pay for my friend here."

That was the first time Ben turned and looked directly at Lou. He and Lou had never before that occasion so much as guessed that the other existed.

Mr Plow got into the act again. "We don't take IOUs."

"I'll pay in whiskey," Ben said.

You see, not one of those seventy passengers had guessed that a ship might run out of whiskey. Every passenger on board had a grubstake in the hold, down where the *Delta Queen* was going to leak if we moved at full speed. Every man on the trip had with him something like a year's supply of food and goods, because the police on the Canadian side of the Yukon border said you had to. If you didn't have a year's grubstake you couldn't go to the Klondike — for the simple reason that you might starve to death before the winter was out.

Those passengers had the hold full of shovels and pans and sacks of flour and bags of beans and sides of bacon. But not one passenger had guessed that a ship might run out of booze on its way to the booziest town on the whole coast.

"How many bottles you talking about, Ben?"

"I'm talking about kegs."

Ben smiled a little at the sound of astonishment that greeted his remark. "I'm talking an even two kegs."

"Two kegs?" Captain Poole finally got his voice into the air.

"Two kegs would get us to Skagway. We don't have that far to go."

"Bring on the whiskey," someone said.

"And somebody lower a boat," Mr Plow added. He was out for blood and he was determined to draw some.

"Yes," Ben said. "Please. Lower a boat this minute."

From my perch I could see the shoreline. There wasn't much of a place for a rowboat to land, except where a gravel bar marked the mouth of a creek that seemed to spill out of a solid wall of forest. Behind the forest there were mountains. They were the straight-up variety, with glaciers on top.

That's when I started to climb down out of the lifeboat.

Those stampeders were waiting for a whiskey apparition. Instead, I put in an appearance, showing them first the back end of my only pair of trousers.

Lou pointed as if she was ordering me back into the lifeboat. "Peek, you idiot. Bring our stuff."

There wasn't a whole lot of bringing to do. When you stow away on a ship you don't get to take along your steamer trunks and your hatboxes. I scrambled back into the lifeboat and in two shakes I was down on deck with a pair of worn leather bags and two damp quilts.

The ruckus caused by my showing up gave Ben time to go on negotiating. He insisted he must take his grubstake with him, or he and his two charges would starve there on shore, and then the captain and the whole damned shipload of people, passengers and crew alike, would be up on murder charges.

Captain Poole said he thought something could be arranged. He could taste the whiskey already. He signalled the wheelhouse, asking for the man at the wheel to ring from slow to dead stop.

Old Captain Poole suddenly remembered how to be a

captain. He set about ten men to bringing up Ben's outfit from the hold, which was directly beneath our feet. He ordered his deckhands to lower a dinghy.

That dinghy looked about the size of a bathtub. Those cheechakos dropped sacks and boxes into it as if they couldn't decide to make it capsize or sink. The two deckhands receiving the goods were risking their lives.

Ben opened one wooden box right there on the steamer's deck. It had in it two wooden kegs, which was fine. But the print on each keg said BENJAMIN REDD SALT HERRING.

"What kind of a goddamned joke is this?" Mr Plow said.

"See for yourself," Ben told him.

Mr Plow, not to be bluffed, hopped to it. He and a couple of other men knocked in the bung on one keg. Mr Plow inserted a finger and pulled it out and put it into his mouth.

His face transformed into something resembling ecstasy. He took that same finger and inserted it into the mouth of a bystander.

That man nodded his head in a gesture of unspeakable bliss.

At least three men went scrambling to find tin cups. Another twenty began to argue about how to do the distributing.

They would dilute the whiskey with some of their scarce water supply and dole it out like grog to sailors. They would turn the keg of whiskey into a tub of whiskey, the tub into a fountain, the fountain into a deluge.

That old steamer, with her engines stopped, rolled just slightly in the small waves. But it seemed like a storm to me.

I was at the rail, trying to figure out how to go down a rope ladder with my eyes shut and my hands sweating.

Someone gave Ben a hat.

I went over the side.

Lou followed down after me, with Ben trying to steady her, which wasn't easy. When she paused to thumb her nose at the whole mob of stampeders up there on the steamer's deck, they were too busy proposing toasts to each other to notice. Ben told her to never mind, we should skedaddle while we had half a chance.

2

So much for my birthday party. If I'd known I had another hundred to attend or avoid, I'd have taken better care of myself. But this is not about regrets. Or aching joints. What I want to set straight before I kick the bucket is the matter of Mr Robert Service and his saying that Lou pinched the stranger's poke — the corpse's poke — and all the gold that was in it. Poets are liars. We know that. They'll say just about anything to make themselves sound good.

Lou was not a thief. She was many things, and not all of them to the poet's liking, but she was not a thief.

I thought I'd come to the story's end, not its beginning. I thought the jig was up. As a result, my arms were dangling loose from my shoulders.

I looked better then than I do now. No hump in my back. No wheelchair. I had clay-coloured hair. Taffy-coloured, Lou called it. Most of it in my eyes, in spite of my old tweed cap. I was gangly tall and sullen-looking, at least according to Lou, and sometimes I walked with a slouch, which also got on her nerves. She said I tried to make myself look as if I was missing a few bones.

We were standing on a patch of gravel by the mouth of a creek, Lou and Ben and I, with the morning sun glancing off a glacier right smack bang into our eyes.

"Straighten up," Lou said. To me.

Ben sat down on one of his packing boxes.

I went on staring around us, partly in gratitude, partly in simple bowel-churning unease. And I'm referring to empty bowels.

Ben hadn't said a word since he stepped out of the dinghy into the ice-cold knee-deep water and began to accept cargo from the two deckhands who had rowed us ashore but who wouldn't step ashore themselves. He was seated on a box, staring at the heap of boxes and canvas sacks we had stacked a yard beyond the water line before the deckhands rowed away from us and back to the *Delta Queen*.

It was Ben who noticed the water was rising. Lou saw him staring at his new boots. He could feel the water rising. She looked at Ben and then at his new ankle-high workboots and then at the rising sea water and said, "Well? Are we going to stand here all day?"

"I'm sitting," Ben said.

He could be picky too, in his way.

"In that case why be uncomfortable? Why not stretch out and take a nap? The tide won't swamp your supplies for another twenty minutes."

Lou had lived a hard life. She wasn't into displays of gratitude, mostly because she was always on the lookout for hidden motives.

"I was hoping the tide might be going out." Ben spoke to me instead of to Lou. He pointed at the water. He was new to the coast, it turned out, and not really used to the idea that the sea might take a notion to rise twenty feet above his ankles.

Lou wasn't ready to leave bad enough alone. Sometimes she had great faith in repetition, especially when talking to, what she liked to call, a mere man. "When the water is rising it's a sign that the tide's coming in."

We were off to a rocky start in more ways than one.

Ben gestured toward the east, not at the high and distant glaciers, but at the green wall of absolutely towering trees. Then he indicated the line of grey rock at the base of the trees.

"Go on up there, Peek, would you? Rustle up some dry wood while I move our supplies. Get a fire going where people can see it."

He was trying to pretend he knew what to do. That was good enough for me. I heard myself groaning with every breath I drew and tried to stop. I was ready to go tearing across the beach like Hiawatha himself. But I had to wait for Lou's okay.

She wouldn't look toward the forest. At the same time she was being careful not to look at the spot where the steamer had disappeared behind a headland. I think she was listening for it to turn around.

A new kind of silence was falling as the last sound of the ship faded into nothing. I whispered when I asked Ben for matches.

"Matches? It only takes one match to light a fire. We've got one can and one can only of dry matches to get us to Dawson City."

He had been reading up on how to get to the goldfields.

"Us?" Lou said.

"If you're coming with me, it's us."

"Listen, Mr Redd. Mr Benjamin Redd. You get yourself to Dawson. I'll get myself to Dawson."

Ben's name was printed in careful black letters on each and every one of his boxes and sacks.

"Fair enough," he said.

"Don't fair enough me. And don't start getting ideas."

Ben brushed some sawdust from the right sleeve of his green mackinaw, then settled the broad-brimmed grey hat more firmly on his head. "I've already had one idea too many." That was about as sassy as he was likely to get.

"I mean —" Lou wasn't quite finding the opening she needed. She'd spent a few days realizing she was traveling with a horde of excited men. "Don't start getting any ideas just because you saved our hides." She pointed at me to indicate that I was included in the mess that Ben had got himself into.

"I'll get that bonfire built," I said. I took off straight across the rocks toward high ground. Toward a rock ledge. And higher trees, whatever they were. Hemlock. Cedar.

I found a huge tree. And I mean huge. I walked all the way around it, picking up dry branches and needles and bark. Then I built a small teepee of dry bark and branches out on a rock ledge that faced the water. I struck the match. I thought I would die, inhaling all that smoke. Then the bark caught and I was scrambling to find more dry wood because I'd forgotten to prepare to turn my fire into a beacon.

Lou and Ben came across the rocks, each of them carrying a sack and trying to find a foothold without being able to see. They set down the sacks near my fledgling fire.

"Looks like I can make us some breakfast," Lou said, "now that Peek has a fire going."

She was softening up. Or she was trying to. The trouble came with Ben's reply.

"We don't have a whole lot of food."

Lou pointed at the sack she'd carried as if the man had to be out of his mind. "'Flour,' it says. I take it you've got a year's supply of grub, as required by the Canadian police. Surely we can eat a mouthful or two before we get to the Klondike."

Lou and I had something like four slices of mouldy cheddar in the bottom of one of our two leather bags.

Ben was shaking his head before Lou had finished her lecture.

"Well excuse me for living," Lou said.

That would have taken me out of the argument. But not so for Ben. Silently, he tapped the sack that was marked flour.

"Flour," Lou said. "It says flour right there on the sack." She spelled the word out for him, and actually got it right. Lou was no great speller.

"Whiskey," Ben said.

"No way." She was trying not to understand him. "Not on an empty stomach. And we've got to feed this boy."

That was another thing — sometimes when she was in a tight corner I became "this boy."

"I wasn't asking a question," Ben said. "I'm trying to tell you something."

Lou bent toward the sack as if it, not Ben, would clarify matters.

Ben was a little short of breath when he spoke. "Whiskey, Lou. I'm telling you. It's whiskey. It's all whiskey. The real thing. Genuine bourbon from Bourbon County. Hard liquor. Kentucky corn mash whiskey."

"What are you trying to tell me?"

Even I was getting the message.

"I'm just explaining that all my boxes and sacks are mostly full of kegs of whiskey packed in sawdust. Kegs. Little oak casks."

Lou backed away from the sack and from Ben and nearly tripped into my fire.

"Fifteen kegs of whiskey. Thirteen now." Ben let out a kind of a crazy, resigned laugh. "All of them packed in sawdust. Replacing flour. And beans. And rice." He couldn't stop. "Replacing sugar," he said. "And tea. And cornmeal. And sides of bacon. And tins of corned beef. And pepper. And mustard. And salt. And dehydrated apples —"

Gold fever, I thought to myself. That's one of the ways it sounds. It sounds like a grubstake. I had heard the men on the steamer, reciting lists to each other, checking, rechecking. Listing and then listing again.

Ben might have gone on if Lou hadn't interrupted. "And it's all for *you*?"

"I haven't got any of it," Ben said. "That's what I'm telling you."

"I mean the whiskey," Lou said.

She had worked in a pawnshop in downtown Seattle for her five dollars a week. I helped out now and then for fifty cents a day. We couldn't imagine what kind of a stock of food would last a person through more than seven days.

Ben wasn't to be stopped. "I have a friend up there in the Klondike. He's there now. He's waiting for me. All I have to do is buy into one of his claims and in six months I'll be a rich man. Filthy rich. You too. You can get rich with me."

"We don't have any food? You're telling me, Ben —"

Lou was recognizing that she'd chosen starvation over drowning, and she was having second thoughts. She looked to where the ship had been and saw the flat expanse of water.

Ben all of a sudden had to reassure her. Not that he'd had any more breakfast than the rest of us.

"We'll get by. We'll scrape up enough for a meal or two. By sundown we'll be off this beach and heading for the Klondike again."

He avoided the look on Lou's face by appearing to address me. "I need three thousand dollars to buy into McGrew's operation. All I had, back home in Iowa, after I sold everything I owned, was eight hundred dollars spot cash and my new boots. I'm a cooper. Or I was. So I made myself fifteen solid oak kegs and got a good deal on some whiskey."

He remembered then. He turned and went running back toward the water as hard as he could go. Lou and I went running after him to lend a hand.

3

Ben Redd was a wet cooper from Davenport, Iowa, on the Mississippi River. A wet cooper, he explained, makes casks and barrels for liquids. For vinegars and jams. For dill pickles and Worcestershire sauce. For beer and wine and bourbon whiskey. That is, Ben had been a cooper. Up until one month ago. Then he got a letter from Dan McGrew. Now he had a scheme, as he kept on explaining to Lou, for becoming filthy rich.

Not that Lou didn't have a scheme of her own. She had a scheme too. Her scheme was to come up with a scheme while she was on her way to Dawson City and the Klondike.

"Out there on the boat," Ben said, "I heard about a woman who took four hundred dollars worth of needles and thread and patches into the Yukon and made a fortune." He stopped to consider. "And buttons," he added, as if he'd almost neglected that detail and told a terrible lie.

Lou wasn't impressed.

We had managed, the three of us, to haul everything up onto high ground. Wooden packing boxes. Canvas sacks containing sacks that were supposed to contain flour and rice. A mining pan and a shovel and six tarps. We found comfortable rocks and sat down, trying to catch our breath.

Lou still wasn't grasping the obvious logic of Ben's scheme.

"If we get to Dawson City by Christmas," he said, elaborating once more, "we won't know what to do with all our profit. We'll sell the whiskey to the men in the creeks. We'll buy into McGrew's claims and start weighing the nuggets."

Lou had stopped quarreling with Ben's pronouns, I noticed. We and us no longer gave her a conniption fit. It was his arithmetic that was bothering her. She was quick with figures.

"You keep giving your whiskey away —" She pointed toward the water as if the *Delta Queen* was still sitting there at dead stop. "You'll be in the poorhouse."

"I had to act fast," Ben said, "didn't I?"

Lou bent over and rapped at a sack and then at another with her knuckles. From inside each sack we heard a knocked-wood sound.

"You *gave* the stuff away, you idiot."

Ben set a sack on its bottom and started trying to undo the knots at the top.

Lou pretended not to notice. "You could have sold that whiskey at so much a drink for a small fortune. Did you see how those men turned into children at the mention of your whiskey?"

"We were in a hurry, Lou. Remember?" Ben had somehow managed to tie up his own left hand instead of undoing the knot. "I've got to find my cooking utensils."

Lou gave vent to something that was a cross between a sigh and a snort. "Now why on earth would you want your cooking utensils?" But she stood up to help. "Wouldn't your — cooking utensils — be in a box?"

"Of course. Of course."

Lou was beginning to realize she was on a deserted shore on the coast of Alaska with a vaguely competent stranger and her one and only son. Ben might even be less than vaguely competent. And yet when he picked up a large rock she felt she should give the talk she had on the tip of her tongue.

"And don't get it into your head that I owe you any favours. I could have got out of that fix by myself."

Ben wacked at a wooden box with the rock. "Sure. You could have." He went on knocking. "By walking off the end of that gangplank. You could have figured out what to do next. Just before you hit the water."

The lid came loose from the packing case.

We were looking into a case that had in it a whole lot of sawdust and one oak keg.

Lou had her own opinion of whiskey and bars and men. When you're thirty-four years old and working in a pawnshop and your husband hasn't put in an appearance for fourteen years and you're trying to feed yourself and your son and somehow keep body and soul together, you develop attitudes. You get to be wary. On top of that, Lou had pawned everything we owned in order to equip us to be stampeders. Or stowaways. Or, as it was turning out, castaways.

For the moment she was at a loss. She was developing an awful sense that Ben really and truly didn't know what she was talking about. "Favours," she said. "I mean, no favours." Then she noticed the blankness in his wondering blue eyes and she tried again. "I mean, Ben — we could be here quite a while."

"Like two hours. If our luck doesn't improve."

Lou desperately wanted to believe him. "Even so. We should rig up a shelter or something." She tilted her green felt hat down over her eyes. "Even if we don't have anything to eat."

Ben was puzzled by her concern. "It's morning. We'll be picked up by noon. Half the boats in Seattle are heading north."

Lou raised her right arm and pointed defiantly this time at the empty channel. If you looked far enough, and concentrated, you could make out a couple of seals playing hide-and-seek around a drifting log.

"Where's your axe, Ben?" I wanted to change the subject, I guess.

"I didn't bring an axe."

Lou was on her high horse again. "You're on your way to the Yukon and you didn't bring an axe?"

"I explained, Lou. McGrew has everything. Up there in Dawson City. All he needs is cash. Dollars and cents cash. Capital. The town is full of miners going broke or falling sick or breaking their bones. You offer them the price of a ticket out for their claims, they'll take it. McGrew explained in his letter. All we need is a bundle of cash."

Lou pointed at the open wooden box and the keg of whiskey. "Explain again about the bundle of cash, would you, Ben?"

Ben gave her a look of resigned patience. "We don't have to do the dirty work. Get it? We invest."

"Sounds like a nice guy, this Dan fellow. If you like two-bit chisellers."

Ben played his ace. "I met him seven years ago. He was in trouble. I did him a favour. Now he's doing me one. Turn about is fair play."

Lou held her tongue for something approaching thirty seconds. Then she said, "What are we going to eat, Ben?"

She wasn't getting back at him. She was inquiring.

I hate to see people upset. And watching them try to make up is even worse, especially when one of them isn't very good at it.

"I'll go look for some gold," I said. I thought that would make them smile.

Ben had taken the precaution of looking the way he thought a prospector should look. He had with him a gold pan and a pick and a shovel, even if he didn't have an axe.

"You better go find more wood," Lou said, "if all those hundreds of people out there on the water are going to see this blazing fire of yours."

She dropped some twigs onto my fire.

Ben offered me the mining pan. "Good luck," he said.

I hesitated. I heard the groaning in my breath again. I took the pan instead of going to look for wood.

Ben was talking to Lou. "I'll wrestle some of that driftwood up here onto the rocks." He pointed down at the line of drift-wood, then at his heaped supplies. "Lou, why don't you unfold one of those tarps and see if you can rig us up a shelter?"

4

A mining pan has a good feel about it. If you hold it with both hands it makes you feel like stepping forward. It's maybe a foot across at the bottom, a foot and a half across at the top, with flared sides that give the water a swirling motion when you let your body dance the gold down to the pan's bottom and the sand out over the tilted lip.

I began to get it, on about the thirtieth try.

The tide was rising, coming in at the creek's mouth, covering the gravel. I had to keep moving inland.

I carried the pan upside down as a hat on top of my cap on top of my head. That was why I didn't see the bear. The morning was all sun and dried berries and salal and the pleasant mystery of a creek that seemed to flow uphill.

I smelled the bear before I saw it. The morning breeze was moving down the valley. I was taking in the hemlock aroma, the thickness of moss, the pleasant rot-smell of dead tree trunks, things like that. And then I got hit by a smell that fell over my gold pan and my head like a hood.

It scared me. But I liked it too.

When I opened my eyes and saw the grizzly it was in a lagoon that had in it hundreds of trapped salmon. Silvery-grey salmon. Red salmon just on the edge of turning black. I could see them in the perfectly clear water, riding over the gravel. I insisted on looking at the salmon, bear or no bear. They were milling around, waiting for the water to rise so they could resume their journey up the creek toward their distant gravel beds and the shallows where they would spawn.

But for the moment they were trapped. And that grizzly was having the time of its life. I saw how quick it could move.

I dropped the gold pan and turned around and made tracks. The funny thing was, I only ran about a hundred yards. Then I slowed to a walk. Then the walk became what you might call a limp. And the closer I got to our camp, the more fondly I remembered the grizzly.

I could hear Lou's voice before I stepped beyond the tree line. She and Ben were too busy talking to notice me. They were talking while they worked.

Ben didn't know how to raise his voice. He was whispering in response to what Lou was shouting at him.

"No, we are not in this together," Lou said. "Stop kidding yourself, Ben."

Ben muttered something that I couldn't hear.

"I know we don't have anything to eat," was Lou's reply. "It doesn't take a genius to figure that out." She gestured at three kegs that Ben had unpacked. They were, each and every one of them, according to the large print on their sides, full of salt herring.

"Pour yourself a drink, Ben. Celebrate our good fortune."

Ben shook his head. And this time I could hear him. "We can't afford to drink this whiskey," he said. "We need it, partner."

There was a silence you could hear all the way up the creek

and past the grizzly and on up to the blue-green face of the nearest glacier and back again.

Apparently that was the first time he'd used the word.

Partner.

He didn't so much use it as try it on, as if he had blistered heels and was trying on a new pair of shoes.

All the newspaper advice that Lou had read back in Seattle — the only advice she'd paused to get — insisted that you shouldn't try going to the Klondike all by yourself. She read the advice aloud to me and told me that she and I had to stick together, come hell or high water.

Lou kicked the end of a small log, pushing it farther into the fire.

"So we're going to be partners, are we?"

Ben was mumbling again.

"So where's *your* partner, Ben?"

I edged closer, trusting they wouldn't notice me.

"I told you. He's up there now. He's in Dawson City. Dan McGrew. He's expecting me."

"So why are you suggesting that you and I might be partners if you already have a partner?"

"I told you. Because it's quite a distance from here to Dawson City. Like maybe seven hundred miles of ocean and mountain and river and bush and muskeg and rock. Or maybe you hadn't heard."

Lou ignored his feeble attempt at sarcasm.

"And what will this partnership cost me?" Lou swatted with both hands at some sparks that came up onto the long sleeves of her blouse. "All I have to do is cook and sew and clean and mend? And bow and scrape?" She delivered those statements as questions. When it came to sarcasm, Ben wasn't in the running. She didn't pause to let him answer. "And if it isn't supposed to cost me anything, why were you so eager to come ashore with me?"

"With you and your boy," Ben said.

"Okay, with me and my boy."

"I came along, Lou, because, given another ten minutes, the stampeders on that steamer would have figured out that I had more whiskey where those two kegs came from. You get it?"

Lou was trying not to get it.

"I'm saying," Ben said, "that once I shot off my big mouth I was left with no choice but to come ashore with you. Get it?"

Lou got busy fixing the fire so the hundreds of invisible travellers out on the water in invisible boats would be sure to see us.

"That is the whole complete kettle of fish I got myself into. Do you get it, Lou? Those stampeders are looking for gold but there on that boat, given a choice of gold or whiskey, they would have, every damned one of them, chosen whiskey."

Ben was wound up. I liked that. I didn't have to see Lou's face to know that she was biting her lip. She had a way of biting her lower lip, toward the left side, when she was flummoxed. I knew she wasn't about to say either sorry or thank you. But at least she was listening.

"Whiskey," Ben said. "Wanting gold is one thing, and it drives them all crazy. But then there's thirst. That's about staying alive."

Ben seemed to be confusing mere water and alcoholic spirits. That's why I cleared out again. I knew they hadn't seen me. The two of them had a gift for not seeing me, once they started looking at each other. I went back to the grizzly with the feeling that grizzlies weren't such bad company.

On top of that, it turned out to be a young grizzly. You could tell by how stupid it was. It was making a lot of plunges and splashes and coming up soaking wet. But without a salmon.

I stood right out in the open and watched, what the hell.

On about the fortieth try that bear caught a salmon in its jaws and came bouncing back to shore as if it had managed to catch the creek itself. It held the salmon under its right paw and tore off the head with a single yank that I could feel all the way to my testicles.

The grizzly looked up and saw me.

This is it, I thought. But so what?

That young silvertip got quite a start. It tried to stand up on its hind legs but got scared instead. I knew how it felt. It left the headless salmon lying on the rocks and turned around and positively leapt back into the water and for a moment disappeared, sank right out of sight. When it came up it was busy trying to find its breath.

I had left the mining pan there on the rocks the first time I saw the grizzly. Now it was my turn to fish.

I loaded the salmon into the pan. I didn't run this time. I said thank you to the young grizzly and gave a little bow and turned and marched away, not once glancing over my shoulder. I had to show the bear I trusted it.

I made a racket when I got close to our camp. I started to hum one of the tunes that Lou liked to hear me play on a piano there in the pawnshop when we weren't busy. "Absence Makes the Heart Grow Fonder."

Lou looked up from where she was trying to make two pieces of driftwood lean against each other. She studied the fish and then studied me and then studied the fish again.

"Where'd you get that?" she said.

So much for gratitude.

I turned around as if I was going to take the salmon back to the grizzly.

"Just hang on there," Lou said. Then she turned to Ben.

"Peek has a fish," she said.

"Good," Ben said. It was the sort of thing a person who has just lost an argument might say.

"I don't suppose, Ben, you have a fish knife, along with not having anything else."

I didn't even try to understand. I was looking into the mining pan. It must have weighed fifteen pounds, that salmon, even without its head. Ben came and stood beside me and studied it. I guess it was sort of a mess, what with tooth marks and claw marks and the head ripped off and blood all over the place.

Lou took a closer look. "At least it has a tail," she said.

Not so much as a thank you to me for risking life and limb and showing up with fresh salmon. No, the question was, apparently, why didn't the fish come complete with china plates and silver cutlery. Lou liked to borrow those things from the pawnshop once in a while, and then we'd use them for a couple of days, and then she'd take them back. But no such luck this time.

She took the pan out of my hands and gave me new orders. "Go over there and bring me that leather bag. The one with our tin plates in it. And my jackknife. Then we'll get some wet bark."

I let her get her own wet bark. I sort of lay down and stretched out and relaxed for a minute, the hunter back from the hunt, the fisherman home from the sea. Ben went along the shore to try and scare up a few dry-looking berries.

The smell of salmon baking somewhere deep in hot coals

was a breakfast in itself. We had to share one jackknife and two forks and two tin plates and two tin cups, the three of us. Lou sent me back up the creek for fresh water. I found a small spring before I got as far as the bear.

Handing things back and forth got us to laughing.

"Peek," Lou said, "I should explain. Ben and I are going to be partners. You can't make it alone in this country. We've made an agreement. We're sticking together until we set foot in Dawson City. Then it's goodbye and thank you."

Ben was fishing with his tongue for a bone that he'd got into his mouth.

"You understand?" Lou said to me.

"I guess so," I said. "You're saying that you and Ben are going to be partners."

"Can't you hear, Peek? What else did I say?"

"You said you'll be partners until you get to Dawson City. Then it's goodbye and thank you."

"Excellent, Peek. That's right." The salmon was giving her back her strength. "Partners. Until we set foot in Dawson City."

I gave a little gulp and a nod.

Then she turned to Ben. "You got it, Ben?"

"I told you before," he said. "I get it."

Would you believe, the two of them stood up from the herring kegs — or whiskey kegs I should say — they were sitting on. They stood up, facing each other. And there in the warmth of the fire, under the noon sun, on that lovely October day in the middle of absolutely nowhere, they shook hands.

"It's a deal," Ben said.

"It's a deal," Lou said.

She turned away to get on with finishing her meal. Bending over her salmon, she spoke to herself. Only to herself, I swear.

"None of that love shit," she said. She might have been looking in at a pawnshop window. Then she pointed a finger at me. "Peek, pass me that jackknife again."

5

I was trying to make our fire smoke. That way we'd be easier to spot from a passing ship. In a little while the sun would be going down, and then I'd want a clear fire with no smoke at all, but for the moment I wanted it to smoke. I was figuring out how we might get rescued, in the event that something other than a walrus came by.

I've always liked the expression, bed-partners. Lou and I were bed-partners, in a way, there in our lifeboat on the *Delta Queen*. We slept curled up together wearing all our clothes and huddled in the two quilts she'd managed to bring along on the pretence that she was going to leave them with her husband, who, she told the officials, was somewhere on that steamer.

She hadn't heard from the man since a few months before I was born, as she reminded me more than once. One time I asked her why he left us. "Because I just went on throwing up and throwing up," she said. "Come on," I said. "Well then you tell me," she said.

I tossed some seaweed onto the fire and damned near put it out. I couldn't quite tell if it was smoking or steaming.

There wasn't a sign of any sort of ship or fishing boat at all, in the narrow channel in front of us. Two bald eagles took turns waiting for us to keel over. I swear I saw a pod of whales, but neither Lou nor Ben could see it. Ben speculated that Captain Poole, along with not knowing how to deal with passengers on a steamer that was carrying more than its legal load, didn't quite know how to read a navigational map in fog or rain.

"He was covering his ass is more like it," Lou said. "Dumb like a fox. Take the wrong channel on purpose. Stay out of the path of the law."

When the rain began, they set to work, Lou and Ben, as if they were about to found a city there on that bare rock ledge. They hardly seemed like two people hellbent on escaping the isolation of an uninhabited wilderness. First off, they covered Ben's supplies with three of the tarps he'd brought along. I argued for using them to waterproof the lean-to they'd built, but no, they wanted to protect our outfit. I don't know what we thought would get wet, maybe the sawdust. While I was trying to keep the fire alive in the rain, they stacked more firewood under the nearest hemlock.

There was the small matter of Lou's two quilts and three people. Lou, who had curled up with me for eight nights in a lifeboat on the *Delta Queen,* now declared I was big enough to sleep by myself wrapped up in a quilt of my own. That left the difficult mathematical question of one remaining quilt and two remaining sleepers.

"Well, partner, how are we going to work this?" was Lou's way of stating the issue.

It turned out that Ben, at forty-two, was a bachelor. He had got hold of the notion that women disappear around eight in the evening and reappear just before breakfast the following morning. He seemed dumbfounded by the idea that Lou was not going to up and vanish.

"Ben can use my quilt," I said. "I'll make myself a bed of hemlock and cedar boughs."

"Good thinking," Ben said.

Lou said that was not a half-bad idea. She and Ben and I set to work cutting off branches with Lou's jackknife, gathering together the softest hemlock boughs we could find.

My bed was a foot thick. I want to tell you, sleeping on top of and under those branches and with that smell was heaven. So much for wool and eiderdown. I simply wanted to stay awake all night and inhale.

6

Lou told me next morning I had fallen asleep in one minute flat. I slept so deeply I didn't hear a sound until Ben fell off a log he was jumping up and down on, under the mistaken illusion that he was going to break it in two. Startled awake, I thought I was back on the steamer, listening to horses that were trying to break out of their narrow stalls.

It was Ben's morning fire that drew the attention of the men out on the water.

You'd think we'd have rushed down to the beach to greet them. But we didn't. We went maybe twenty yards toward them and then we stopped.

Their boat was an old war canoe or whatever — a huge cedar log hollowed out and shaped into a perfect boat that slid right through the water hardly leaving a wake. They had rigged a square sail onto a makeshift mast.

There were four men in the boat. When they touched the beach they got out and pulled the bow of their canoe onto gravel. They came up the beach toward us like four totem poles that had decided to go for a stroll. It looked as if they were trying to be each other and themselves at the same time. They were wearing mixtures of blankets and jeans and yellow mackinaws and slickers and red plaid shirts and boots and moccasins and cowboy hats and some kind of cedar bark hats that were pointed on top.

"Ben," Ben said, as if he thought one of those guys was Ben.

"Ben," one of them replied. It was hard to tell which one. They weren't much into opening their mouths too far when they spoke. "Isaac."

We thought maybe we were trespassing. Before we could explain our predicament Isaac asked if he and his friends could boil some tea and make some bannock on our fire.

It didn't take us long to say yes.

Lou had been trying to bake a mixture of flour and sawdust and water on the end of a stick. Something to go with the salmon that was still warm, buried in warm coals. She had managed to find a little flour in the seams of one of the flour sacks that was full of sawdust and whiskey.

Four Tlingits they were, those men. We thought we were rescued.

Isaac asked if we had any sugar.

Ben explained that we didn't.

Isaac allowed himself just a hint of a sceptical smile. He wore a thin little goatee.

We walked over the rocks and back to the fire, the seven of us, one of the Tlingits carrying a cardboard box full of supplies and food. While we were walking Ben explained that he and Lou and I wanted to get to Skagway. Isaac simply looked at all of our sacks and boxes and asked again about the sugar.

Ben was rushing things. He had to learn to sit down and wait. In fact he sat down on a sack that said on it, SUGAR. I was hoping that Isaac couldn't read, but no such luck. He was puzzling out the letters, I could tell.

"We don't have any sugar," Ben said.

"You got any tobacco?" Isaac asked, without so much as a blink.

Again Ben had to say no.

Our fire was too big for cooking purposes. One of the Tlingits pulled a burning stick out of the fire and started a smaller fire of his own. Adam was his name. While he tended the fire the guy named Peter set to work mixing flour and water and salt in a frying pan.

"Pass me that bear grease," he said to the fourth man.

While they were sampling their tea, with canned milk, without sugar, Ben once again brought up the subject of a ride to Skagway.

Isaac listened patiently to Ben and then said, "Skagway. Not on your life."

"Now wait a minute, Isaac. How come?"

"We just left Skagway. Two days ago."

I was pleased to realize we were fairly close to our first destination.

Ben was losing ground. "I could make it worth your while."

"No way." It was Peter's turn to try and get the point across. He had squatted down to make the bannock and hadn't bothered to straighten up. "We aren't going back to Skagway. No way."

Ben tried again to explain that we were in a hurry to get through Skagway and onto the trail up over the mountains.

"You'll get killed there," Isaac said. Then he added, "In Skagway. There were five of us."

That put a stop to the conversation. Or rather, the Tlingits chatted with each other instead of with us. In Tlingit. After a while Peter used his monstrous hunting knife to divide up the bannock. He stuck the knife into a piece and offered it to Lou.

He said a word to Lou but Lou didn't understand. I thought he was trying to teach her a word in Tlingit. But when she didn't understand Isaac intervened. He said the same word.

"South," Isaac said. He said it, then repeated it. He pointed south each time he spoke. He took a chunk of bannock from Peter and handed it to me and watched me take my first bite. I chewed and nodded at the same time. I'd never tasted anything better.

"South," he said again.

It was his turn to make a speech. He said that Lou and Ben and I could go south with them. To Juneau or some such place. They had lots of space in their canoe. From Juneau, he said, we could make our way to Seattle. Those were his exact words. We could make our way.

That's when Lou turned and went into our shelter. She came back with the chunk of bannock held between her teeth and a tin cup in either hand.

I could smell the whiskey over the bannock.

I guess Lou thought two cups of whiskey would be a fair trade in exchange for a ride to Skagway. What happened was, Isaac accepted the whiskey and then spoke to the man named Joseph, who hadn't been doing anything at all. Joseph walked down from our camp and across the beach to their boat. Very shortly he came back with another cardboard box, bringing three salmon and a small bag of flour and some tea and a tin of evaporated milk.

"We are going south," Isaac said. He was being conspicuously patient. "We must find a new place for our people to fish for coho." He took one of the salmon out of the cardboard box and opened its mouth and showed us the white gums, the white mouth. "Coho," he said. He could tell we didn't know much. He put down the coho and waited.

That's when it became clear to me that Lou was just as stubborn as Ben and Ben was just as stubborn as Lou. They had a chance, right there, to give up and turn around and go back home.

Poker faces all around. They were playing a kind of poker, the whole bunch of them. The Tlingits had guessed there was a good reason why we didn't have anything to eat. They wanted more whiskey. A lot more. Lou and Ben wanted a ride to Skagway. To and into the jaws of certain death, the way the Tlingits were telling it. I was neutral myself.

Those four Tlingits were cool customers. They had a complicated way of drinking whiskey out of our two cups, handing them back and forth, circulating them, exchanging them. It made me half dizzy. They each took measured sips without glancing down into the cup. At the same time they were passing around their own chipped granite cups, full of tea, and Lou and Ben and I got the hang of taking sips.

When the two tin cups were empty Isaac handed both of them, using both hands, to Ben. I could see that Ben was getting ready to say a few words. Making actual speeches was seldom his thing. He stood there looking into the two empty tin cups, trying to loosen up his facial muscles by protruding his lips out and then pulling them back across his teeth. Ben had very white teeth for a man of forty-two.

The four Tlingits, as if Ben in moving his lips had given them a signal, turned around and walked away, leaving the coho and the flour and tea and milk on the rocks. They remembered to take their own cups and their own cardboard box.

They went down across the rocks in single file without one of them glancing back. They pushed their boat into the water and got in and left without waving.

"That's a good sign," Lou said.

There were times when she saw the bright side of things.

"The way they up and left us?" Ben asked.

"The way they didn't say goodbye. They're coming back."

"Too bad for them," Ben said. "We'll be long gone before they show up. And I was getting ready to make them an offer."

"That's what I was afraid of," Lou said.

7

The only ship that went by that day was a small coastal ferry, close enough to shore so that we didn't need a fire to get attention. A couple of men in the crowd on the forward deck of the ferry waved briefly in response to our frantic waving and leaping.

"May your mothers' milk turn to poison," I shouted after the departing vessel.

"Damn it, Peek," Lou said. "Honestly. Sometimes I wonder."

By night we had dragged a whole pile of beached logs up into the first woods above the tidewater line. Ben told us a lot about how to bend and shape wood and wished he had some of his tools with him. Under his direction we put together a snug-enough shelter. At least it was drier than our lean-to. We figured out how to build a small cooking and heating fire in front of the three-sided shelter without choking ourselves to death in smoke. We set up some of Ben's kegs as chairs and then needed a table, so we took four more kegs out of hiding, so to speak, and made a table by pushing them together and setting two packing box lids on top of the kegs. The kegs were three-gallons each, made of oak, maybe sixteen inches high, nicely bellied. They made for a homey sight.

"Three gallons," Lou said. "You are talking one hundred and twenty-eight fluid ounces to the customary gallon."

"I made them just a little bit bigger," Ben said. "The kegs. They tend to shrink."

"How much bigger, Ben?"

He gave her a look that said he was letting her in on a secret. "Maybe a quart."

I could see Lou was pleased. "Ben," she said. "Nothing's going to shrink that much."

They were flirting, I knew that. They flirted by exchanging numbers. They scratched numbers on the kegs themselves, using Lou's knife. Three times one hundred and twenty-eight. Add another quart to each keg for good measure. Count all the kegs. Two forever gone. But thirteen remaining. Allow for shrinkage. Guess the sale price. Multiply by the unknowable. Here, you try. No, you.

That's what made me long for the company of the bear. Their ignorance. Ben's and Lou's, I mean. Ben had never been in the bush for a day of his life. And Lou for less. Yet they sat by the fire talking whiskey and talking Klondike, calculating, guessing, journeying over white mountains and down swollen rivers. Ben had read a guidebook. One that came out a month after the gold was discovered. Lou had read the Seattle papers. She and Ben weren't making the slightest effort to get us there, but they went on speculating about which route they should take when returning with their gold. Ben said he would come back the way we were going. Lou said she would take the rich man's route, riding a riverboat all the way down the Yukon from Dawson City, boarding a steamship in St. Michael, sailing across the open Pacific to Seattle and home.

I went out next morning just as the sun came up. There were ten grizzlies at the fishing spot. Part of their fishing activity involved taking swipes at each other's heads. Mostly it was the older bears taking swipes at the smaller and younger bears, teaching them to stay out of reach and to wait. I recognized that one of those swipes would have pretty much sent me to the Klondike unaided. The bald eagles and the ravens were hanging around, playing a game of patience, keeping their distance and yet showing they weren't about to go away. I looked for some berries to pick, but without any luck.

The good weather was just about over, and winter was on its way. They had to get fat in a hurry, those bears. It was their hurrying that made me anxious.

Ben had gone from thinking we'd be rescued in an hour to thinking we'd never be rescued at all. He went out to dig for clams. He took off his wet boots and socks in the evening and put his bare feet up on a whiskey keg. He started planning a cabin.

"That should be fun," Lou told him, "building a cabin without an axe or a saw."

But there wasn't any reprimand in her voice.

By the fifth morning the Tlingits whose return she had prophesied had not shown up. And nor had anyone else. If there were boats or steamers by the dozen heading for Skagway and Dyea, they were using a different channel than ours. There were two bustling, booming ports somewhere north of us, hardly more than a day's travel away. And we were going nowhere.

We had pretty much used up all of our food supply. The grubstake that was supposed to carry Ben through a year in the Klondike yielded up a cupful of dried beans. Ben and I took to clamming at low tide. We had salmon again and bannock again and tea again. Actually, we didn't have bannock. We had pancakes. Lou called what she made pancakes. And once in a while for a change we had beans and sawdust and a baked clam each.

After breakfast on that fifth morning I took the shovel and walked south along the shoreline by myself. I hit it lucky. In no time at all I had my cap full of clams.

When I returned to our lean-to, Lou and Ben weren't on duty, watching for passing ships. They were inside the lean-to. I half listened. They were having a different kind of conversation. Somehow they weren't telling Klondike stories.

"I still can't believe my good fortune," Ben said.

I thought he was trying his hand at sarcasm again. Then I realized he was serious.

"Are you complaining or bragging?"

"I'm trying to understand."

"Understand?" Lou often said as much. But this time she was somewhere in between laughing and teasing. "What is there to *understand*? For God's sake, Ben. You *are* something." The same old words. Except that they came out soft and gentle.

Ben tried to explain, but halfway through his sentence he sounded as if he'd swallowed his tongue. Just when I was about to make some noise Ben downright giggled. "I want to understand all this good luck I'm having."

If I hadn't been stopped in my tracks, that would have done it for me. We were starving, dying of exposure, and about to become grizzly food, once the salmon were gone.

Then they were both laughing, Ben and Lou. Not big laughs. Small little intimate laughs, with a kind of helpless quality to them. But even so, laughs of any sort were a treat for Lou. I was pleased for her. I heard her catch her breath. Then she said, "Good luck, nothing. That was charity. At your age, Ben. A virgin."

"Like they say," Ben said. "Charity begins at home."

Apparently that was a thigh-slapper. When they caught their breaths again, Lou said, "Well, I guess one good deed deserves another."

Ben giggled again. "I was going for the record."

"You weren't going for it. You had it. It was yours."

"What on earth comes next?" Ben asked.

"What comes after first?" Lou said.

Ben was quick on that one too. "Practice makes perfect, they say."

Some people would claim that, technically at least, I'm a virgin myself. At the age of one hundred and fourteen. So much for Ben's piddling record. But I don't see it that way. I'd say I'm the person who got it all. The luck, I mean. Love sought me out and never let me go.

I went out onto the rock ledge to look for ships. The water was calm and pale. Across the channel an island threatened to sink into its own reflection. Beyond the island more clouds were practising up to rain. As for ships — I might as well have been watching for a gold brick to come floating by.

After a considerable time I picked up my capful of clams again and went stumbling loudly toward the shelter. The pair inside apparently heard me. Lou was pouring me a cup of tea when I bungled and thumped my way around the tarp that was a doorway and a door at the same time. But Ben carried on their conversation, as brazen as ever.

"You were married," he was saying. "You had an advantage. I never got off the starting mark."

Lou changed her voice in my presence. I could hear her making the change.

"I *am* married, Ben."

Before I had sipped my tea she was explaining that she and Ben had put their two quilts together to make one bed. Not that I hadn't noticed. I suggested they cut fresh cedar branches to make their bed more comfortable. Then I said it was such a nice night, I might try sleeping outside for a change.

8

It was pissing rain next morning. Thank heavens the Tlingits showed up when they did. They didn't even pretend to be surprised at our still being there. Lou and Ben weren't especially glad to see them, even though we were on the verge of extinction.

Isaac explained that he and his crew had done a lot of looking before they found a new site for their fishing camp.

Ben was hardly listening. "Which way you headed?"

"We're going north to pick up our families. We could stop in Skagway."

Ben should have been flabbergasted. He should have jumped up and down the way he had at our one sighting of a passing ship. Fortune smiling on him again. Instead he looked a little glum.

Lou whispered to Ben, "They've probably been camped over on that far island, waiting for us to run out of food."

Ben came up with a whisper of his own. "Don't be so cynical, Lou."

And yet, in some way, I was just as unexcited as Lou and Ben about being rescued. I wasn't in any hurry to leave our little home. Being rescued didn't seem to me such a great thing. It was just that the bears had hinted something about a forthcoming winter, and that was hard to ignore.

They squatted down, those four Tlingits, as if they planned to stay until spring. I thought at first that ours was the site they had picked for their fishing camp. They smelled of damp wool and of moosehide and cedar and salmon. I liked the smells. I wanted to ask if they belonged to something called the bear clan, but I didn't know how to begin the conversation.

We had got used to keg furniture. We had arranged three kegs in front of our shelter, where we had a pleasant view of the channel. Those Tlingits, squatting on their haunches, used the kegs as places where they would set whatever drinks that might be offered. They had brought with them up from their boat their own large drinking cups. To give credit where credit is due, they had also brought their tea pail. And tea and milk.

After three hours of slurping tea and spitting tea leaves and talking about the salmon run and how to dry salmon and how to store them for winter, Ben figured out that those men had come back, not just to rescue us, but to collect a specific price for passages as offered. They had come back for the mother-lode itself, and they weren't in a hurry. They were willing to wait. Just plain wait.

After three hours of tea and iron bladder control, Ben blurted out something about kegs. He didn't say kegs of what. But there we all were, seated on kegs, leaning on kegs, surrounded by kegs.

Ben's use of the actual word, keg, set Lou into motion. Just that suddenly she was her old self. She was ready and willing to try and beat those Tlingits at their own game.

It was she who invited them to stay the night. That took Isaac by surprise. Not to mention Ben. Lou saw the surprise on Isaac's face and went on to suggest the four visitors make preparations to stay for a day or two. She mentioned that I had seen no end of coho moving into the creek's mouth.

Ben, instead of guessing what she was up to, panicked. I suppose he had a vision in his mind of seven people sleeping in his shelter. "How much whiskey," he asked, speaking directly to Isaac, "would you guys want in exchange for that trip to Skagway that you mentioned, just to drop us in the harbour and run?"

Just like that, Isaac had him. The game was over. A snap of the wrist, the hook was set. I swear, my jaw ached all the way down to my groin.

Isaac spoke not to Ben at all but rather to one of his companions. They spoke for a long time in Tlingit. They looked extremely serious while they talked, never raising their voices, seldom moving their lips.

Isaac turned from the conversation as if to translate.

"Joseph says that the weather will change soon."

It had taken those Tlingits forty minutes to come up with that remarkable speculation. The chances of the weather's not changing were something less than zero.

I was hanging around, keeping the tea pail hot and full. I tried to go to Ben's rescue. "We should spike this tea," I whispered.

Lou gave me a killer look. "Just sit tight."

She wasn't much at reading or writing, but she certainly could do figures in her head. She had calculated Ben's kegs as being worth, at the very most, two hundred dollars each, especially on New Year's Eve in a city where the streets were paved with gold. Fifteen kegs would have taken Ben right up to the required three thousand dollars. The trouble was, he had squandered two kegs when one would have done the trick, out there on the *Delta Queen*. And now he was in a corner again.

"If the weather is changing," Lou said to Isaac, "I believe we should prepare to stay here until it changes again."

Lou got a kick out of that kind of talk. Her dark brown eyes were shining. There was a little sheen of sweat on her upper lip.

"The bears," she said, "are not yet fat enough for winter."

She hadn't laid eyes on a single bear, as far as I knew. The Tlingits gave each other a puzzled look.

Isaac spoke with his fellow sailors again in their language. After a while he said, "We have been gone a few days from our village. The elders would appreciate a gift."

Isaac allowed himself his usual little smile and touched his goatee. He liked the way Lou bargained. It was obvious he could smell whiskey right through the staves and headings of Ben's exquisitely made kegs. Ben had made each keg himself and then filled each with whiskey himself and then printed on the outside of each keg, BENJAMIN REDD SALT HERRING, on the assumption that not even a starving man would steal something called salt herring. He had fooled a ship's crew and seventy thirsty stampeders. But he was having no luck whatsoever with those Tlingits.

"We're in trouble," Ben whispered to Lou.

"We're doing fine," she said. Then she raised her voice. "Peek, you go into the shelter and bring us a tin cup of something to wet our whistles with." I could tell she was pleased with her bargaining powers. She liked talking that way. "Then you and Ben start packing our things," she added.

I filled one cup out of the keg that was open and hidden away in the shelter. After that Ben and I got busy, repacking everything. We used cedar boughs where we needed extra packing material. I went to the boat and borrowed an axe. We knocked the nails back into the wood with the head of Isaac's axe while Lou went on with her negotiations. We found some fishing line in the boat and helped ourselves to a few yards of line for wrapping and tying.

This went on for a good part of the afternoon. Ben and I worked like two donkeys while Lou and her four friends drank their mixture of tea and whiskey and chatted. I took away the kegs the Tlingits were resting their elbows on. Or at least I took away all but the one Isaac was leaning on. I didn't have the nerve to ask him to raise his elbows. He had upper arms like little barrels.

When Ben told Lou that the packing up was done, she looked at him and said, "Well. The boat won't load itself."

Trust our luck, the tide had gone out about as far as it could go. It couldn't decide whether or not to return. We had to haul

Ben's outfit across a few hundred yards of rocks and gravel and tidal flat. Nobody lifted a hand to help us. Even the little crabs hardly bothered to scramble out of our way. A raven took to making rude noises. The sand dollars, instead of looking like dollars, looked like eye holes in a skull.

When we finished we hollered up to the rock cliff that the boat was loaded.

"Hope she's planning to take us with her," Ben said. He had just about broken a leg when he slipped on some kelp by the water's edge. Then he thought I may have misunderstood so he added, "She's having a great time."

"The time of her life," I said.

She and the four Tlingits, after another half hour, deigned to approach us. They were all pretty well looped. Plastered. You could tell by the trouble they were having with the rocks and the seaweed and the razor-edged barnacles. But they were being dignified nevertheless. Isaac was carrying on his left shoulder the keg he'd been leaning on. Joseph held in warm embrace the keg they'd been dipping into all afternoon, while Ben and I slaved.

Peter and Adam were acting as flunkies to Lou, carrying the few things that Ben and I, in our gross carelessness, had neglected to pack. We had missed one tin spoon and a small handkerchief.

"The open keg," she said, "is for the crew to drink while we travel. The closed keg is a gift to our Tlingit elders."

She had picked up a way of talking that made it difficult for Ben and me to move our lips. Besides, we were too tired to say much. But we were both scrambling through our statistics, trying to figure out how Ben might, there in Dawson, sell eleven kegs of whiskey for three thousand dollars.

"Everything has been arranged," Lou said. "They have extra

paddles. Peek, you take a paddle and sit up there in the bow with Peter. Ben, you can sit beside Adam with your paddle."

Lou sat down in the middle of that old war canoe.

I'd had no idea until right then how much she looked like a queen. I had to keep glancing back. Her green felt hat, sitting slightly askew, appointed to keep her heaped hair out of the way, could have been a crown. She wore draped over her shoulders Ben's green mackinaw. He'd taken it off while he and I were sweating and had almost left it behind. Lou had at some-time in the past few days hemmed up her skirt by a foot at least. She wore her laced-up shoes as if they were golden slippers. She wasn't all that tall. It was the way she sat that did it. She sat straight up as if she was on a throne, looking tough and busty and wise.

She looked interested. That was it. She was interested in everything. She studied every cove and inlet. Every eagle's nest. Every drifting log. Every distant glacier. She just sat there ignoring Ben and me completely, and all the while she was sizing up the waves and measuring headlands and checking currents and watching for whales and studying the high, fast drift of the clouds. And gauging distances.

9

We paddled and sailed all night. I damned near pulled my arms right out of their sockets. Those Tlingits didn't see the sun go down, apparently. They just went on paddling. Pad-dling and drinking and, would you believe, singing. Every so often they sang some kind of a strange song. I think Lou pretended they were singing for her.

We went ashore at sunrise to make tea and bannock. All that day we sailed and paddled hard again, with a good wind behind us most of the time. It was such a good wind that we should have guessed what was coming. That second night the snow overtook us. I mean heavy, wet snow, snow coming down by the tonne. Apparently those Tlingits couldn't see it, even when it covered their heads and arms and legs. We just kept on travelling. Most of the time we couldn't see a thing. Apparently we were into the long fjord that led to Skagway and Dyea.

We arrived in Skagway, on the second morning of our ride, under cover of snowflakes that were the size of silver dollars. It was like a dream of money. I had blisters about the same size as the snowflakes.

We could smell the wharves before we saw them. We couldn't see them at first, because of the falling snow. The wind had let up. But we could smell the new lumber and the tarred ropes. And the dried apricots. I swear, dried apricots, I could smell them. I was hungry. Then I began to think I could smell dried apples and black pepper. And then I thought of cured hams and great slabs of smoked bacon and sacks of split peas. I thought of bags of onions and gunnysacks full of potatoes that still smelled of soil from home.

The Tlingits wouldn't approach the wharf, there in Skagway. No way. They pulled up instead beside a barge that was lightering supplies ashore from a steamer anchored in the channel. There wasn't space at the only completed wharf for all the ships that were in port with stampeders and supplies and equipment bound for the Klondike.

Those four Tlingits didn't so much as give Ben a chance to

negotiate with the captain of the barge; they heaved our sacks and boxes onto the crowded deck — everything except for their two kegs marked salt herring — and they would have heaved us as well, if we hadn't jumped in a hurry. Or they would have heaved Ben and me. They, all four of them, worked to hold their canoe steady while Lou made her regal ascent onto the deck of the barge.

I caught my balance on the deck and turned to wave to those Tlingits. But they were nowhere to be seen. Just like that, they had disappeared into the snow. I guess it wasn't a war canoe really. It was some kind of a whaling canoe, forty feet long, shaped out of a single cedar log. A few strokes of their paddles, and our friends had vanished.

The half-dozen men working on the barge, we soon heard, were on their way to wealth and indolence. They had, each and every one of them, just for the moment, run out of money; each one of them was temporarily bulling freight.

I was brazen enough to ask one of them what they were making.

"Five dollars for a ten-hour day. After that it's overtime."

I could hardly believe my ears.

"Let's stay here and get jobs," I said to Lou.

"That's just wages," Lou said.

I thought of the five bucks a week she earned back in Seattle, but I held my tongue. I was reminded that she had a scheme. Or she was going to have one.

She and I sat on some stacked bags of oatmeal there on the barge while four men in a rowboat towed us toward shore. She started to talk about the meal she'd prepare if she could get into those sacks and boxes. "A nice roast of beef," she said, "with creamed corn and mashed potatoes and gravy."

After Ben had looked around he went to sit down too. Facing Lou and me was a row of stacked, identical wooden boxes. Ben moved a couple of boxes to make himself a bench. It was then he noticed the boxes were full of bottled whiskey.

You could see his face sag. Just for a moment there, he didn't want to believe what he was reading: **CORN MASH WHISKEY AGED IN OAK BOURBON COUNTY KENTUCKY**.

Lou saw his anxiety. "Rotgut," she said. "That stuff is rotgut. You ever drink any of that brand?"

Ben explained that it was such an expensive brand he hadn't ever tried it.

We were put to work unloading freight, Ben and Lou and I. That's how we paid for our short ride. Lou's reign as a queen was looking shaky. Even breathing cost money in that town, it seemed. We had to help unload the barge into the chaos on the shore. I was put to work carrying the boxes of whiskey down a long, steep, slippery gangplank onto the beach.

"Drop one of those," the barge captain told me, "you're a dead duck. Soapy Smith will be here soon to claim his share. He'd rather have you shot than argue."

It was hard to hear in all that din and racket. But I got the message. You talk about walking carefully.

Two stampeders, unsteady after days on a ship, roped off the small space on the crowded beach where we were working. They stationed themselves with shotguns on opposite sides of their newly arriving supplies. It was that kind of town. Those two guards cussed at each other and at no one. They cussed, I could tell by the sounds in their voices, to give themselves courage. They were greenhorns like myself.

Out on their steamer, in the falling snow, a bunch of men were driving a herd of horses over the side, whipping them and shouting, forcing them to leap into the water. Maybe twenty horses were swimming toward shore. More men, where the water got shallow, were trying to capture the frightened horses as they found their hooves under them and began to wade. The panicking horses ran right over our two guards. No one paid much attention.

There were hawkers selling everything, there on the beach. Men, and a few women too, bawling out their wares. You could rent a room or buy a tent. You could buy a whole outfit from some stampeder who was ready to turn around and go back. You could buy buckskin jackets from old Indian women or you could negotiate with pimps. Or more directly. You could buy rifles and fishing nets and coils of rope and stacks of lumber and boxes of cigars and quarters of beef and tubs of butter. And you could buy booze. Any kind of booze. No end of people would tell you where to go to get whatever you thought it was your heart desired. And all you needed to offer in return was a fistful of spot cash.

When everything was off the barge, the barge captain let us unload our outfit. I say ours because Ben insisted we call it ours, not just his. No one helped us. All those men from the barge, once they'd unloaded, instead of rushing back to the steamer for more freight, fell into a kind of trance. I could see they were waiting.

Soapy Smith rode up on a tall white horse. He had a rifle in a scabbard on his saddle and a black hat with snow on it on his head. He had a sloping moustache like a little roof over his mouth, and when he spoke the men on horses behind him fell silent.

Soapy Smith counted the whiskey boxes himself. Then he ordered a sidekick on a bay horse to give commands. Two men wearing solid black appeared out of nowhere and started lifting some of the boxes onto a wagon. I didn't see where that came from either. Soapy pointed his finger and moved his lips again. Apparently, he could only count out loud.

Protection. Soapy Smith was offering protection, a stranger explained to me in a whisper. The trouble was, he said, the chief danger was from Soapy Smith and his gang of thugs and thieves.

The man who did the explaining turned out to be a packer. The moment Soapy and his men and the wagon loaded with a share of the whiskey left the beach, the place was jumping again. Packers swarmed all over the freight, like crows moving in after a grizzly had its fill.

People were arguing here and there. Whose freight was whose. Who was a packer going to serve first. Tempers flared. Prices went up.

The man who had told me about protection money said his name was Lemon Ed. People must have named him that because his face looked as if he'd just eaten a whole lemon without stopping to so much as peel it. He agreed to haul freight for two newly arrived stampeders. Then he told Ben that he'd haul our freight as well, later, if Ben would help him now.

We needed to save money. The packers were charging a couple of dollars, just to move a tonne of supplies away from the water line.

Ben and I helped load Lemon Ed's wagon while Lou guarded our freight. Then Ben went with Lemon Ed while I stayed with Lou to help out with the guarding. I could see that Lou was worried.

What we were really doing, I suppose, was watching for Ben to come back. We'd been waiting for what seemed a long time when I asked Lou if her partnership with Ben was to take her to Dawson or only as far as Skagway. I pretended I didn't quite remember.

She pretended she hadn't heard me. She just sat there on one of our boxes, while the snow fell like feathers off a distant bird. Or a whole flock of birds. I looked around. Most of the outfits were disappearing as fast as they hit the beach, stampeders and packers loading wagons and carts, heading into town. Some of the stampeders just loaded their own backs and walked straight into the jumble of tents and shacks and frame buildings that were more or less arranged along tracks in the mud that were supposed to be streets.

"Maybe I should go look for him," I said.

Lou shook the snow off her gloves. She hadn't moved for quite a while. "He's a grown man. I'm not his mother." Then she turned her gaze away from the jumble of streets. "Go down along the beach and see if you can find us something to eat that isn't salmon."

I could tell she was distracted. I had hardly started out when she called after me, "Be careful, Peek."

You might think I got my name from peeking. That wasn't quite the case. My mother was no great speller, even though she got through grade eight before her parents sent her out to work. She thought she was naming me after Mount Baker, the peak that glowed white and beautiful up there in the sky above her childhood. Obviously, she couldn't name me Mount Baker. Maybe she'd been hoping for a girl. Anyway, somewhere in a government office she wrote down my name as Peek, and that was that.

I walked down the beach a ways, looking at all the freight and supplies stacked and heaped there just beyond the water line. Or sometimes in the water. A few men had fallen asleep right there on their outfits. They looked as if they were dead. Other men were staring around as if they'd just awakened and couldn't get their bearings. One man was sitting under a red umbrella in the falling snow, writing a letter. He had a dog with him. A retriever.

I found a little stand that was selling pretzels, out there in the cold. Pretzels with crystals of salt baked right into the brown crust. Great big warm-looking knotted pretzels dripping hot mustard.

Lou hadn't given me any money. I'll tell you what I did. I stole a pretzel. I mean, I wasn't underhanded or anything. I just grabbed a pretzel off the stand, one that had mustard on it, and I was gone into the crowd. I ran as if Soapy Smith and his white horse were hot on my trail.

I took the pretzel to Lou. She needed some cheering up.

She was sitting on our heap of sacks that didn't have any food in them. When I handed her the pretzel she didn't notice it at first, she was staring into the snow. Then she saw what was in her hand and she said, "Where'd you get the money for this?"

I was stuck. I didn't want to lie. I couldn't tell her the truth. I don't think I ever told Lou a lie in my whole life. It was worth your life to try. That's why, even now, I have to lay out everything exactly the way it happened. But standing there, then, I couldn't just outright say I'd stolen the pretzel, because I knew she'd make me take it back and apologize to the owner.

Just as I was about to take the belt off my pants and hand it to her, Ben and Lemon Ed and Ed's team of horses and the empty wagon came rattling and steaming out of the snow. It was that kind of day. You could steam and freeze at the same time.

Lou handed me the pretzel and jumped up as if she was

looking at a miracle. Then she caught herself and tried to look mildly surprised. "That was fast," she said.

Ben was all apologies. "I'm sorry."

"Sorry for what?" Lou asked him.

"For being gone so long."

"Was it that long?" Lou said. "I was just sneaking in a little snooze. That whaling canoe just about broke my back."

I guess it just about broke her back. Trying to look like the Queen of Sheba will do that for you.

I managed to gulp down the pretzel while Ben told Lou about his good fortune. He had found a place where we could stay for a couple of nights, while we got ready to tackle the mountain pass.

But that wasn't the only news.

Lemon Ed, it turned out, not three weeks earlier, had packed in six casino tables and a dismantled oak bar that a guy named Dan McGrew had ordered for a saloon in Dawson City. Lemon Ed made so much money on the deal he bought all the extra packhorses he had borrowed, and after that, as he told us in no uncertain terms, he said to hell with the Klondike, there was money enough to be made on the fools who didn't know when to quit.

Ben could hardly contain himself. "You see?" he said to Lou. "Dan McGrew probably owns half the damned city up there."

"I hope he's short of whiskey," Lou said.

She was her old self again I could see. She could do that to you, just when you were warming up to your own story.

"Did you haul in any whiskey?" I said to Lemon Ed.

"No such luck." He tried to laugh. But his face looked as if he'd just sucked another lemon.

Lemon Ed hadn't been around family for a long time. He got a kick out of joshing with Lou and Ben. In no time we had our outfit loaded and were on our way.

A man in front of our hotel was whipping his horses with a bull whip and screaming and swearing. We had to wait until he got his wagon out of a mudhole. Then we pulled up. There were three hotels going up in a row, all of them facing onto a wooden sidewalk that ran along a street that was two feet deep in mud and tree roots. Ours was the middle one. The Nugget. The woman who owned it said we could bring our grubstake in with us.

"Must be a mansion inside," Lou said.

The place was swarming with stampeders, and we weren't the only new arrivals with lots of supplies to move. The floor was being finished up enough so people could walk on it. Or sleep on it. Mrs Keeler was putting an addition onto the clap-board building that was the old hotel — it was a month old. Ben gave the carpenters a hand and in twenty minutes we had a section of floor of our own.

"If those guys are carpenters," Ben said, "I'm a goose." He had enough cash on him to take our room for two nights and to pay for a few meals. Mrs Keeler provided two mattresses, which we had to carry. Not that it's hard to carry a mattress that's one inch thick. Mrs Keeler herself hung cotton sheets on wires around our space.

"There," she said. "Sleep tight. Don't let the bedbugs bite."

"What about our outfit?" Lou wanted to know.

"Oh." Mrs Keeler acted as if she'd forgotten. "That will be extra." She began moving a couple of the cotton sheets to give us more floor.

The hotel was something of a warehouse at the same time

that it was a hotel. I was all for falling asleep right there on the bare boards. But Lou and Ben insisted we haul in our whole outfit and stack it square all around us like a palisade.

Supper was a huge bowl of vegetable soup and more fresh bread than I could eat and dill pickles and mashed potatoes with gravy and slabs of what I thought was dark roast beef but turned out to be moose.

We were seated along with a few other people at what might have been a dining room table in its better days. It felt good, just to be seated on a bench, even if there were ten people crowded together around a table that was designed for a setting of six. I was into my third helping of everything when a new customer sat down at the table beside me and across from Lou.

The man who sat down was none other than Mr Plow.

He didn't recognize me. But he recognized Ben and Lou.

"Good to see you." He reached across the table as if he planned to shake hands with both of them at once. The man had no end of gall. Good to see you all right. Surprised as all hell to see you.

"Mr Plow." Ben put down his knife and fork as if he was going to reach out. Lou gave him an elbow in the ribs.

Mr Plow, seeing as much, directed his proffered hand at Lou. I was afraid she might lean across the table and bite his arm. Lou ignored the hand and said, "You fart."

Ben, quickly, tried to pass her the potato bowl. She ignored that too.

"Mr Plow, you're a flea-bitten excuse for a dead dog. Let alone for a man."

Mr Plow, just slightly, was wiggling his ears. He had to grind his teeth to do it. "I know how you must feel. Mis-understandings. The world is rife with misunderstandings."

It was obvious he wasn't about to apologize. So what did I do, I plunged in where Ben had failed. I asked a question.

"Did the whiskey last?" I said.

Mr Plow noticed his own right hand extended into the open air above the table. He hauled it back. He turned to give me a serious look. He looked at me twice.

"How old are you, talking about whiskey like that?"

He didn't wait for an answer. "I've got a job for this boy of yours," he said to Lou. "Yes, the whiskey got us here, thank heavens." He was obviously dying to talk. His need to talk was stronger than any fear of retribution or torture. He was wearing his spotless leather hat and his tight racoon coat right there at the table. "Quite a party, quite a party. But we got here. Old Poole was as crooked as a snake's belly. But revenge has its day. Half his crew jumped ship while we were waiting for a berth at the wharf. The first mate went with them. Made himself a small fortune. The blasting powder he'd smuggled aboard. Some outfit trying to improve the White Pass Trail. Then two of the horses hanged themselves, trying to jump off the boat."

He gestured up at the wooden beams over our heads as if they might be a gallows.

"I'm in real bad trouble," he said.

I thought he was going to mention his attempt at killing me and my mother by having us walk the gangplank. Maybe Captain Poole or someone had reported him.

"Deep-shit awful trouble," he said.

I could see that Lou had a few more things she wanted to say. But she was listening. She was interested. "Gangplank trouble?" she said.

Mr Plow seemed to have no idea what Lou was talking

about. "Soapy Smith," he said. "Soapy and his boys. I owe them some money."

Ben shook his head. "He's a bad one. We saw that with our own eyes. You borrowed money from Soapy Smith?"

"I wish," Mr Plow said. "I only wish." He reached for a slice of bread and dragged his right sleeve through the gravy boat. "I got into a card game in one of Soapy Smith's saloons. I was losing a little. I signed an IOU."

"You did?" I was fascinated. I thought that from Skagway north everything would be gold dust or nuggets.

Mr Plow ignored me. "He can have my wages."

"How so?" Ben asked.

"How so? Because one of his goons meets me on payday, that's how so. He takes my wages from me."

Mr Plow bent across the table again, toward Lou and Ben. "But I'll tell you one thing. That bastard ain't going to get one penny of my grubstake money. That's for the trip to Dawson."

He made that pronouncement sound final.

"When are you leaving for Dawson, Mr Plow?" Lou said.

Mr Plow's ears were twitching again. "I can't leave. Damn it. Goddamn the luck. Soapy's buzzards are watching me. I can't set foot outside this town. I can't quit my job. I can't go into the bush to take a piss."

A couple of strangers came in at the front door and Mr Plow put his face down into his large bowl of vegetable soup. "Are they looking this way?" he asked me.

I gave my head just the slightest shake to assure him.

Lou had moved into mere disdain. "They seem to want something to eat. This is a restaurant."

That's the way it was in Skagway. Mr Plow was running scared. He was working as a labourer on a wharf that was under construction, pretending that he was trying to save up enough money so he could pay his debt to Soapy Smith. But all the time he was planning to make a run for it, just as soon as everything looked safe. He had a scheme.

It was the price of the meal that made Ben and Lou ask about the costs of transportation from Skagway north. Mr Plow explained that the cost of packing an outfit up over the White Pass Trail could be double and then some the cost of buying an outfit in Seattle or San Francisco or Victoria. Five hundred dollars, he explained, right at the moment, might get three people and their outfit over the pass, if they were dead lucky, no sudden blizzards, no washouts from rain, no horses with broken legs.

"Shit and be damned," Ben said. He didn't ordinarily swear, but he'd been listening to Lou.

10

By noon the next day Ben was pushing a wheelbarrow. Mr Plow knew people and got him the job. Lou, by suppertime, was working for Mrs Keeler in the kitchen of the Ole Nugget Saloon. She claimed she was cooking. Any time I looked into the kitchen she was washing dishes.

The job that Mr Plow had for me involved hanging around The Nugget and pretending I was just loafing. When he described it I thought I was about to get the best job on earth.

Mr Plow hired me at four bits a day to keep an eye on his

outfit, which was stored in his room. He also gave me a wad of money, all that he had, to carry around in a canvas belt around my waist, under my shirt and trousers. It was enough money to pay off the debt to the Soapy Smith gang. Which was fine. Except that paying off the debt would have left Mr Plow flat broke and a long ways from the Klondike. He explained that to me. Then he made me promise not to tell, even if someone threatened to break both my arms.

Ben and Lou arranged for me to move my rented mattress into Mr Plow's so-called room, which was in what they called the old hotel and a bit the worse for wear. I didn't mind that, though. I had the room to myself most of the time, because Mr Plow didn't dare sleep there. He explained that if he did the goons might guess that his outfit was his and come and steal it. By steal it he meant they might take it by brute force in payment of debts incurred.

By that arrangement Ben and Lou had a room to themselves, which pleased them a lot, even though they claimed to miss my company at night.

I wasn't scared in my room alone. I had Mr Plow's grubstake to examine. It was a real grubstake, not a bunch of whiskey kegs. It had everything in it. Enough to keep a person alive for a year in the Klondike. Assuming you got there. It was like having your own grocery store. Mr Plow said that if I touched anything he'd cut my hands off, but even so it was nice to go through the boxes and sacks. I told him I was taking inventory. It was something like working in a pawnshop. I checked this and counted that. Ten flour sacks at 50 pounds each. Dry salt pork 60 pounds. Rice 50 pounds. Dried beef 20 pounds. Sugar 50 pounds. It went on like that. Dried fruits. Tea. Coffee. Rolled oats. Baking powder. Soda. Yeast cakes. Pepper. Mustard.

Ginger. Tar soap. Castile soap. Evaporated potatoes. Evaporated onions. Beef extract. On and on. And that was only the food. That didn't include the frying pan and the kettle and the bucket and the cutlery and the knives. And the cooking equipment didn't include the gold pan and the axes and the shovels and the pickaxes and the scales for weighing gold.

It crossed my mind that we might travel with Mr Plow. If we ever got together enough money to pay a packer. I thought I might talk to Mr Plow about it. He certainly was well equipped.

Ben and Lou claimed they were making pretty good money, and saving as much as they could. That meant that in something like six months we'd be able to afford the trip over the White Pass Trail.

There were so many dead horses in the high gulches that people had taken to calling the whole pass the Dead Horse Trail. Lemon Ed said it was a crime, people who didn't know one end of a horse from another using the poor dumb animals as pack animals on a trail that would make a mountain goat stumble and slide. He said that on one trip he counted four hundred dead horses in the course of an hour's travel on a corduroy road over muskeg and then up into a gulch. He also said he saw a packhorse walk out over a cliff and commit suicide.

The packers were robbing people blind. Lemon Ed almost said as much himself. One night at supper I heard him say to Ben and Lou, "I hate to tell you this, folks, but the packers' prices are going up just about as fast as your stack of silver coins."

Ben just laughed when he heard that. He sounded so comfortable with his terrible situation that it made me totally miserable.

He was in no hurry at all to set out. After supper that same night I asked him why he didn't sell some of his whiskey so we could be on our way.

"First of all," he said, "my whole damned stock of whiskey wouldn't raise enough cash to get us over Dead Horse Pass. Second of all, if Soapy Smith found out I was peddling booze in this territory, I'd be taken out into the fjord for a midnight swim with the seals."

"I guess we'll be here forever," I ventured.

Ben was becoming defensive. "Looks that way, doesn't it?" Then he softened up a little. "We'll get there, Peek. You mark my words."

He gave me a grin. "Like they say — time flies when you're having fun."

That got to be our little joke. I said it to him when he went out in the morning to push his wheelbarrow. The November mornings were close to pitch black and close to ice cold. I made the same joke to Lou when she came back from the kitchen too tired to take off her shoes.

Then I'd sit down on the floor in front of her and take off her shoes and rub the soles of her feet and massage her toes. She'd watch me while I did that, and sometimes she'd say, "Ben says I have beautiful legs."

I guess you can be scared and happy at the same time. The weather was coming down on us fast. Each morning seemed colder than the one the day before. Each nightfall seemed to come earlier than the one of the previous short day. It spread out into the streets and alleys like a bruise, the dark. The loafers who hung around the hotel looked more and more like shadows. Mean shadows. Shadows that stumbled over mine. I got to feeling a lot less happy and quite a bit more scared.

Not so for Ben and Lou though. They turned their small space on the floor in their room in The Nugget into a cozy den of sorts. I was the only one counting days. Or counting objects, for that matter. They were holed up as if to stay for the winter. They pretended to be busy, trying to lighten up their load so they could afford a packer. Take the long underwear. Leave the mining pan. Take the tea billy. Leave Ben's old tweed winter coat. Buy a parka. Leave the shovel. Leave the kerosene lantern. Get more candles.

The trouble was, most of the weight was in the eleven oaken kegs. Ben wondered about that.

"Maybe just the three of us," he said. He sounded as if we were planning a picnic for the afternoon.

"Leave the whiskey?" Lou said.

"That's what I'm thinking."

"You numbskull, Ben."

Then she reached across the heap of blankets there on the mattress on the floor and tousled his hair and he toppled over, putting his head on her lap.

11

After thirty-four days of squeezing nickels and talking big money with packers, and my having to decide whether to stand on my left leg or my right while looking in two directions at once, we had to act in a matter of minutes. It was poor Mr Plow who caused us to jump to it fast.

He and Ben were both pushing wheelbarrows. But they didn't actually see each other until the end of the day.

On the evening of that thirty-fourth day it was cold and miserable down by the water. That was nothing new. The wind filled your eyes with tears. It was bone-chilling cold.

It was an early December kind of nightfall. The harbour was full of boats newly arrived from the south, and the bars on the waterfront were full of stampeders trying to persuade themselves that the weather outside wasn't as bad as it appeared to be.

What made that usual December night special was the fact that it was payday. Mr Plow suggested to Ben that they stop for a drink.

"You have to make your payment," Ben said.

"Let's have a whiskey first. At least I'll get that much out of my pay."

"Have you thought about this?" Ben said.

"All day. Let's go."

That's how Mr Plow was.

"I have a matter to settle," he added. "I'd sort of like to have a witness, in case push comes to shove."

It was snowing again. The two men walked on along the crowded waterfront street. It was hardly a street, really. It was a mishmash and tangle of tents and shacks that called themselves bars and bars that called themselves hotels. There were outfitters set up to do their buying and selling right on the wharf, and packers backing their wagons almost right off its edge and down into the black water. You could hardly find room to walk.

The man who stopped Mr Plow was one of Mr Smith's henchmen, a gentleman who introduced himself as Gob.

"I know you," Mr Plow said. "You were at the table when I was foolish enough to sit into a faro game with a bunch of strangers. At least they were strangers to me."

"Mr Plow," Gob said, "you had been drinking pretty heavily at the time. We were told you had been drinking pretty heavily for forty-eight hours."

Mr Plow acknowledged that possibility. "I had come into contact with some excellent whiskey. It was not the whiskey, however, that marked the cards we were playing with. I'm sure you know that."

"Your accusations at the time, Mr Plow, did not stand up to Mr Jefferson Randolph Smith's interrogation."

Mr Plow demurred again. "Interrogation. Well. Let us try to be precise. My accusations did not stand up to the sight of the business end of Soapy Smith's revolver."

"You did sign the IOU, Mr Plow."

"I did indeed. Signing seemed preferable to being dead. Even if I came to recognize I was being cheated by the worst kinds of thieves and scoundrels."

Gob drew from a pocket the IOU and showed it to Mr Plow as if he might not remember having signed it.

"I have been asked by Mr Smith to collect the weekly interest on this IOU that bears your signature."

Mr Plow, instead of looking at the IOU, looked around at the darkness and the men hurrying along the wharf.

"Step over here, Gob. I don't like to flash money in public."

Gob and Mr Plow stepped off the wooden deck of the wharf and into a muddy alley that was hardly as wide as the wagon ruts filled with water and ice. Ben, reluctantly, tagged along.

"I would like to make a new arrangement, Gob."

Gob himself looked at the IOU.

Mr Plow took off his right glove and fidgeted with the flap on the right-hand pocket of his once elegant racoon coat. It was then Ben had the horrible realization that Mr Plow might be carrying a gun.

"Mr Plow," Gob said, "my employer calculates that you are paying the interest on your debt each week, which is commendable. But you haven't touched the principal. I might add that prior to arriving in Skagway I was something of an accountant."

"Then you will understand," Mr Plow said, "why I would like to renegotiate the arrangement. I would be happy to agree to send you further payments from Dawson City. Bullion or dust as you prefer."

Gob leaned toward Mr Plow. "There is a rumour abroad in this town, Mr Plow, that says you acquired your excess of whiskey by a process that might not endure the scrutiny of the law."

Mr Plow became indignant. "Would you like to know how I got the whiskey? Would you care to hear the story from the horse's mouth?"

Ben thought he was a goner. He thought he was about to be found out as a smuggler and a bootlegger with eleven kegs of whiskey in his possession, a cheat who dared enter into the domain of Soapy Smith and his thugs without paying head tax or extortion money.

"I am not interested in your explanations," Gob said. "I am interested in the rumour that says you are wealthy enough to travel with a considerable grubstake."

"Gob, listen. I was grubstaked to go to the Klondike, not to work here in Skagway at the building of a wharf for everyone else who is going to the Klondike. I was grubstaked by my brother, who had to mortgage his house to send me on this mission."

Gob, very slowly, very deliberately, unbuttoned his leather coat. He drew a six-shooter from what had been a concealed holster.

"Mr Plow, my friend, I am here to collect the money you were paid for this past week's work. That will constitute the interest on your debt. Then I would like to discuss the principal. Right here and now."

"Fair enough, Gob, fair enough."

Mr Plow reached into his right overcoat pocket as if about to make the usual weekly payment. Instead, he drew from his pocket a revolver.

The two men might have been, casually, in a friendly fashion, comparing weapons.

"As I say," Mr Plow said, "I would prefer that you consider an arrangement that will allow me to proceed to the Klondike. I have connections in the Klondike. I expect to flourish."

Gob looked into the barrel of his own gun as if by that curious gesture he might check and see if indeed Mr Plow did have connections. "You see," he said, "I could shoot you right now."

"Quite right," Mr Plow said, "But at your own peril. The chances are I would shoot you at exactly the same time."

"Is that a threat, Mr Plow?"

"It might be construed as a threat, yes."

It was dark enough there in the snow and mud, Ben felt, that both men might shoot and miss. He chose to believe in that possibility. And yet he chose also to step up and stand protectively beside Mr Plow.

"Okay, boys," Ben said. "Let's calm down a little. Let's talk this over."

Gob, as if persuaded by Ben, put down his gun.

It was then that the shot rang out.

It was not Mr Plow who fired the shot.

Ben was standing slightly ahead of and to the left of Mr Plow. He saw Mr Plow's hat rise dimly into the air as if lifted by a gust of wind. Then, a split second later, he realized that he was wearing some of the warm contents of Mr Plow's head on his own face.

Mr Plow was lying dead in the mud.

Gob bent down to frisk the clothing of the corpse.

Ben stooped down at the same time. He reached down and fished out of the water in a wagon rut the revolver that had been Mr Plow's. He wanted to make certain it was not used against his dead companion in any so-called court of law that Soapy Smith and his friends might convene.

Stepping away from the scene of the death, turning a corner in the snow and the dark, Ben ran smack into Soapy Smith and another man.

It was Ben who was holding a gun, not either Soapy Smith or his accomplice.

Soapy Smith was famous for his courtesy and charm. "Now don't tell me, sir," he said, "that I see before me a smoking gun."

What Ben remembered hearing next was the sound of heavy breathing, which turned out to be his own. Then he heard the pounding of boots on the wooden deck of the wharf, a pounding that sounded like footsteps following after him. The sound of the boots, like the sound of heavy breathing, was of his own making. He bumped against men running toward the place where they thought the sound of the gunshot had come from. Someone slammed into him and knocked him down and he leapt to his feet and went on running.

There were no street lights in Skagway. Ben ran through mud and through the haze of falling snow and into black darkness. The shadows of men on the walls of tents that were lit from inside seemed to lurch out and try to grab him and he ran harder. He found a wooden sidewalk.

Lou and I were in the kitchen doing dishes when Ben fell in from the night, breathless and speechless. To his own apparent surprise, he was carrying a gun. It was a single-action Colt .45, the famous Peacemaker. A beauty. I'd only seen two in all my time in the pawnshop.

Without being able to catch his breath and speak, Ben opened the revolver, spilled out the cartridges, lifted each cartridge to show us that the gun had not been fired.

He was gasping for air.

"What on earth," Lou said, "are you doing with that thing, Ben?"

Ben was gasping in the unbearably hot room. "I didn't shoot him."

"Calm down, Ben," Lou said.

"This is his gun," Ben told her.

"It isn't a horseshoe. I can see that."

"This is Mr Plow's revolver."

"And where," Lou said, "is the insufferable Mr Plow?"

"We're leaving," Ben said.

Lou sometimes became irked at Ben's inability to hear a simple question. "I asked you about Mr Plow."

"They shot him. Soapy Smith or somebody."

"Soapy Smith or somebody?"

Then the horror of what Ben was trying to say hit Lou. She recoiled from the gun and from Ben.

"Mr Plow was shot? Is he dead?"

She put down her dishtowel and took hold of me as if to protect me from I don't know what.

"Ouch," I said. She was holding me too tight.

Ben buried the Peacemaker in one of his pockets. He gave a gutteral croak that suggested he was pleased at the way he had made the revolver disappear.

I was wearing the canvas belt that had in it all of Mr Plow's money, the money that he had intended would take him and his outfit over the mountains and into Klondike country.

Lou was trying to get Ben to talk. He was gasping and gagging and explaining what had happened and Lou was asking him to please explain. There was no one else in the kitchen. Or there wasn't until a waitress stuck her head in.

"What's all the ruckus?" she said.

"Swallowed a wishbone," I said. "Ben did. He's okay."

"I need some clean plates," the waitress said.

I was cool as a cucumber. I took a stack of plates into the eating area and set maybe twenty places for the waitress. She was so busy she didn't have time to say thank you.

Not only did I have Mr Plow's money. I was in charge of his grubstake as well. His brother in Cincinnati had grubstaked the whole venture. You might say that Mr Plow hadn't actually owned the outfit or the money he was going to use to transport the outfit.

I was about to explain all that to Lou and Ben. I was back in the kitchen, trying to get a chance to say something. Ben was talking. He couldn't stop talking. Just before I opened my mouth I noticed a couple of black hairs pasted to his left cheek. His own hair was sort of greyish. He had gone a bit grey very young, the grey mixed in with the brown.

Lou was wiping plates one by one, carefully, instead of

working with a stack the way she usually did. Somehow she had gone on wiping dishes while she talked and while she listened to Ben and while I was out of the room.

"Ben —" I said. I couldn't stand it. I was going to tell him about the money and the outfit. But instead of that I said, "You should go wash your face, Ben."

He looked puzzled.

Then Lou noticed what I was noticing. "Good God, Ben."

The hairs looked silly, plastered to Ben's wet face. Then I noticed that some of the grey wasn't Ben's own grey hair. It was Mr Plow's brains.

It's a crazy thing. I wondered about Mr Plow's black leather hat. It was the only thing he ever made an effort to keep clean.

Lou put down the plate that she was drying. Out of force of habit she looked to make sure it was clean as well as dry. She used the wet dishtowel to wipe the brains off Ben's cheek.

12

It was less than half an hour from the time Mr Plow was shot dead until Ben went to find Lemon Ed. We had to clear out. While Ben was gone Lou and I got busy packing. While we packed we talked. I discussed Mr Plow's nest egg. I suggested that in a way we were doing him a favour, saving his money and his grubstake from Soapy Smith and a gang of hoodlums.

Ben and Lemon Ed showed up within an hour. They showed up with a packtrain.

Lemon Ed explained that Soapy and his men controlled the White Pass Trail, and there was a good chance they were looking for Ben with the intention of blaming him for the third murder of the week in Skagway.

"The smart thing to do," Lemon Ed suggested, "would be to travel as fast as we can around the head of the fjord and get to the port of Dyea and the beginning of the Chilkoot Trail."

"That'll cost more money?" Lou said.

"I'm afraid so, ma'am."

Lou looked at Ben and then at me. She looked at the lump of the canvas wallet under my shirt. Then she whispered something to Ben. She was afraid for his life.

"Like I say, ma'am," Lemon Ed went on, "Ben told me about his situation. I'm just saying that Soapy will have his men out watching at the entrance to the White Pass. He likes to show his support for law and order."

Ben became indignant. "But Soapy Smith or his henchman did the shooting."

Lemon Ed was fidgeting. "This happens, here in Skagway."

We didn't dare wait until morning.

"Let's go," Ben said

"Travelling at night will be expensive," Lemon Ed explained again.

Ben smacked his right hind pocket as if the money was there instead of under my shirt.

Word of the so-called gunfight had spread. Mrs Keeler, when she collected for the rooms, including Mr Plow's, told us with no hesitation that Mr Plow had started everything by pulling a gun on Gob. Otherwise, she said, she'd be ashamed to collect what was due on his room and meals. But, she added, the murderer ought to be shot too.

We rode into the darkness two hours and fifty minutes after Mr Plow came to his destiny. Or at least Lemon Ed and Lou rode, at the head of our column of eight packhorses. Ben and I walked behind.

All of a sudden we had enough picks and axes and shovels and and hammers and gold pans to go into the grubstaking business ourselves. We had everything I'd counted and a lot more that I hadn't got around to looking at closely. We had two cases of candles, with 120 candles in each case. We had mosquito netting. We had a three-gallon keg of sauerkraut and forty pounds of dried macaroni and a whole case of two-pound cans of corned beef and no end of canned tomatoes and cabbage. You name it. We had enough food to last the three of us through the worst kind of winter.

We set out from Skagway as if we were going to attempt the White Pass route. The Dead Horse Trail, as it was known. Packers reported there were now three thousand dead horses along the trail, and more dying every hour. We told people in the hotel we were going to go as far as the first stretch of corduroy road and wait there for an early start.

We set out as we said we would. The sky had cleared. We could pretty much see our way by moonlight, because of the glare off the snow and ice. We were moving along a well-travelled track when Lemon Ed gave a low whistle that Ben and I could hear, over the creaking, clacking sounds of the packtrain. At that signal we took a turn onto a path that led into dark forest.

It was six miles, by Lemon Ed's route, from that turn-off to Dyea. Die. Eee. Like two words. The other boomtown, there at the head of the fjord. The jumping-off place for the Chilkoot Trail.

We were travelling through rain forest. Some of the time we couldn't see the moon at all. Sometimes we couldn't see our own feet. Lemon Ed and Lou, on their saddle horses, set a pretty good pace in spite of everything. Ben and I kicked our share of horse turds. A couple of times we heard wolves howling up a chorus that sounded to me like they were saying grace before a meal.

Lemon Ed knew how to make a dollar. We would have paid him just about anything for a glimpse of Dyea. What kept us going forward was the thought that Soapy Smith and his hooligans might be hot on our trail. Ben walked behind the horses and I walked behind Ben, listening to every tree that creaked in the forest, every slide and plop of snow from a branch.

Dyea was mile zero of the Chilkoot Trail. I was never so happy in my life to see a light in a window.

Lemon Ed called a halt to our travels. Ben and I walked up past the pack animals.

"I'll be go to hell." Lemon Ed was talking and pointing.

We didn't know how we were supposed to respond.

"A hotel," he said.

There was, obviously enough, a hotel at the side of the path. A square, two-storey building. We could see that much, for all the darkness around us. We could smell the new lumber.

"Weren't there two weeks ago," Lemon Ed said.

That's how it was, around Dyea, there at the foot of the Chilkoot Trail. Buildings seemed to grow in the dark. There was an actual, genuine hotel right there ahead of us, a clapboard hotel that must have iron beds in the rooms, and blankets and sheets on the beds.

"Wish we had the money to stay," Lemon Ed said. You could hear a terrible nostalgia in his voice. He'd been sleeping for so long with a tarp wrapped around him and his head on a saddle that he'd almost forgotten how to wake up in the morning without being damp and stiff.

I was dead tired. I was absolutely dead tired. Walking there in that black forest made me think not only of Soapy Smith, but of grizzlies too. And there weren't any salmon around to keep them happy. I knew they were supposed to be holed up for the winter, but one or two might be out looking for a late-night snack. I felt like standing Lemon Ed a treat.

"We do have the money," I said.

Lou wasn't too impressed with my extravagance. But she was just as anxious as I was, I suspect. There in the space they called a lobby — the hotel was so new it didn't have a name — I turned the canvas wallet over to her to let her make the arrangements.

I had a room of my own. There was a washstand in one corner and a hatrack in another and a wardrobe in between where I actually hung up my clothes, after I actually undressed. I used the pitcher and the basin of water to take a bath. I slept in a bed, not beginning to guess how long it would be before I slept in another one. The bed had on it a real straw mattress and enough woolen blankets to smother me alive.

But, trust my luck, Lemon Ed had us up before the sun. He was in a hurry. All he had to do was deliver us to Sheep Camp, thirteen miles away, and then turn around and ride back. But he was in a big hurry nevertheless. He told us again that he could made a pot of money without ever laying eyes on the Klondike. It was like he was giving us one last chance. We were having a breakfast of bacon and fried eggs and potatoes and sausages and just a sliver of ham and stacks of toast, white and rye, and strawberry jam and maple syrup and coffee.

"Let's hit it," Lou said, before I could ask for one final egg and one last piece of toast and jam.

She and Ben and I reloaded the packhorses. Lemon Ed looked after the feed. He said that the whole trick to running packhorses in the mountains was keeping the horses fed. Half the cheechakos on the trail didn't know there was no food for a horse anywhere in the forest or on the mountain slopes and boulders up ahead.

It was thirty-three miles from Dyea to Lake Bennett and the headwaters of the Yukon River. A mere thirty-three miles. We were paying Lemon Ed an arm and a leg to take us to Mile 13.

Horses couldn't travel any farther than Sheep Camp, because after that the boulders and the slopes won out. After that we'd be on our own, Lemon Ed explained twice over, to make sure we understood. A lot of people didn't understand, he said. They were dumbfounded when they got to Sheep Camp and looked straight up at the cliffs and snow and the glacier ahead of them. No horse alive, he explained, could go up the Chilkoot Pass to the summit of the Coastal Range. Either you hired Chilkat packers there in Sheep Camp or you carried the goods yourself.

Lemon Ed made quite a show of being a forthright man. "Might be the death of you, up there," he said. "Unless Soapy Smith gets you first."

He gave Ben a slap on the back. Ben had bought himself a new blue twill parka and couldn't see too well when he had the hood up. Lou was wearing Ben's green mackinaw. I was wearing an excellent parka I found in Mr Plow's outfit.

"Just joking," Lemon Ed said. "We fooled those crooks." He reached over and tugged my cap down over my eyes. "Say goodbye to the world, young feller."

He made his giddyup sound to the horses.

And there for the first five miles I didn't quite know what all the fuss was about. We stopped for tea in a tent that called itself Finnegan's Point Cafe. The going was almost easy. Or at least it was easy for those of us using packhorses. Everywhere along the trail were the people who couldn't afford pack animals. They had on their own backs wooden boxes and canvas sacks and shovels and pans. But more than that. They were carrying everything from raw lumber to mattresses to framed pictures. One man was carrying a rocking chair. Another had on his back what looked like the front half of a boat. Two women were carrying between them a portable stove with a sign on it that said COFFEE AND DOUGHNUTS 25 CENTS.

We were all of us moving slowly, steadily, gradually going uphill on a trail that was crowded with people who seemed to feel they were setting out on a picnic.

The canyon was a surprise. To climb through the canyon we had to step over or around something like forty dead horses. Lemon Ed launched into one of his sermons again. Damned fool owners didn't realize that bigger horses were worse, not better, on the trail. But some of the horses weren't really big, they were just swollen from being dead.

We got to Canyon City in four hours, with all our freight. There were maybe a thousand people already there. I was all for pitching our tent and having a look around.

Perhaps Ben was still worried about Soapy Smith. "You getting tired?" he asked me.

"No way," I said. "I'm just getting limbered up."

"Are you game to go on?"

I answered by starting to walk on straight ahead.

The next four miles were a pretty steep climb. On top of that we decided to step up our pace. Lemon Ed said that if we hurried we could beat the next snow squall to Sheep Camp. It was the last camping place before you left the forest and headed up onto the treeless mountain slopes with their boulders and ice.

The snow squall won the race by about ten minutes. Lemon Ed called a halt just as we entered into that tent city. We needed to give the horses a rest. I wasn't all that sorry to give my legs a rest as well.

Lemon Ed was explaining that right now two thousand people were doing what we were about to do. They were engaged in the climb. They were taking their outfits up the pass one back-breaking load at a time. Lemon Ed was explaining all that when Ben interrupted to ask what was happening just twenty yards off the trail, in front of one of the first tents.

Nine or ten men were going at another man with long-handled shovels and chunks of firewood. The surrounded man cowered inside his parka. He tried to break out of the circle and was knocked back into the middle with blows from a shovel. Those blows made him fall down. Two men went into the circle and kicked him, forcing him back onto his feet.

No one was saying a word, not even the man in the middle of the circle. All you could hear was the thudding of wallops onto the man's muffled body.

Ben wanted to rush in and stop the fight.

"I wouldn't do that if I was you," Lemon Ed said.

"How so?" I said. I could hardly bear to look. "Why are they doing that?"

"A grub snatcher," Lemon Ed said. He said it without emotion. The matter was settled by his three words.

I had to ask him three or four times before he would say anything else.

He hooked his right leg around the horn of his saddle so he could sit and watch in comfort. "You noticed, Peek. Most of these people can't afford packhorses the way you can."

"I noticed that."

"You carry seventy pounds of your supplies up this far, all of it on your aching back, right?"

"Right," I said.

"You bring a load this far. Then you go back for another load."

"Right," I said again. Though the very thought made my legs ache.

"Think of your own grubstake, Peek. You and Ben and Lou. Just to bring it up this far. Seventy pounds at a time. Then walk back. Then seventy pounds more. Then walk back. Then another seventy pounds."

"It would be plain hell," I said.

"And when you get here — one time you get here — you just make it — and the food you cached the time before is missing."

I heard him. The snow was falling lightly.

"You get here, Peek. You're starving hungry and so dead tired you can hardly walk." Lemon Ed let his body slump where he sat there in his saddle. "And your food is all gone. Every last ounce of it. Gone. Plumb stolen."

Lemon Ed paused. He was letting his message sink in.

"Even a camp of a couple thousand people ain't all that big. Sometimes you don't find what you're missing. Sometimes you do."

I just waited.

"What you see there is one of the times they found it," Lemon Ed said.

Someone hit the grub snatcher on the head with a stick of wood. He staggered to his feet so he could be hit again. Some of his teeth went flying and he fell down once more. I saw that his face was mashed and bloody. When he refused to get up another time someone walked closer and gave him a swift kick in the balls to get him back onto his feet, but he couldn't make it.

Lemon Ed gave me a stern look that was intended to show his disapproval. "Shouldn't kick a man when he's down." He clicked his tongue and the horses started.

That tent city looked like a railroad accident without a railroad track. Lemon Ed led us through the noise and the scattered heaps of supplies and the tangle of tents going up or coming down or just standing there. It looked as if the whole camp had been pitched in the dark of night during a blizzard. I began to recognize that the trail we were following had been turned into a kind of crooked and unpredictable main street. A kind of uncertain main drag. People had set up stores and cafes and saloons and what they advertised as hotels. The Palace Hotel and Saloon. Mush-On Saloon. Frisco Store. Seattle Hotel. But all those places were big wall tents, with their signs half buried in snow.

Lemon Ed said that we might want a place that was a distance away from the racket, and after a while he found one. It was almost a private place, in between two scraggly spruce trees. While he was lifting a sack off one of the packhorses, he casually remarked that the sack of flour seemed to gurgle when he lifted it.

Lou saw what was coming.

Let's face it, in a way we were grub snatchers. The sack that Lemon Ed was testing for sound was ours. It was Ben's. But most of everything else wasn't. We were downright grub snatchers, even if the man we robbed was stone dead when we robbed him. Lemon Ed had a hunch that came close to the truth, even if he was holding the wrong sack.

We pitched Mr Plow's beautiful new white canvas tent right there in the snow about two blocks off main street. The tent had never been unfolded. It was called a six-man tent. Mr Plow had planned to travel in style, you had to give him that.

We were all delaying, mostly because we felt there was more to be said. More to be settled. Lemon Ed, just by saying nothing, had all of us holding our breaths. Lou was trying to deal with the crisis by coming up with a scheme. Ben was trying to figure out what the crisis was.

Lou and Ben got their wires crossed. Lou took me into the tent while the men were outside in the snow tying extra lines to the two spruce. She had Mr Plow's wallet but somehow was pretending that the money in it was mine. She suggested that maybe we should offer Lemon Ed a bonus. She didn't actually call it a bonus. She called it hush money. "Something to seal his lips," she said.

We were whispering like that to each other inside the tent, Lou and I, and meanwhile Lemon Ed and Ben were talking outside.

"I hate Soapy Smith," Lemon Ed said. "I hate the ground he walks on. Or rides on. I hate his contempt for everything that is decent and good."

We could hear Lemon Ed speaking. Lou was counting bills into stacks in the snow that was supposed to be our new floor.

Lemon Ed went on again. "And the only thing I hate worse is a grub snatcher. If we let grub snatchers get off scot-free, then we might as well shut down this trail. You get what I mean?"

Ben responded by saying that, yes, he understood. Then out of nowhere he added, "There's a drop or two of something that will cure what ails you in that sack you just took off that horse."

It was as if he'd fired a starting gun. Lou swept up the stacks of bills and headed for the tent flaps. The trouble was, her fingers were stiff from the cold. We weren't yet used to the mountain cold. She dropped the bills. I scrambled to scoop them into one fist.

We got out of the tent just in time to hear Ben tell Lemon Ed, in a hearty voice, that maybe he would like to throw that one sack back onto the sawbuck packsaddle on one of the pack-horses, on the condition, of course, that he, Lemon Ed, would forget where and how he accidentally came into possession of such precious medicine.

"Mum is the word," Lemon Ed grunted, giving the sack a hoist.

Lou grabbed at my shoulder. But it was too late to stop me. By then I was handing Lemon Ed full payment for the little bit of packing he'd done, and a bonus as well.

Lemon Ed was gone. He was gone into the light snow with his horses and a keg of whiskey and a pocketful of loose bills.

Transportation fees had a way of going up on the Chilkoot Trail. More than one stampeder, halfway over the Chilkoot, discovered that the price per pound was different from what he'd understood a day earlier and lower down on the trail. Or he discovered that the estimated weight of his outfit had a way of increasing with altitude. I tried to explain all that to Lou, by way of suggesting we hadn't done badly at all, in spite of everything.

Lou was figuring again. "We have to arrive on the other side of this damned mountain with enough money to build or buy some kind of a boat."

While I did the arguing, and all in vain, Ben set up our new woodstove. It had never been used. Ben figured out how to assemble it, with the new tin pipes leading to an opening in the top of the tent.

We all worked together, finding some wood, stoking up a fire, cooking up a meal of corned beef and canned cabbage and canned tomatoes After that we felt better. Mr Plow knew how to live. I was finishing up a cupful of raisins when Ben said he would go walk along main street and make some inquiries.

He wanted to know what it would cost to have packers carry our outfit up to The Scales, at the base of Chilkoot Pass, and then up The Golden Stairs — the last and steepest part of the climb to The Summit.

That's when Lou counted our money again. It didn't take her long.

"Your friend Lemon Ed," she said, "left us with exactly one hundred and two dollars."

Ben had just had a good meal. "Not bad," he said. "Not bad. I only had one hundred even when I left Seattle. We've already made two dollars."

I managed to laugh, but Lou didn't.

13

What princely sum wouldn't have hired enough packers to carry our outfit to the bottom of The Golden Stairs, there in Chilkoot Pass, let alone to the top. To begin with, thanks to our good fortune, we had two outfits to move.

Lou had an idea. She got me to shovel every last flake of snow out of the tent. Then she got Ben to put down our tarps to make a dry floor.

Sheep Camp was crowded with stampeders who didn't have a warm, dry space to sleep in. It was cold up there, at night. Sheep Camp wasn't named after your common run of mutton and wool sheep. It was named after the mountain sheep that called the place home. They like rocks and slopes that are so mean and steep that even the toughest wolves can't get at them.

Lou went out along main street and in less than an hour she had rented sleeping space for the night to eight stampeders. We slept like spoons in a drawer.

But it wasn't so bad, having roomers with us there in our tent.

Each morning the roomers headed for a tent that called itself a restaurant, and then loaded their backs with freight. Each morning Lou and Ben and I fed ourselves and then loaded our backs with freight.

The professional packers were charging ten cents a pound just to guess what your outfit might weigh. We shouldered our packs each morning and walked the first four miles, climbing all the way, to the place called The Scales.

The Scales was the last stop at the base of Chilkoot Pass. There actually was a scales at The Scales. It was there the packers weighed their loads again and discovered they'd gone up in weight and in price per pound.

The last half mile of the climb, from The Scales to the top of the mountain range, was mostly straight up. Stampeders and packers had cut into the packed snow and the ice a flight of twelve hundred steps. The Golden Stairs, we called them.

Exhausted stampeders had cut little niches into the snow and ice at the side of the steps. White spaces about the size of a grave. You could step into one of those niches to rest. The catch was, it might take you four hours to find a gap where you could step back into the line of climbers. That's the way it was. From sunrise to dark. And day after day.

I never once stepped into one of those niches. Lou had to, more than once. Ben did, three times. I never once stepped out of my place in that godawful line of climbers. I figured that a dead man, given the determination of those stampeders, would be pushed to the top before anyone noticed he was dead.

We made a trip each day right from Sheep Camp to The Scales and up The Golden Stairs to The Summit. Sometimes just Ben and I went, when an overnighter woke up too weak or too sick to set out.

On our best days, the three of us together, we delivered two hundred pounds of goods to The Summit. We cached our provisions there at the white top of the world, leaving everything unguarded. We simply put up a long stick in the falling snow.

The good part was going back down.

It was a wild slide, going down Chilkoot Pass. Stampeders had made chutes down the mountainside and in a matter of minutes you went shooting down the slope it had cost you one or two or four or six hours to climb, depending on the snow and the wind. I loved that slide. Lou and Ben loved it too. Sometimes they hung on to each other and went sliding down out of control, screaming with exhilaration like two little kids. Sometimes Lou had tears in her eyes from all the flying snow and her laughing. She had a sudden, unexpected laugh that set other people to laughing along with her.

After that slide we would trudge back to Sheep Camp to eat

and to fall into a deep sleep. We were so tired we could have slept in a den full of skunks. I say skunks because eleven people who haven't had time to wash, or to take off the clothes they wore all day, keep a tent more than warm. Even the mice gave up on us after a few of days. They were suffocating.

Each time we got to The Summit we found our goods still there, buried deeper in snow, surrounded by more and more outfits. Once in a while a stack of supplies disappeared and you knew someone had got all his outfit up to The Summit and had struck out for whatever waited beyond.

It was the blizzards, not the packing itself, that caused our delay. Some days it was storming so hard there in Sheep Camp that we couldn't stick our noses out of the tent.

It was the blizzards that made people take chances. You stood a good chance of getting lost trying to walk from your tent to a place where you could unbutton your fly. The funny thing was, Ben stopped worrying about his whiskey. We simply hauled the sacks and boxes up to The Summit and stacked them in the falling snow then turned around and slid down the chute.

We had just a couple of more trips to make when I got sick. Nothing serious. Just a fever. Other people were getting things like cholera and scurvy. I had trouble breathing. Ben and Lou decided to stay with me in the tent instead of leaving me by myself. They asked the last of our overnighters to move out, and we had the tent all to ourselves.

Actually, the overnighters moved out on their own. I had the shits, along with my fever. I had the real thing. The pure, unadulterated shits. I was too weak to go outside. Ben made me a little one-holer bench that he set over a mining pan. It was very comfortable. At least until my asshole got so sore I thought it had caught fire.

One of Lou's mottos was, Starve a cold, feed a fever. For four days running, in addition to bread, beans and bacon, I was forced to down chicken soup and johnnycake and something called gruel. That was followed by a double dose of cod liver oil, which, by some amazing contradiction, was supposed to stop me from shitting myself blind. I claimed Lou was trying to kill me but she said no.

She went through camp and found two men who had been doctors until they became stampeders. She told them I had the total, catastrophic, carbolic shits. They claimed they were run off their feet. Tell me about it, Lou said. So they had a good laugh and then came and looked at me.

"Try putting a bung in him," one of them said. Perhaps he'd heard that Ben was a cooper.

The other one said, "We've got cholera, typhoid, meningitis, hepatitis, two kinds of pneumonia, ringworm, bedbugs and crabs in this camp." He seemed to be offering me a choice. Then he added, "We sent a guy back to Dyea yesterday. Chest pains. I hear he didn't get there."

It was the first one's turn again. I expected him to write out a prescription. Instead he announced, along with the fee for a house call, "The only medicine we have left is for distemper. In horses."

Those two guys were making a fortune.

Lou thanked them and made some more chicken soup. At least she said it was chicken. I hope it wasn't rabbit. I've never been fussy about rabbit. She scrounged up more cornmeal and made me enough johnnycake to see us through a famine. Ben rummaged around and came up with a firken of butter and a small keg of strawberry jam.

It was New Year's Eve the night I nearly died. I couldn't

breathe. Ben was for filling me up with whiskey and trying to sled me down to Dyea. I told him I liked the whiskey part of his remedy. Lou reminded both of us that every last drop of our whiskey was up at The Summit, along with any rags or soft paper that I might have made use of.

She fired up the stove until it was red hot. She had a little oven she could set on top of the stove. Despite the surplus of johnnycake, she made enough baking-soda biscuits to keep us for a week. Or it would have, except that around midnight, when I took a turn for the better, Ben got into her cache.

"Happy New Year," they said to me, Ben and Lou, the two of them smacking strawberry jam onto each other's cheeks while I groaned.

You could hear the gunfire from outside, men shooting off their revolvers and rifles and shotguns, joyously welcoming in the new year.

1898

14

Thanks to my being under the weather, we weren't on the trail out of Sheep Camp when the avalanche hit. We were snug in our tent, the three of us, that afternoon. It was two days after the first blizzard of the new year.

We heard the avalanche. But hearing avalanches was nothing especially new, not there. You heard the crack and the rumble, and that was that. There were glaciers and mountain slopes all around us. And too much fresh snow on both.

It was hardly twenty minutes after we heard the rumbling sound that men came down the trail and into Sheep Camp, hollering and shouting. High above us, the avalanche had hit the trail. Dead on and fast. The first stampeders back into camp called for help and picked up shovels and cut long poles and turned around and went back up the trail.

Ben rushed out to help with the search.

Lou and I were alone with each other that day. I guess I expected it would be pretty great. I mean, I was still recuperating, and Lou said she'd look after me. She opened a tin of pickled hogs' feet that she knew I'd like. Ben had never been absent in quite that way. I expected things would be different.

Different all right. Lou hardly spoke a word all day, except to ask if I thought the avalanche danger was over, or would one be followed by another, or could a man ride on top of an avalanche, sort of like he was swimming? How was I to know? She didn't talk much, but every time we heard the faraway roar of another cliff or slope of snow breaking loose, she clenched her eyes shut.

As it turned out, she had nothing to worry about. Ben showed up a little after dark, which came early up there inside that pass. He didn't say much. He wasn't all that hungry. He just said we wouldn't be packing next day, he would help again with the search for survivors.

By noon of the next day the searchers and three or four sled-dogs had found forty-one bodies. It was hard to do a head count in a town where almost the whole population was on the move, but obviously a lot more people were missing. Friends reported on friends and inquired about strangers they had seen setting out or loading packs and getting ready to set out on the day of the avalanche. There were bodies, people said, like the bodies of dead horses, that wouldn't be found until spring.

The Mounted Police from the Canadian side of the border had come down from The Summit to assist in the search. It was the Mounties who sent word through Sheep Camp, asking people to come and help identify the bodies that had been found and to try to guess who was missing. I was feeling too miserable to go with Lou, so she went by herself. She knew quite a few people in camp because so many had rented a space on our tent floor for a night or two or even for a week.

About two hours later Lou came back to our tent. She looked pale and exhausted.

"I want you to come with me."

I didn't feel like going anywhere, because of my high fever. I was running quite a fever again. "I don't want to go out, Lou. And you look like you should climb right into bed instead of climbing around in the snow."

"Just get up and into your clothes."

It was the voice she used to indicate that I had no choice in the matter. I was sleeping in most of my clothes to begin with. I crawled out of my blankets and put on my moccasins and my parka and my mitts, stubbornly taking my time. Lou was ignoring my delay tactics. She was hurrying me along, but she wasn't hurrying herself. She just plain sat still in our easy chair, made of lengths of poplar and covered with a tarp.

"Are we in a hurry or what?" I said.

"I suppose not. I suppose it doesn't matter."

That didn't sound at all like Lou. I stopped in the doorway of the tent. "What's eating you?"

"Nothing."

"Something's eating you."

"Nothing's eating me. Just keep quiet."

I didn't want to pester her. I started out through the doorframe of our tent as if I was tired of waiting for her. We'd built a frame inside the tent, because of the weight and the force of the blizzards. That's when she said, "They found your father."

I stood outside the tent for a long time, listening to the cold and the stillness. Everything was so still that it hurt my ears. Even the dogs had stopped barking, it seemed to me.

Lou came out of the tent and carefully closed the shiplap door and the tent flaps behind her. She was carrying one of our quilts, the one that had on it, in pieces of cloth that had once been yellow, the shape of a five-dollar gold piece. At least that's what it always looked like to me. Lou claimed it was some kind of a picture of the sun.

While we were slogging our way through the snow, up toward the mountain slope above us, I managed finally to get my breath.

"You never mentioned my having a father."

"I told you. Everybody has a father."

"That's not what I mean."

"What do you mean then?"

The climb was making us gasp in the cold air. If you aren't careful in that kind of icy cold air you can get frostburn in your lungs.

"I mean — you never told me about *my* father."

"There's nothing to tell you."

"You said you found him."

"He was in the avalanche. *They* found him."

I waited for a while, watching my moccasins' progress through the loose, dry snow.

"Is he alive?"

"Of course not, stupid. If he's dead he's not alive."

"You didn't say he was dead. You said they found him."

"Well he's dead. Okay?"

I was running quite a fever. Lou had to walk slowly so I could keep up. She was impatient. It was a pretty stiff climb, up to the open space on the upper boundary of Sheep Camp. We could see where a crowd had gathered. We saw two rescuers coming down the trail from above the crowd. It looked at first as if they were pulling a sled.

They had laid out the bodies in crooked rows as they brought them in. Each body had been frozen into its own unique posture or shape, up there on the slope, after the avalanche did its thing. Some of the men looked as if they were wrestling with figures you couldn't see. They were folded up like dough in a bakery or twisted up like pretzels. Their faces were full of different looks, some still trying to scream, some trying to call out for help. Some were in pain, you could see. You could almost feel the pain. Some were peaceful-looking.

My father was of average height and about Lou's age. Or maybe a little older. Maybe it was his face that made him look older. He needed a shave. He had stringy brown hair. I saw where I got mine. I studied him for quite a while. Or at least it felt like quite a while. I could see where I got my strong nose and my rather bold ears. I didn't feel like crying, partly because his mouth seemed to invite me to smile. He looked as if he was preparing to have his picture taken and was only for the moment holding still. His arms were frozen in the shape of an embrace. One of his mitts was missing. I wanted to take off one of my own and pull it over his naked hand, there in that fierce weather.

The searchers had found my father still hanging on to his partner's knees. They had managed to separate the two men without breaking any of their limbs. The searchers had gone through my father's pockets. All they found, along with a bill addressed to him at a street number in Vancouver, was a pack of playing cards. There were pictures of naked women on the backs of the cards, so no one had kept them for us. Someone explained this to Lou and me. Then someone added that he seemed to have filled his pants when the avalanche hit, but everything was frozen.

Lou didn't speak for a long time. When she finally said something she said, "I never knew the man to change clothes."

I gave her a look. It was then I noticed that she and I were holding hands. We had our mitts on.

Then she added, "I only knew him for four months." She pulled her hand out of the mitt I was hanging onto and showed me four fingers. "Two months of courtship. Two months of marriage."

"Where did he go?" I asked.

"I never found out."

It was then I gave him a little poke with the toe of my right moccasin, as if he might speak up and do some answering. I stubbed my toe. The whole entire body was frozen stiff as a board. That's when I said to Lou, without looking away from the frozen corpse, "I guess you aren't a married woman any more."

"Just say goodbye, Peek."

"How am I supposed to say goodbye to someone I never met?"

"You've got his stupid way of asking questions." She was bending forward, to study his face. She was talking to me. I wanted to hop up and down a little, to keep warm, but I thought it would look bad.

"Why don't you say goodbye? At least you knew him."

She started to speak and then thought better of it.

"You must have loved him," I said.

"You said that before."

"When did I say that before?"

She was looking straight at the corpse. You could tell, she wanted a little sign. Just any little signal. "The trouble was, I didn't know him."

"You married him."

People all around us were bending close to look at bodies, straightening up, then bending again, as if that little change of distance made a difference. Grown men were crying.

"I was pregnant after our second date. I could tell."

I had to keep at her. "That doesn't mean you didn't love him."

"Okay," she said. "It doesn't. Clever boy."

An old guy sitting in the snow right next to the third corpse up from us was bawling his head off. That fellow's crying got to me. I started to get bleary-eyed myself.

Stone-faced Lou noticed my tears. "You feeling sick?"

"I feel fine," I said.

"You look sick."

We just stood there.

"Why did you haul me up here if I look sick?"

I could tell that Lou was getting tired of my nattering. She had a way of letting me know. She had a way of looking as if she was gathering up her energy so she could jump into action.

"Peek," she said. "I wanted you to see something. That's why I — as you put it — *hauled* you up here."

"I see that you loved him."

The old guy crying his head off sounded as if he was going to seize up and die himself. It was getting to me.

"Yes, Peek. I loved him. Does that make you feel any better?"

"It does," I said.

"Don't get sassy," she said. She pointed at the corpse. "And that's what love does for you."

I didn't quite follow, but I pretended I did. "Say your good-bye," I said.

"I tried that a long time ago. How many times do I have to do it?"

Some of the bodies were to be loaded immediately onto packhorses that were heading back to Dyea. The police wanted us to hurry. One of them explained to Lou that she should take charge of her husband's belongings. He assumed that Lou and J Badger were travelling together.

Lou didn't let on that she hadn't been travelling with the corpse there in front of us, nor with his dead partner who lay right next to him, flat out and stiff, as if making a joke. When she wouldn't claim anything from either of the two men, the Mountie just said, "Probably stolen by now anyhow."

Somebody located a bible and offered to conduct a quick service over the bodies that were being wrapped in whatever anyone could find. Lou had brought along the quilt for J. We tried to wrap up the corpse but didn't have much luck, because of the arms.

The packhorses were accustomed to going back down to Dyea light, so to speak. They didn't like being loaded again. The horse that was to carry J's body bucked him off. Finally we took advantage of the frozen arms and made them embrace the packsaddle and threw the quilt over J's back and somebody tied a diamond hitch.

"He never was much of a rider," Lou said.

The men gathered around had a good laugh.

The fellow who claimed to be reading from the bible went on reading through all this. He was long-winded as well as a liar. I noticed he was reading — taking care to mumble as much as possible — from a copy of *The Farmer's Almanac*. He read some weather forecasts, which were good. That pleased everyone.

Lou, waiting for the service to end and more corpses to be loaded onto horses, looked down over the camp. She gave me a nudge a couple of times. You could see stampeders robbing the tents of the men who had died in the avalanche. The professional packers wouldn't do that. They were always careful never to carry too little or too much.

The first packtrain started out with the first fifteen corpses, each in the posture it had assumed in the slide. Some of the corpses weren't covered at all. I mean with blankets or tarps. For that matter, some of them had been deprived of their parkas and boots. One was seated backwards, as if he was studying the horse's rear end. One man was seated upright wearing nothing but his winter underwear and an old pair of boots that no one wanted. One fellow looked as if he was flapping his arms and trying to fly. Another seemed to be examining his own private parts for crab lice, which weren't too hard to find in that camp.

I recognized the corpse of a man I had slid down the chute with, returning from The Summit after a hard climb. We'd waved and shouted and actually clung to each other all the way down. I almost said hello. I went and patted the horse that was carrying him.

Ben was somewhere up on the slope, looking for more bodies, or even for a survivor or two. Fever or not, I had to stay there with Lou and wait. Someone had built a fire near the remaining corpses, so we were able to keep half warm.

Finally Ben and two other men appeared high up on the trail. We could see they were empty-handed.

"Poor Ben," Lou said. "More bad luck."

She told me to stay by the fire and wait. My eyes were watering a lot, partly because of my fever, so she thought I should try to keep warm. She went up the trail to meet Ben. And to give him the news, I expect. About J Badger.

Ben looked exhausted when he came to where I was waiting by the fire. Lou told him it would soon be too dark for anyone to go back up the slope to continue digging and searching, so he agreed to call it a day.

We weren't halfway back to our own tent when Lou said, "You aren't going up there tomorrow, Ben."

"We know of four missing stampeders for sure. They might still be alive."

"Either," Lou said, "we're out of here by tomorrow morning, or you can get me a straitjacket."

That took me by surprise. She seemed so calm.

Ben walked on for a while. I was behind him. I saw him start to put an arm around Lou. Then he hesitated. Sometimes Lou didn't like to be touched by anyone.

I heard Ben say, "I'm sorry."

"It's okay," she said. "I mean, you know. I'm sorry. It's okay."

That's the way we talked to each other, sometimes. One of us would say something and the other person would sort of repeat it.

"Are you warm enough?" Lou called back to me.

"I'm warm enough," I said.

It was fairly dark by the time we got to our tent. I lit a couple of Mr Plow's candles, and then I set about stoking up the fire. Ben and Lou were sitting side by side on a bench that Ben had put together. They were half touching each other. I opened a can of corned beef and a can of cabbage. I knew that was always a favourite meal for both of them.

15

We all three of us fell into a deep sleep and slept for something like twelve hours. I felt a good deal better the next morning. My fever was gone. We ate a big breakfast of bacon and sourdough pancakes and the usual strawberry jam, and then I finished off the pan of johnnycake that Lou had made the previous morning.

We took down our tent. We made up three packs. We gave what food we couldn't carry to a couple in a neighbouring tent that had a baby girl. She was the only baby in the whole camp.

We set out toward The Scales one last time.

There was no stopping us. We went through the avalanche area without hardly looking to left or right. Stampeders had reopened the trail in a matter of hours after the slide. I did notice three men poking at the snow with long poles. Someone said they were still looking for a partner who had disappeared.

Without so much as a breather, we took our places in line. I was carrying the stove and a few odds and ends. Lou was carrying some bedding. Ben had the tent. We couldn't stop, once we got into that line. After a while I tried climbing with my eyes shut, then open, then shut. J Badger, I thought to myself. I wondered what the J stood for? I was afraid to ask Lou for fear she didn't know. I wondered if he knew he had a grown son somewhere in the world. I wondered if maybe he found out Lou was pregnant and realized he couldn't support his wife and family and ran away. We met people in the pawnshop, fairly often, who were in a similar fix. Maybe he'd heard that I was on my way to the Klondike and had set out himself, hoping he might catch up with me. I wondered about that. But Lou was up ahead of me and I didn't want her to waste her breath on any more of my silly questions. What you heard mostly in that line was the sound of men puffing and coughing and spitting. And blowing their noses with the thumb of a mitten up against one side of the nose. And farting. And swearing.

Lou was incredible. She used a walking stick. She led the

way with me in the middle and Ben behind. Sometimes we were pushing or pulling each other, sometimes we were just giving support or balance.

I didn't know until then that a body could hurt that badly and still go on. My fever was completely gone, and in its place I had a bag of nails wedged in behind each eyeball. It hurt to breathe. My nostrils felt numb. I could feel them not having any feeling.

The steps we were climbing were chiselled into solid ice. Twelve hundred steps, with snow heaped as high as our shoulders on either side. Not that I hadn't been up them a few times already. But this time the ache was different. I felt dizzy. I tried to keep my balance by counting. I wasn't trying to get anywhere, I was simply counting steps. With every step I felt that I was raising up every ounce of my pack and every ounce of my body out of a place that was deeper than a grave. It wasn't a dark place. There was too much light for that. It was something else.

Sometimes I saw urine stains. Once or twice I saw blood, right down there where my moccasins gripped the ice. I was up to 599, counting, when my mind just said to hell with it, leave me alone, why bother?

It seemed it was hours later, days later, when Lou turned around to me and smiled through the frost on the yellow scarf she had wrapped over her hat and under her chin. She didn't say a word. She was breathing hard, with her mouth open. But she managed to give me a complete smile.

When we fell out of line and stopped, there at The Summit on our last trip up, I was almost angry to see that not a single item of our possessions had disappeared. I kicked my way down into the snow. Everything that we had packed up to the top of that pass was still there. Every last ounce of food. Every keg of whiskey. Every shovel and every tarp and every kettle and frying pan. I looked at all the stuff, and I wanted to be absolutely free of earthly possessions.

The wind was howling, up at Chilkoot Summit. One of the Mounties who had been down in Sheep Camp to look after bodies recognized Lou. He was huddled inside a buffalo coat and a matching cap. He motioned for her and me to proceed directly ahead without going into the little shack that looked as if it might blow away if two Mounties didn't sit inside to hold it down.

It looked as if we had enough food and equipment to see us through a year inside or on top of or under a glacier. Ben went into the shack to deal with Customs and to write our names on the list of arrivals. He had just finished that chore and rejoined us when a Mountie came out of the shack to call him back in.

"There goes our whiskey," Lou whispered to me. "Shit. How did they know? After all the goddamned work that we did."

I could hardly hear her, for the wind.

She and I spent a long ten minutes, freezing to death, waiting to find out if Ben was going to be deprived of all our belongings or sent directly to jail or both. When he came back out of the headquarters shack he pushed his parka hood off his head and his hair tried to fly away. He was wearing a sheepish but delighted grin.

Lou and I were huddled on the lee side of our huge stack of supplies, where the wind wouldn't suffocate us by taking our breath away.

"A message," Ben said, shaping his mouth against the wind. He had got a bit warm in the police headquarters, and now he was colder than ever. His whole body gave a shiver. He pulled the hood of his parka back up.

Lou was unwilling to believe her ears. "You got a *message? Here?*"

She had a look of plain shock on her frosted, stiff face.

"A message. You better believe it."

"I suppose it's something about J Badger. Even now, he's going to haunt me."

I couldn't tell if Lou was being serious. I was so cold my mind could only be literal. I thought maybe the Mounties had the corpse itself, there in the Customs shack. Someone had found it and was returning it to its rightful owner.

Ben shook his head. "It's been here six weeks."

"*What* has?" I said.

I thought of how my father looked. Frozen. Hanging on for dear life to a packhorse's back. I thought of Lemon Ed. The packtrain carrying all those corpses was his. He knew a good thing when he saw it. That guy could turn ice into money.

"Listen to this," Ben said.

He tried to fish the sheet of paper out of his pocket without taking off a mitt. Then he gave up and pulled the mitt off his right hand with his mittened left hand and quickly dug into a pocket.

"Dear Benjamin Redd,'"

"Get on with it, Ben."

Ben was, you might say, savouring his moment of recognition. "It's from a woman named Gussie Meadows. She left it here six weeks ago, when she went through Customs. It's for me."

"What does it say?" I said.

Lou overrode me. "Who the hell is Gussie Meadows?"

"I have no idea."

"Then the message probably isn't for you."

"It's for me all right. Listen to this. 'Dangerous Dan is worried about my travelling alone. He says I should try to partner up with you.'"

"That's the message?" Lou said.

"That's it. That's the whole thing. Signed, 'Gussie Meadows. P.S., I expect I'll be in Dawson before you read this. Good luck.'"

That was the first time ever that Ben heard McGrew referred to as Dangerous Dan. He read the name again and chuckled. "Dan McGrew," he said, hardly able to contain himself, "must be known as Dangerous Dan up there in Dawson City." He shook his head. "Well I'll be danged."

"You'll be sorry," Lou said. She didn't quite have Ben's enthusiasm for the message. "All we need is some namby-pamby fancy doll of Dan McGrew's tagging along. We're in a hurry, Ben."

Ben wasn't listening. "The Mounties said she might still be at Lake Lindeman. The river froze early last fall. No boats have left there for nearly two months."

Lake Lindeman was hardly nine miles away.

"I suppose the Mounties told you what she looks like too," Lou said. I could tell she wasn't all that pleased. But Ben wasn't noticing.

"They did indeed. I didn't ask them, but they did. They said she's a looker. They said she was wearing enough gold to start a gold rush of her own."

"I take it she passed through here on a warmer day than this one." Lou surveyed our heap of worldly possessions and then looked at Ben and me and then looked at our outfit again.

"Maybe you could get her to pay the packers' bill on this stuff. I'm not going to carry another pound anywhere for anybody ever again. You boys hear me?"

16

You've seen those famous photographs of Chilkoot Pass. Nothing but snow. Except for a line of stampeders climbing from the bottom left corner of each photograph up toward the top right. A long thin line of humped figures, each small dark shape bending against the snow-covered mountain. Eric Hegg captured it all by being there and climbing with us. And by taking photographs which he later let us have at a considerable price.

Lou and Ben and I are in the line in the one I own. I keep it on the wall in the parlour, here in my cabin. If you look closely you can make out, just above the middle of the line, a place where two men have stepped into a niche in the snow beside The Golden Stairs. Lou and Ben and I are the three figures just below that small gap in the column. It was we who let those two exhausted men back into the long, slow misery of the climb.

What the photo doesn't show you is how it felt when we thought we'd made it to the top of the world and deserved a reward. Ben and Lou and I looked out over The Summit, into the interior. We peeked out over the divide. We looked out toward the headwaters of the Yukon River. And all we saw was more rock and more snow and more glaciers — when the wind and the blowing snow allowed us to see anything at all.

Ben and I heard what Lou said. The trouble was, every packer up there at The Summit had been contracted for. Not that Ben was to be delayed by that small hitch in his plans. We had to get to Lake Lindeman at once and find Gussie Meadows, and find out what was going on with Dangerous Dan and his Klondike investments.

It was Gussie Meadows who lured us on. Ben was full of guesses about why Dan was so eager to get his crowd together, there in Dawson.

"The message," Lou suggested, "doesn't say anything about getting a crowd together. Your friend Dan seems desperately intent on getting Gussie Meadows to Dawson. Full stop. That's it. That's what you ought to hear in your precious message. Your friend Dangerous Dan is worried about his precious Gussie. He wants you to deliver the goods."

Lou went on like that while Ben went on trying to forecast his own future fortune. I reread the message again myself. As far as I could tell, Gussie Meadows was on her way to Dawson and probably, right then, seated in a saloon, sipping champagne and eating smoked oysters.

Lou got tired of waiting for Ben to do something. She found two men who were comfortably asleep on dogsleds, with dogteams nearby, curled up in the blowing snow. She tiptoed past the dogs and woke both men by poking at the fur parka hoods that covered their heads.

They were trappers who were doing some packing.

Ben took over the negotiations. "We'll pay you spot cash," he said. "Name your price."

One of the trappers introduced himself. Boner, or something

like that. I believe he introduced us to his dogs as well. It was hard to hear him, there in the wind. His face was lost inside the fur hood of his fur parka. "What would we buy with more money?" he asked.

That one seemed to stump Ben. But not Lou. "Lots," she said.

Boner's partner introduced himself. I thought I heard him say his name was Lou.

Lou?" I said.

"Lou," he repeated. He spelled it out, "L-o-u-p." It wasn't the first time he'd done it, you could tell. He introduced himself again. But I still couldn't hear the *p* .

"It's French," Ben said. I don't know how he knew that. "Like wolf," he said. Ben knew that sort of thing.

Loop was the name I gave the man. He wasn't so much a man as a caribou parka hood that had a voice. "We've made more damned money in two months" Loop said, "than we know how to count. So what good does it do us?" He turned over as if to go back to sleep, under his blanket of snow.

The wind was going right clean through me. I wanted Ben to speak up and argue. Instead, he went to our cache and lifted a sack out of the snow.

"There's a keg of whiskey in this sack," he said. He was desperate to please Lou.

Boner and Loop seemed to respond. Or at least the wolverine trim on their parka hoods moved. Ben went on with the offer. He mentioned the quality and quantity of whiskey in one of his oak kegs.

Boner actually stood up off his dogsled. "If you're that damned fool determined to get to a dump like Lindeman, we'll take you."

"Only," Ben insisted, "if you let us pay you."

"It doesn't matter," Loop said, from where he was lying. But he sat up.

Ben stuck to his guns. "You have to let us pay you."

"It doesn't matter," Boner said. "We're headed that way."

Ben wouldn't take no for an answer. "I absolutely insist." Once again Lou and I were mystified by his logic.

"Just help us load the sleds," Boner said

Those two trappers, in one fast run, took us down the steep slope to Crater Lake and then on another few miles to Lake Lindeman. The trail was downhill and smooth all the way, with seven dogs to a sled, harnessed in a row Indian-style, and each dog good for three hundred pounds of freight. The big job was to hold the sleds back, not to get the dogs to pull. Ben and Lou and I could hardly keep up. We could have made the whole move ourselves, pulling by hand three of the abandoned sleds that were stacked up there at The Summit. More than one stampeder had stared in disbelief out toward the Yukon and turned around and gone back to Skagway.

Lake Lindeman looked like a mirage. Or a bad dream. White tents on white snow scattered every which way along the margin of a frozen blank reach of whiteness that must be a lake. There were something like four thousand people camped and getting ready for the ice to go out. Which might happen in four months.

It only took us twenty minutes to find out that Gussie Meadows wasn't in Lindeman City. "As far as I know," a man told us from under the boat he was building, "she's in Bennett. I've heard she's a crackerjack businesswoman."

Lou wasn't about to fooled by that. "I'll bet she's a *business-* woman."

The sleds were loaded and the dogs still fresh. It was my suggestion, not Ben's, that we head for Bennett. The lake was five miles north of where we were standing. The trappers agreed to deliver our outfit the rest of the way, if we didn't mind an overnight detour to their trapline. They had work to do.

"If it's free," Lou said, afraid that Ben would offer them another keg.

I could see they were doing us a favour because they enjoyed Lou's company, even if she was being snippy. "Spunk," Boner said, when I tried to apologize on her behalf. "I like spunk."

We travelled for an hour before we made camp. And we did it trapper-style. None of that sissy tent stuff for those guys. In no time they'd cut a few spruce branches and set up a lean-to. They built a fire that reflected its heat off the wall of branches. Then they set to work feeding their dogs. All fourteen of them. They let me help, and I tried to throw a chunk of fish to a hungry malamute without losing an arm.

Lou cooked up some of the frozen caribou that Loop chopped off a carcass he was carrying on his sled. He and Boner served Ben and Lou some of the whiskey they'd received as payment for the packing.

I asked those two trappers if they ever saw any bears in the country around us.

"I got two last fall," Boner said. "Prices the way they are now, it was hardly worth the trouble of skinning them."

But he saw I was interested. He went to his sled and came back with a bearskin. "Great thing for sleeping on. You curl up inside this, you'll sleep like somebody hit you on the head."

I held up the bearskin. "It must have been a big one."

Boner shook his head. "Pretty big, I guess. For a grizzly that young."

Ben and Lou and the trappers put down their tarps and blankets on some spruce branches on the snow, so close to the fire I thought they'd all be baked by morning. I went and spread out the bearskin near one of the sleds. I fell asleep curled up inside it, with a malamute on either side of me.

I don't know if I was awake all night or dreaming all night. I was inside the bearskin and I was warm, I know that much. And I was back in the pawnshop where I played as a kid, because Lou had to work and she didn't have anywhere to leave me. I twanged at guitars and crawled behind sofas and under tables, and I broke a few wineglasses and china cups and then caught holy hell and then was forgiven. I hammered away at pianos. I counted gold rings and gold watches, not ever guessing where all the damned gold came from. I hid in the racks of clothing left by people who pawned their Sunday clothes on Monday morning and redeemed them Saturday afternoon. It was the best school I ever attended. And just about the only one, as far as that goes.

Next morning I might have stayed right there in the bearskin — I had half a mind to steal it — except that my friends the malamutes decided to practise up on how to kill a bear. They damned near killed me by mistake.

We pushed out across a frozen creek bed that would take us to Lake Bennett. Loop and Boner stopped to check their cache and some of their traps. They found a lynx and two otters in their traps. They left their whiskey in the log cache, up high in some trees.

We were making good time when Loop spotted a pack of five wolves, out in the open on a frozen lake. He stopped his team. He offered me his Winchester. "Collect yourself a wolf hide. Pick off that leader before it gets to the bush."

I had to tell him I'd never fired a gun in my whole life.

"No time like the present to learn," he said.

"Lou wouldn't let me," I said.

That's when Loop said, from out of nowhere, "You're here to stay, a serious tenderfoot like you. You better start learning."

I was flabbergasted. "I'm here like everybody else. Get rich and get out."

Loop produced a belly laugh. "Want to bet on that?"

I liked Loop. I hadn't really taken to him at first, but I'd come to like him. He was more furs than anything else, trotting along behind his dogteam and sled. But he had me sized up. He had all of us sized up. He was telling me the truth. He saw inside me the way I saw inside Ben, back when, on the *Delta Queen*. I would never leave the Yukon.

Instead of letting on that I got the message I asked if I could try driving his dogteam the rest of the way to Lake Bennett, and he let me. Not that I did a whole lot of driving. I said "mush" in a commanding voice. The dogs just kept their noses to the trail and I followed along behind, running sometimes, sometimes riding on the ends of the sled's runners. But I was thinking all the while. I realized I was was going in and not ever coming out.

Bennett City was a tent camp of seven thousand people, with more arriving every day. The hundreds and more hundreds of tents were scattered along the frozen shore of the frozen and snow-covered lake. Each white tent had a black stovepipe, and each stovepipe was sending up a column of smoke.

"Too many people for my taste," Boner said. He was talking to Lou. He'd let her ride in his sled most of the trip. "We're going to have to dump you here."

The trick was to be as close to the shore as possible, even if it was hard to guess where that might be. All of those stampeders had one intention in life. They were intent on building boats.

What we heard first, when the dogs stopped running, was the sound of hammers. Then we saw, through the haze of smoke, hundreds and more hundred of hulls and frames and stacks of lumber that would become boats before breakup. We saw hundreds of men, hammering, sawing, carrying lumber, or just standing still while they stared out at the white lake and its frame of white mountains.

Men who had never been in a small boat, let alone built one, were trying to put together something that would float 560 miles downriver through floes and rapids and darkness and springtime flooding.

We found a camping space and started to unload the sleds. Just as we were finishing up a stampeder carrying some oakum and a mallet stopped by to say hello

"You're too far from the water." He indicated the frozen lake with a motion of his fur cap.

Ben indicated all the tents. There was no room for us.

"What kind of a boat you planning to build?" the stampeder wanted to know.

Lou spoke when Ben wouldn't. "That's up to Ben."

I could see Boner and Loop getting ready to flee. I had the feeling right then that I'd never really seen either man's face, inside its fur hood. Those two trappers couldn't stand what was going on. Loop said goodbye to Ben. Boner said goodbye to Lou and then without waiting for a reply gave his dogs a command. Loop still hadn't left. He put the thick arms of his fur parka around my shoulders. But he spoke to Lou instead of to me.

"This lad Peek has the makings of a sourdough. Kind of a warm streak in him. He's here to stay."

"Not on your life," Lou said. "He's going out when I go out."

17

I don't think it had really penetrated Ben's head until then that he was about to build a boat. He was a cooper, not a shipwright. He could have built a barrel that would float all the way down the Yukon system, past Dawson, across Alaska, all the way to the Bering Sea. A boat was a different matter.

"Whatever you need," the stampeder said, "Gussie Meadows will have it. She runs quite a place."

"Maybe," Lou said, appearing to address the stampeder but speaking to Ben and me, "we'll set up our tent before we run off to break into high society." She pointed around at the snow and then out toward the lake, with its four-foot covering of ice. "We'll have time."

That stampeder went hightailing for wherever it was he was headed.

"I could go find her place now," I dared to suggest.

Lou got hold of the hood of my twill parka from behind. "Just you mind your own business. And see if you can unfold that tent without filling it with snow this time."

They fell into a pretty heavy silence, Ben and Lou. Ben was obeying orders that Lou hadn't given. She was dying for a chance to speak her mind. Our tent bore the brunt of the irritations. By the time we admitted that we couldn't drive a tent peg with a sledge hammer into that frozen ground, Ben and I had run lines to the nearest but distant trees and under sacks and stacked boxes and boulders.

"It looks like we've invented a bear trap," I said.

Ben crawled into the tent and flopped down flat on a tarp. "Keeping up with those dogteams did me in. I'm too damned tired to do any visiting."

I guessed that he was making peace rather than describing any genuine exhaustion.

"Set up the stove, Peek," Lou said, "and I'll try to see if I can whip up some of those buckwheat pancakes that Ben likes."

Two days went by and still we hadn't got around to paying a visit to Gussie Meadows. That's when I took the law into my own hands. Maybe Lou didn't want to meet her and Ben didn't feel like it, for reasons beyond my understanding, but I had neither restriction to deal with. The two of them were fussing and arranging, creating such a comfortable place in our tent that I guessed they were planning to hibernate right there until spring.

On the morning of our third day there in Bennett City I said I was going for a walk. And I was. I walked along the frozen, snow-buried beach. I was looking for Gussie Meadows.

The sun was low and red in the southern sky, even in late morning. Every man in camp fancied himself a master boat builder. What a sight and what a sound. Some men were heating pitch on smoky fires. Some were whipsawing lumber out of logs. They couldn't dig saw pits in the frozen ground so they'd set up pole frames. Scaffolds. One man stood above the horizontal saw log, another underneath. They pushed and pulled, pushed and pulled at the whipsaw, turning the log into boat lumber. And swearing.

A man who was standing on a scaffold, trying to take a piss without falling off and breaking his neck, pointed his free hand when I called up a question. "That way. A great big tent with a wooden sign. You can't miss it."

And he was right. I walked past maybe two hundred tents, dodging around starving dogs and stacks of firewood. Someone had hung out laundry in that weather and the upside-down plaid shirts and denim pants were frozen stiff.

The big wooden sign had painted on it **GUSSIE MEADOWS HARDWARE**.

I guess I had listened too much to Lou. I expected the sign to be a front for a brothel. And there were lots of men going in and coming out. After a while I screwed up my courage. It was something like thirty below that morning. Standing still wasn't all that comfortable. I stepped into the gloom of that big tent. I stood still again, waiting for my eyes to adjust.

Gussie Meadows was wearing a flat-topped, wide-brimmed straw hat, as if we were in the middle of summer. She moved through the narrow aisles, brushing against axe handles and saw blades and kegs of nails and coils of rope. The customers were about as colourless as saw blades, in their wool pants and parkas and fur caps. Gussie had on a full woolen sweater that had in it, if you took a close look, all the colours of the rainbow. Her dark brown skirt was too long and full and wide for the narrow aisles. She had on white gloves. But the show stopper was her hat.

That's what men looked at. The hat. It made her taller than she already was, and she was taller than most of the men who slouched around in the store, pretending they were looking for something they couldn't remember while they were looking at her.

The one thing she wasn't wearing was gold. She didn't have any rings on her fingers. She wasn't wearing earrings. She didn't wear a necklace or a brooch on the front of her sweater.

I stood for a good while inside the door, letting the warm air soothe my lungs. The stove set there on a sheet of tin was close to being red.

Some of the customers were talking. Gussie this and Gussie that. "Gussie, have you got any six-inch nails?" "Gussie, have you got any quarter-inch line?" She didn't do the heavy work. She did some of the weighing. She gave orders. A couple of men with obviously sore backs were trying to jump to it every time she gave a command. She handled the stacks of paper money and the taller stacks of gold and silver coins.

And she talked. She talked to every customer. I saw that, and I hoped my turn was coming. At the same time, I wanted to run away. But my feet weighed eighty pounds each.

It was a hardware store all right. But it didn't just smell of rope and oakum and kegs of nails and rifles and oilskins and pitch and kerosene and linseed oil.

Gussie walked a customer to the door of the tent and held the framed door open while he went out carrying about a tonne of supplies. Then she turned to me.

"Well, young man? Don't tell me you're building a boat too."

The smell of roses made me dizzy.

"No ma'am," I said.

"You stampeding on your own? What is it you need?"

I wasn't looking at her. I was looking at her hat. I was tall even at that age, but I had to glance up at the hat as if avoiding her green eyes. She had a corsage of roses fastened to the hat's crown. I swear they were real roses. They smelled exactly real.

She turned to listen to another customer's request. She gave one of her stooped men an order and he tried to hop to it. The trouble was, with a bad back he wasn't moving very fast. Then she gave me a look that melted my knees.

"You looking for work?" she said.

I didn't quite know how to answer.

"Fine," she said. "Fine. Just take off your parka. Then I'll show you how to weigh and measure." She allowed me a hint of a laugh instead of a smile. "And how to lift. And fetch. And stack. And cut."

"I know all that," I said. "I worked in a store for years."

That's how it started. She didn't ask me where I'd worked or what I'd done. Her two helpers had been injured so badly they were almost useless. Besides that, anyone with two good legs and two good arms and a strong back was building a boat, not working in a hardware store.

I took off my parka and she told me to throw it into the room back of the main counter. That's how I got my first glimpse of her living quarters. She had partitioned off part of the huge tent by hanging up two large Oriental carpets. No cotton sheets on wires for her.

She put me to work, I'll tell you. It was strictly learn on the job, do or die. Get me four pounds of two-inch nails and three pounds of four-inch nails and eighty feet of the heaviest chain we have in stock. Try keeping that in your head while the smell of roses fills the air. I had to learn the prices of things. That sounds easy. Except that nothing was marked. Prices were flexible. Gussie had a way of sizing up a customer. She sent me to haul tools up to where she held court at the main counter. Three kinds of axe heads. Braces along with nine sizes of bits. Chisels. Hatchets and drawknives. Squares. Rules. Caulking irons. Adzes and planes. Gussie just started speaking her quick, beautiful words and before she was half finished I jumped.

She and I finally found time to have a bite to eat. I was sitting on the counter and she was putting slabs of cheddar onto two thick slices of brown bread, when who walked in but Ben and Lou.

"Where on earth have you been?" Lou said, as if I wasn't sitting all relaxed in front of her.

I introduced Ben and Lou. "Ben," I said, "this is Gussie Meadows. Lou, this is Gussie Meadows."

"Ben?" Gussie said. "Ben Redd?" She looked at Ben and then she looked at me and then she looked at Ben. It was as if something had clicked for her.

"The same," Ben said.

Gussie hardly gave Lou a glance. "Ben Redd?" She was studying Ben as if he was a piece of hardware that she didn't quite recognize. "I've been expecting you. Did you ever get my message?"

Ben didn't trust his voice. He nodded.

"Dan McGrew thinks the world of you."

"Thank you," Ben said.

"Don't thank me, thank him. He thinks you're it and then some. You're the cat's meow. You're the milk of human kindness itself."

Ben scratched the top of his left ear. Lou gave him his haircuts. You could tell. Lou herself was chewing just slightly at the left corner of her mouth.

Gussie went on talking while I lit into my sandwich. She gave Ben the answers before he had time to ask the questions. No, she wasn't disappointed that he hadn't showed up. Dangerous Dan was a schemer, he always had a scheme. Ben must know that, she said, from his experience back in Iowa. She knew about Ben and Dan and how they met in Iowa. She had arrived here herself six weeks earlier, she explained. Or was it two months ago? Time flies. And right off the bat she'd seen her chance. It was right here, right under her nose. In Bennett City, of all places. She traded her gold jewellery for a hardware business that was going broke. The man who owned it was lonesome for his wife back in Montreal. He was having nightmares. His business was going to pot. He couldn't stand it any more, he was going crazy and charging the wrong prices and forgetting to collect for items purchased. He took Gussie's gold in exchange for the business, tent and stock and all, and melted the gold down to make it look like nuggets and headed for home.

Gussie had a laugh that made me tingle all over. She went on talking and eating and Ben went on listening. She chewed her food with vigour. I could tell that Lou had taken an instant dislike to my new friend.

I leaned to where Lou was standing straight up and I whispered, asking, could she smell roses? She whispered back in a voice you could hear down on the lakeshore, "That smell isn't roses, dearie, it's the stink of ill-gotten gains."

Gussie had stories about Dan McGrew. "He's a fine man," she said, "until he gets his hands on a deck of cards."

"I sort of gathered that," Ben said.

"Once he sits down he's useless." She turned from Ben and gave Lou a wink. "Once he lies down he improves."

I noticed that Lou didn't crack a smile.

Gussie had large, glowing eyes about the colour of Ben's, now Lou's, green mackinaw. Lustrous is the word. She laughed that wicked laugh that permitted you to say anything you wanted to say.

I was surprised myself at what I said. "You must love him."

"Love?" Gussie pretended to make a face. Even then she was beautiful. "What would you know about love, Peek, you rascal?"

I kind of liked it when she called me rascal.

"I'll bet *he* loves you," I said. "Dangerous Dan," I added. I wasn't reminding her. I was trying out the word, dangerous.

Gussie looked serious for a moment. I suppose she was having a read at my mind before I had read it myself. "Does a man love a woman if he asks her to sail from Frisco to Skagway and then doesn't bother to wait in Skagway to meet her ship?" She offered me the portion of her sandwich that was still in her hand. She could see I was starving. "If a man prefers a gambling table to — well, to — " She glanced again at Lou.

"Love," I said, completing her thought.

Before Gussie could so much as nod her agreement Lou was whispering again in a loud voice. "You just mind your tongue or I'll send you back where you came from."

"He can't leave," Gussie said. She was all business again. "Not till quitting time. And that comes after dark here."

That's how Lou and Ben found out that I was employed.

There were customers waiting.

Gussie gave me a tap on the hand. "You run put out more of those woolen gloves. And we'll jack up the price by ten cents. It's turning colder."

18

Gussie Meadows made me feel special. There were thousands of men around for her to choose from. Thousands. Like ants. They were everywhere. I could have, without half trying, taken a dislike to the whole lot. There was a kind of smell to them. I don't mean a sweat and smoke and tar smell. I mean the smell of their wanting to get to Dawson City and the Klondike River and dig deep holes in the frozen gravel and muck.

I got back home a bit after sundown. Lou was waiting for me inside the tent flaps. I'd expected as much. But before she could open her mouth I asked how she liked my new boss.

"Boss?" she said. "I guess so. Let's call a spade a spade, young man. Dan McGrew's whore. That's who she is. Or at least one of them. Whore." She pronounced whore as who-er, with a strong emphasis on the first syllable.

Having won the first round, she added, "You have anything to eat?"

Obviously, she had seen me eating in Gussie Meadows' hardware store. I had prepared a defence that I didn't get to use. Gussie Meadows, I was going to say, is our ticket downriver and a passport into Dangerous Dan McGrew's inner circle of friends. I was ready, but Lou was busy opening a tin can with a hatchet.

I didn't have much of an appetite. Gussie's sandwich had filled me up. My head was swirling with axe handles and coils of line and fishing nets and rifles and saw files.

"Sauerkraut and canned pork hocks," Lou said, bending to our stove. "And just for you I've made some sourdough bread."

She was always catching me off guard like that. I was absolutely stuck for words.

Lou and Ben had, that afternoon, hung up a tarp so I could have a small bedroom of my own. It was just barely big enough for my spruce branches and my bedroll. But it was all mine.

Ben had hired out to work with a boat builder. Over supper he explained that he wasn't one of those stampeders who thought he could buy a hammer and saw and build a boat. He was going to work for a month for Old Van Slyke, there in camp, a boat builder from Holland who was building boats for sale to cheechakos. I was so exhausted I almost fell asleep while Ben was telling me all this. He and Lou guided me into my own little bedroom and pulled off my moccasins for me.

They had another surprise waiting. They covered me with the bearskin I'd slept on when we were with Boner and Loop.

"It's from me and Ben," Lou whispered, pulling the bearskin right up to my nose. "Your birthday present. We're sorry it's so late."

Lou patted me on the head. That was something she didn't often do. She had too much to worry about. After all that time, I'd received the perfect gift for my birthday. They'd traded a case of candles for it.

What dragged me out from under my bearskin next morning was the thought that I should rush off to work. That and the sounds of hammering and sawing. The forest around Bennett was turning into boats. Packers were bringing in lumber from Skagway and Dyea, but the prices they asked were sky high. I thought of the forest coming down, the bears being killed all around us in their dens.

I gulped down some mush and brown sugar and canned

milk and rushed off to the hardware store. Ben went down to the beach to become a boat builder. Lou got busy turning two oak kegs into a bedside table in the space that she and Ben had curtained off as their bedroom. She'd found a few yards of calico for their bedroom walls. Her next job was to go looking for scrap lumber so she could build wooden walls at least a yard high inside the whole tent, and then put down a wooden floor. She was handy that way.

A hardware store has its own kind of coziness, if you think about it. Especially if it's in a big tent that's more like a treasure house than a tent. A treasure trove. I got to work early, each morning. Gussie and I, sometimes, bumped into each other in the narrow aisles. We laughed about that. Or at least she'd laugh. And then I'd give a little laugh too. Sometimes she just plain stuck out her behind and held me wedged against a table or a shelf for a second or two.

One time when she was holding me like that, with her back to me, she said, "What's that, Peek? Why are you poking me like that?"

I was embarrassed half to death.

That night under my bearskin, I, you might say, fiddled while Rome burned. I hardly thought of myself at all. I buried my face in the deep grizzly fur and imagined being under Gussie's folded skirts, a kind of prisoner, entangled in all that warm, heavy cloth. I had to be careful not to make the slightest sound. That's how it was, there, with Lou and Ben maybe dozing off or maybe not. I tumbled and tossed myself into a deep sleep. I woke up sticking to my long johns.

The nights went by, and the days as well. Five days, eight days, ten days. I came to understand how Gussie had lost track. You left time-keeping to the sun, and the sun was nowhere to be seen. Except that one morning on my way to work I noticed that I could see a red rim on the horizon.

Ben persuaded Lou and me that he was catching on fast as a boat builder. One night he came in from work and announced he had quit his job with Old Van Slyke.

Lou had to think about that for a while. "You're sure that's wise, Ben?"

"Damn it all, I'm a cooper by trade, Lou."

"That's what worries me. I'm not sure I want to float down to Dawson City in a cask."

"In a tun," Ben said. "That would be big enough."

"A tun? What's a tun?" I asked

"It's a big cask. A great big cask." He raised a hand high over his head. "That's what Dan McGrew was hiding in when I met him."

"You never told me that, Ben." Lou had a way of believing that people harboured secrets.

"I was just remembering now. When I first talked to Dan McGrew. Back there on the Mississippi. He was hiding in a tun."

"Good heavens, Ben."

"I never saw him, you know."

"But you said you were friends."

"We are friends. I'm just saying, I've never laid eyes on the man."

Lou gave a cocked-head look that more or less questioned Ben's sanity.

"I went to the cooperage one morning. I was always the first person there. I went to work on a mash tun I was repairing for a distillery. I tapped at a hoop on the tun. Something inside tapped back."

I shivered visibly.

Ben allowed himself a grin. "'Hello,' I said. 'It's me,' a voice said. From inside the tun. 'What are you doing in there?' I said. I guess that was kind of a stupid question. 'I'm hiding,' the voice said."

"Kind of a stupid answer," Lou said.

"He asked me to save his life. Was that stupid?"

That was the way it started. The thing with Ben and Dan. The two men introduced themselves as if they were meeting at a party instead of at a potential lynching. Dan McGrew didn't keep any secrets. He was hiding from four men from the riverboat that was tied up not one hundred yards upstream. He was a riverboat gambler. There'd been a misunderstanding. He was on the run.

"So you saved his life?" Lou asked.

"I took him food and water. That's all I did. Three mornings, including that first one. I had to give him my lunch that first day. Then on the fourth morning I went to deliver more of same and the tun was empty."

"He was gone?" I asked.

"Peek," Lou said, "that's a stupid question."

"He could have been dead," I suggested

"He had up and made a run for it," Ben said, agreeing with Lou. "And a lucky thing. That tun was beginning to smell like something more than roses. Even there in the cooperage, with the shavings and fires, and all kinds of wood being cut or steamed."

"And seven lucky years later," Lou said, "he sends you a letter inviting you to come to the Klondike and get rich and you quit your job on a day's notice and head out. Great. Just great, Ben. Congratulations."

"What's wrong with that?" Ben was on the defensive. "He said I'd be rewarded for what I did. Now he's rolling in gold dust. He's returning the favour."

Lou tried her sarcasm again. "I guess you might say he's your ace in the hole."

Ben insisted on being serious. "He's my last chance, Lou."

"Ben, you're exaggerating."

"The trouble is, I'm not. I was just a cooper, making enough money to keep the wolf from the door. This damned depression. Even the distilleries are hurting." He laid his forearms together and touched his elbows. "I apprenticed when I was thirteen. My joints are starting to ache."

Even then Lou wouldn't relent. "Now you're a boat builder. If we can find the price of the supplies you'll need." She didn't stop there. "Or is this shipbuilding venture going to cost us what little whiskey we have left?"

I had to butt in. I had to go to Ben's rescue in some way. "I'm coining money," I said, "there in the hardware store." The bald truth was, I wanted to go on working in the hardware store forever. "Gussie just gave me a raise."

I liked saying her name.

"You didn't tell us that, Peek," Lou said.

"I was going to surprise you."

And I had planned to surprise them. Gussie had given me a two-dollar raise. That meant I was making twelve dollars a day. She said I was worth her other two employees put together. I hadn't told Ben and Lou. I was going to go waltzing into Dawson City with money of my own to invest with Dangerous Dan.

"Some hard cash would help," Lou said. She was doing figures in her head again. "Supplies cost a fortune here." She looked at Ben and then over at me where I was stretched out on a blanket beside the stove, trimming my nails with the family jackknife. "We could call it a loan," she said. "You're working very hard for your money, Peek. We'll pay you back when we get to Dawson."

That's how it came about that I was free, after the night of Ben's announcement that he would build his own boat, to stay with Gussie Meadows for supper on the following evening. As suppertime drew nearer I mentioned to Gussie that I'd probably have to go home and feed myself, since Lou and Ben were planning to stay at their boat-building by firelight, the way a lot of people did. I joked about it. Ben and Lou, I explained, for the next while would be acting as if they were putting together a China clipper. Which would leave me at loose ends.

Gussie said she had enough food on the stove for both of us. She was expecting a packtrain within an hour, and the packers wanted to unload the minute they arrived. She was paying packers big money to bring in her goods from Skagway. Big money. But it paid off hand over fist. She couldn't get supplies in fast enough for all the hundreds of men who fancied themselves to be shipwrights.

By the time we finished supper the packtrain still hadn't arrived. Sometimes the weather was so bad up at The Summit the packers couldn't see the trail. A transportation company had built an aerial tramway that carried freight overhead at The Golden Stairs. Those who had the money got their freight moved up to The Summit in a hurry. And Gussie had the money. But there was still the problem of getting down from The Summit by dogsled or by packtrain.

Gussie said we might as well sit there and wait. We were

in the big room at the back of the store proper, behind the wall of carpets. She had four candles burning. The scent of pure ambrosia made me dizzy. I couldn't tell if it came from the candles or from her clothes or from the bouquet of roses on her straw hat. She had forgotten to remove it while we ate.

We moved from the table and sat down side by side on her big couch. I tried to talk to her about money and gold. Gussie explained that she was making this investment so she would have more to invest in Dan McGrew's enterprises. I didn't feel any great affection for her dear Dan McGrew.

"When did you first meet him?" I asked. I was being polite, giving her a chance to talk about her precious Dan. She seemed to like that. I guess I was sort of giving myself a poke in the head at the same time. Getting Gussie to talk about that somehow hurt me.

"The first time?" she said. She gave me a hesitant look. Then she said, "I met Dan a week after he left Ben."

"That would be in San Francisco," I said. I knew that was what she called home.

"Correct."

I tried to keep quiet. Then I asked, "Where did you meet him? I mean, there in Frisco."

"In a place where I worked."

That made me think of Ben and Dan, meeting where Ben worked. "Imagine," I said, "going to work one day and giving a big tun a rap with your hammer and having the tun say, 'Hello.'"

"Dan told me," Gussie said.

"They never saw each other," I said. "They became friends. But they never laid eyes on each other."

"Maybe Ben was the lucky one."

Gussie sounded sad. Her sadness always made me speak out. "As I understand, his friends were hoping to see him."

"Friends?" Gussie said. "His card partners. They wanted to see him all right. Dead."

I gave a slow nod.

"They had told him they were going to string him up by his cheating thumbs from a beam that was being used to load the riverboat with more supplies."

I fell so quiet I could hear my heart beat. I could hear the candles burning. I couldn't remember if we'd had supper or if we were going to have supper. I mean, I felt that empty inside.

"He cheated on his own partners?" I said.

Gussie reached over and took my right hand.

We were sitting quite far apart, there on a couch at the back of the store. That's where she lived. She had the place fixed up like a real room, with a stove and a table and chairs. With a couch. With fancy carpets on the wooden floor. All it needed was some windows.

"You better let your father explain. He's the one who saved Dan McGrew."

I waited for a while, watching the candles and then looking over at Gussie's hat. I couldn't quite meet her eyes. Then I said, "Ben isn't my father. He and Lou are partners."

Gussie gave my hand a little squeeze. I thought of it as a sad squeeze. But it wasn't simply that. Sometimes a squeeze can be a question. Or even a bald statement. Squeezes are difficult.

I wanted to ask more about Dan McGrew.

"Are you and Dan partners?"

"Not exactly."

"What does that mean?"

"It means I'm here and he's there."

She was gently rubbing the back of my hand. While she did that I said something inadequate, the way people do when they care for each other. "Don't feel bad," I said.

When she didn't answer I wasn't quite sure what to do next. So, trust me, I went ahead and spoke. I must have got that from Lou.

"Why are you going to Dawson, if you and Dan aren't exactly partners?"

"I need money. He owns a big saloon. I'll sing in his saloon. I'll do some dancing."

"You must be a great singer."

"I'm a lousy singer."

"You have a great voice, Gussie."

"I have a great voice. And I couldn't carry a tune in a basket."

I was trying to imagine how she would sound if she sang. She was sitting still, except for her hand that was rubbing mine.

"You must be a great dancer."

"I can dance. Who can't?"

"I can't," I said.

She shrugged. "I can dress up like a dancer. Dan tells me that in Dawson City, if you dress like a dancer, then you're a dancer."

"You don't have to do that." I felt sorry for her. I heard a sorrow in her voice that I hadn't noticed before. She was always telling people how much something weighed or how much it cost. I hadn't really heard her talk about other matters.

"Have you ever been in love?" I asked. I desperately wanted her to answer. I wanted her to say yes so I could ask her to explain. But I also wanted her to say no, not really. Not until now.

"You're a funny man," she said.

That was strange, being called a man there on that couch with the candles giving out their warm, flickering, golden light. That tent wasn't exactly wind-proof. I liked being called a man. But nevertheless I leaned over and put my head on her lap, as if I was still a boy.

She was running her fingers through my hair when she said,

"Have you ever kissed a woman?"

"I've kissed Lou. I used to kiss her. When she was still my mother."

"That's a strange thing to say, Peek. You shouldn't say things like that."

She lifted up my head. She kissed me ever so lightly on the mouth. I tried to return the kiss.

"I like it when you kiss me," she said, "and don't know how. I like that. I really like that."

She pulled my head onto her lap. I buried my face in the warm cloth of her skirt. I suppose I was blushing or something. My face was hot.

She moved her skirt to make my head more comfortable. Then I moved the skirt as well, trying to find a place for my head, and I found my cheek pressing against her stockings. I could tell by the smoothness that they were silk. There was a sort of damp, slick, warm smoothness to the silk, and it smelled just the slightest bit like basil. Or cinnamon. Or a mixture of the two. Our apartment back in Seattle — if you could call it an apartment, Lou's and mine, two rooms — was full of herbs and spices. The spices of life if not the spice, Lou liked to say, when she was trying to make boiled potatoes taste like something else.

The light from the candles was bothering my eyes so I pulled the skirt up between my eyes and the light.

Gussie, playfully, pulled the skirt completely over my head. "Come now," she said. "Enough of our little sorrows."

Just like that, I was into darkness. The skirt was made of some kind of heavy material that was smooth and soft at the same time. I suppose it was very expensive wool. I was confused, turned topsy-turvy.

"No more silly questions from you," she said.

I could hear through the folds of the skirt and something that had to be a petticoat. There in her skirts I could smell oakum and canvas. I could smell the boxes of cartridges we had for sale and the oilskins that came folded into neat squares. I inhaled deeply.

After quite a long time she lifted the skirt off my head.

"I think I hear horses," she said. "The packers have arrived."

19

I woke up next morning with a pain in my groin that hurt so badly I thought I was getting sick. I mentioned to Lou that I had a terrible ache in the pit of my stomach. Trust Lou, her first and only response, after giving me a spoonful of cod liver oil, was to keep me at home in bed. I knew then I could never again ask her for advice.

I lay on my spruce boughs, wrapped in my bearskin, listening for her and Ben to decide to go to work. They were finding out how difficult it is to build a boat. There in our tent at night they drew plans on the rough table that Ben had put together from packing crates from the hardware store. Sitting side by side, they drafted various shapes of various possible boats. They were up and gone in the morning just as soon as there was enough light for the two of them to drive nails.

Except for that morning.

I lay as still as I could thinking of the smell of oakum and canvas and shotgun shells, in a desperate attempt not to think of Gussie. I was sort of in love, I guess. And I had no one I could tell. That was more fatal than any kiss. My testicles ached from my knees to my elbows. I did what I had to do. Three times in a row. Then I started to hurt from that.

I heard Ben and Lou tiptoe out of the tent to go work on their boat. I jumped out of bed and was gone.

For four long days it seemed that Gussie had no recollection whatsoever of our special time together. I began to think I might quit my job and tell Ben and Lou they'd have to pay for supplies on their own. And thanks to me, they were getting supplies and tools at wholesale prices.

On that fourth night, when I hung around at closing time to tell Gussie I was ready to quit, she asked me if I could possibly help out for an hour or two after we had a bite to eat.

We were tired after a long day's work. She brought out a bottle of red wine and asked if I'd like to have a drink with her before she made supper. I offered to help her pour the wine, but I guess she guessed that I didn't know how, so she did it herself. We clinked our glasses together without saying a word.

After we finished supper and most of the bottle of wine she

suggested we move to her couch. She hadn't, even during the meal, taken off her straw hat. I put down my glass on the table, next to the couch. I knelt in front of her and without speaking I put my head on her lap.

She began, softly, to speak of Dan McGrew. I didn't even have to ask.

"It was nighttime that frightened him. Being in the tun, unable to see. Unable so much as to read the face of his pocket watch. Listening for a watchman. Holding dead still for fear the slightest sound he made might give him away."

I raised my head. "He must have felt as if he'd climbed into his own coffin."

That made Gussie laugh. "I wish," she said. She touched my lips. I started to reach for my glass. She reached on my behalf and held the glass to my lips so I could take a sip without moving from where I was. Then she put the glass back on the table along with the dishes we hadn't bothered to move. She always put a dishpan on the table and washed them right there.

She took off her straw hat and placed it on the table beside what little remained of my wine. She was what I would call a strawberry blonde.

I put my head down into her lap again. She moved her skirt so that my face might touch the damp fullness of her skin. Her thighs. She was wearing silk stockings and garters. The buckle on one of the garters cut softly at my right cheek.

It was a few minutes before I realized that Gussie wasn't wearing bloomers. In all my imaginings of the opposite sex they had always been wearing bloomers, that because all my life I had seen Lou's row of bloomers on the line on washday.

"Dan left a message," Gussie said. She said that out of nowhere. "He's a great one for messages."

I held perfectly still. I could actually feel a drop of blood sliding down my right cheek.

"He printed with a piece of Ben's chalk on the outside of the tun. 'Ben Redd, you'll get your just reward.' That's what the message said. He had to make it vague, or he'd get Ben into trouble." Gussie held me closer. "Dan left then. He ran flat out for the train station. It wasn't yet so dark that he couldn't see. He told me about it. Every shadow was a man. He ran for his life. He was carrying so much money he couldn't run all that fast."

I put out my tongue. Gussie moved her thighs so that I might press closer. I liked the hard softness of her thighs, above her stockings. The almost bristly roughness of the first hairs. Gently with my fingers, I invited her close against my teeth. I thought I heard myself talking. Then I realized the voice I heard was Gussie's own, and she was surely whispering to me. I couldn't understand her, what with my head almost buried in layers of cloth. But I nodded my head. You might say, I nodded my face. I was burying my lips, my tongue, and Gussie lifted against my sweating face her own wet touch, her caress, and her voice went out of any sound I had ever heard or felt, ever, in my whole life. I was kissing her.

20

I realized that breakup would soon crack the very ice that held us together and Gussie and I would have to close the hardware store and join in the rush to float down the Yukon to Dawson City. And to Dan McGrew.

Springtime there in Bennett City was fierce because of the blinding light on the snow. The packers came down the trail from The Summit complaining of patches of mud. The snow thawed during the day, froze at night. The packers checked their horses' legs for gashes. They talked of the snowshoe hares and the ermine they'd seen, beginning to lose their white coats in the new light.

In a way it was the growing length of the days that led to my learning to fire a revolver.

Some slow afternoons, while most people were finishing up their boats, Gussie took me out behind the tent and taught me how to shoot. Most of our customers no longer needed a whole lot in the way of supplies. There were quiet times in the hardware store.

Gussie had a six-shooter. A Remington. Self-protection, she said. She put tin cans and empty bottles out on a boulder back of the store and taught me how to aim and fire. I had a real knack for it, she said.

"For what?" I said.

"Plinking," she said. "This kind of shooting. At tin cans and things. There's no better way to learn." She allowed me just a hint of one of those laughs of hers that could melt my limbs. "You have a good hand."

We squandered ammunition. She would load the gun and ask me to try and hit again the can that I had hit and sent bouncing. It wasn't always easy. When I missed she would correct my errors. The two-hand hold, she said, stop trying to be a cowboy. Hold the gun firmly. Not so tight, Peek. There. Don't fight it. Let the front sight move back and forth across the target. It all depends on your trigger squeeze.

We never talked about our connection during the day. All

day long everything was business. Even the target practice had more of an air of business about it than of pleasure. She was showing me, she said, how to build a space around myself. That's what she herself did, she explained. Never forget, she said. She told me to pretend I was taking aim at something evasive and moving and dangerous. Take a deep breath. Let some of it out. Keep your sights in focus, not the target. A kind of distance, she said. Think of it that way. And then the gentle squeeze. You should hardly know when the gun goes off.

Later, at night, especially after I'd hit smack on whatever it was she had told me to hit, she would whisper softly over my bowed head, "You have a deadly aim, Peek."

I was truly happy. I embraced the darkness that scared Dan McGrew half out of his wits. There in Bennett City I was the centre, the fortunate man, in Gussie Meadows' private life. In the winter dark I found a dark of my own, by going under her flared and folded skirts. I liked the whispers of her pleasure, the touch of her fingers on my ears, her slightest moan when she used two hands to pull my head into her slow, hard motion. She bruised my lips, my tongue, and I told Lou and Ben it was the dryness everywhere, the winter cold, that gave my mouth a swollen look.

It was the days that scared me. The days were getting longer at a terrifying rate. Each night seemed shorter by precious minutes than the night before. I could feel as much with every bone in my body and with my hands and my knees and even with my closed eyes.

The last arrived stampeders had to work on their boats for long hours, and as result Gussie and I kept the hardware store open later and later in the evening, just to help out. Some evenings I thought the dark would never set down its sweet lid on my head.

Sometimes she whispered above me, "Can you breathe?" And then she held me closer, as if daring me down into new dangers. We couldn't see each other's faces. Instead of trying to nod my head I took in and then let out a deep breath that she would surely feel against the insides of her thighs.

Ben and Lou were disappointed that I showed so little interest in the boat they were building, but I explained that I had to make money while I could. I didn't have the heart to tell them I wasn't making enough to pay for all the equipment and supplies they were asking for. They weren't too economical in their use of wood. They had to buy more saws and hammers. And draw knives and planes and chisels. Mr Plow, for all his thoroughness, had missed out on a few items.

Gussie wore different stockings and different garters every night. She was on her way to the Klondike not so much with mining pans and picks and shovels as she was with all those stockings and garters. Emerald and sapphire stockings. With garters to match. Spangled with stars. Black. Golden. I liked the way she pulled them taut, the garters, when she moved her long legs. Sometimes all of a sudden she closed her thighs. She seized me into stillness. Held me. I might have died in a surfeit of sweet, wet fire and heavy perfume.

Our whole tent city, there, beside the lake, was getting madly set to vanish. Our single purpose was to disappear. Twenty thousand people. We were all going to become rich. The men on the shore of the lake were completing their sailboats, their rafts, their barges, their dories, their canoes, their whaleboats, their kayaks, their dinghies, their scows. Some of the boats they were trying to build were not boats at all but floating debris. Organized debris. Some of the decks had on them shanties and clotheslines. And stacked firewood and beds of stones for fire and ash. High-up caches for meat and flour as if the bears and cougars and wolverines might follow those lunatic sailors right out onto the first open water.

Warm days and melting snow made the water begin to rise at the lake's boundary. The iced hadn't moved. It floated on the rising water as if content to stay there forever. But that rim of open water tempted some of the builders to launch their boats into a first test.

Ben and Lou called together a group of helpers for a launching bee and hauled and pushed their boat into the water. Our boat, I suppose I should say. But I was busy with Gussie and I couldn't be at the launch. They would christen the boat the *Trump,* Lou and Ben, and had painted the name in red letters on both sides of the unpainted prow. Lou poured an ounce of whiskey and some lake water into a cod liver oil bottle and, on her third try, smashed the bottle on the rough, wooden hull.

Everyone, she told me late that night, cheered. But the *Trump* wallowed as if Lou's drop of whiskey had got it drunk. The stern went up into the air as if resolved to become a sail.

21

We offered Old Van Slyke a whole keg of whiskey for three days' work. That was Lou's idea. He scratched a hole in his beard and then said he'd be more than happy to oblige. He took one look at the *Trump* where it wallowed among the floes, and then he began to recite a list of the items he would need. Items like more lumber and more pitch and more oakum and more nails and more canvas and more rope.

I was at the beach when Ben made the offer. I was there just to show my interest. But Ben put me to work. He told me what Old Van Slyke wanted, as if I hadn't been listening, and then he told me to go talk to Gussie.

Lou got in her two cents' worth. "I will not arrive in Dawson City in debt up to my *ass* to that Gussie Meadows."

Ben was studying his boots, checking the shoreline.

It was a quiet afternoon in the hardware store. Gussie was seated on a nail keg behind the counter nursing a cup of coffee and idly building stacks of five-dollar gold pieces. I poured myself a cup of coffee and sat down to watch. After a while I told her about the problem Ben and Lou were having with their boat.

"Castaways, you might call them," Gussie said. "What on earth will Ben do?"

"Old Van Slyke to the rescue." I caught myself starting to scratch my left ear. "Helping another cheechako. With the difference that this time he's getting a whole keg of whiskey for three days' effort."

Gussie looked up from her counting. "A whole *what*?"

I told her again. "Topnotch," I added. "The best."

She hadn't, until then, heard about Ben's stock of whiskey. Nor, for that matter, had anyone else in camp. We'd kept it out of sight and out of mind.

I got busy telling Gussie what supplies Old Van Slyke had ordered. She put her stacks of coins into a leather bag and dropped it onto the floor. Instead of telling me to start putting together the order, she went back into her private room.

I guess that in some way I was waiting for her to call to me to join her. The store was empty of customers. I busied myself, setting things straight on shelves. We were running low on supplies, mostly because Gussie knew the big demand was over and had stopped ordering in new stock.

She came to where I was stacking and restacking coils of rope.

"Has Ben got any more of that whiskey to get rid of?"

"He has some whiskey I believe."

I was sulking a little, I guess. I was also in between the devil and the deep blue sea.

"Maybe," Gussie said, "he could get rid of enough of it to settle his account with me. How big are those kegs of his?"

I tried to show her by holding up my hands.

"A gallon?" she said. "Two gallons?"

"We're talking three. Ben made the kegs himself. Oak kegs. And every one of them perfect."

Gussie, sometimes when she was counting, counted on her fingers. It was a pleasure to watch. Each finger sort of jumping at her own touch. She started over, touching her left thumb first, counting to five, then with that same left thumb touching her right thumb next, then counting to ten. She did that three times, moving her lips, but silently, and then she said, yes, she was ready to deal. I was off like a flash. I hurried back to the sinking ship, pretending to stroll, and casually I mentioned to Ben and Lou that Gussie had in stock all the supplies asked for by Old Van Slyke. Then I managed to add that she was willing to take whiskey in payment for same.

"*Our* whiskey?" Lou said. "To that hag?"

"You owe her quite a bit of money," I said. "Even after I

give her what I've saved. We're a floating disaster." I changed that. "We're a sinking disaster, Lou."

She gave me one of her fiercer looks. I responded by glancing conspicuously at what was supposed to be a boat.

"How did McGrew's who-er find out about our whiskey?"

"I told her," I said.

Ben intervened, by appearing to address no one in particular. "We're in a fix, folks."

Lou wasn't about to give in that easily. "We aren't building a steamboat. We're trying to build a scow with two pointed ends, with some storage space in between, and a sail overhead."

"And a sweep at one end," Ben said, "on what is presumably the stern. And some sturdy oars and oarlocks. And a mast in the middle that won't snap off when the wind catches the sail. And a hull that isn't a sieve."

"Excuse me for living," Lou said. "We're going to drift down a river. Not enter a race. Not sail or row. *Drift*. That's what you told me."

"We're talking about the Yukon River," Ben said. "It has its mean stretches."

"Ben," Lou said. "We're talking about transporting three people and their miserable godawful outfit. All we have to do is point our boat in the right direction and fall asleep."

I saw that I had to speak up. "Ben is under some obligation to transport Gussie Meadows to Dawson City."

About two hundred stampeders had volunteered to take Gussie Meadows to Dawson City, free of charge. Some had even offered to pay her to be their passenger. I didn't mention that.

"Transport?" Lou said. "There is absolutely no room on our boat to *transport* a hardware store. We're going to be lucky to *transport* what little whiskey Ben has left in his treasure collection."

She was right to raise the transportation issue. I had raised it myself when I talked with Gussie about the size of the vessel that was still under construction, and she had given me an answer which I related to Lou.

"We don't have to transport anything." I said. "Gussie is leaving the hardware store right here."

"What hardware store? You mean that ragged tent of hers?"

"The hardware store. The tent. Everything in it. The whole kit and caboodle. She says she's walking away from it all, taking her personal effects and her bags of money."

I had to mention the money. I was being mean. I wasn't specific about the trunks full of clothing and perfumes and all that. I didn't think Lou would take kindly to transporting a trunkful of silk stockings and garters all the way to Dawson City.

"Bags of money," Lou said. "I guess so."

Ben was shocked at the sheer extravagance of Gussie's intention. I tried to explain. "She says that once the ice is out and the boats set sail, the local beavers and muskrats won't be buying a whole lot of nautical supplies."

"Bags of money," Lou said. "Out of the pockets of people like us."

I had once commented that Gussie's prices were on the steep side, and Lou would never let me forget it. Gussie had a way of looking ahead. She tended to measure money by sheer weight.

"The ice," I explained to Lou, "will be going out all the way down the Yukon. Not just here."

"Thanks for telling me, Peek. I had no idea that would happen. And what is that supposed to mean?"

"It means there'll be steamboats coming up from the mouth of the Yukon, there in Alaska. Dozens of them. Get it?"

Lou had the look that said she was doing figures in her mind.

I kept right on. "They'll be carrying every kind of hardware tht anybody could want, and most of it for mining gold, not building boats."

"If she's so rich, this Gussie of yours" Lou wanted to know all of a sudden, "why does she want our whiskey? Is she going to make a fortune on that too?"

"She didn't explain, Lou. She just said she'd take whiskey in lieu of debts incurred and monies owed. That sounds pretty decent to me."

"Just what the hell is *monies*?" Lou said.

"Give the boy a hearing," Ben said. "It sounds to me like he's got us a pretty fair offer. We've got about twenty dollars cash under the mattress."

"What mattress?" Lou said. But I could see that she was relenting.

22

I went back up to the store and told Gussie that the whiskey deal was on. She told me to take whatever I needed and haul it down to the water, so I loaded up and set out once again with a seventy-pound pack on my back. I was there beside the lake, showing Ben all the new rope and a new square sail, when Old

Van Slyke straightened up all of a sudden and said, "Yup. Here it is. You feel it?"

"Feel what?" I said. I was unfolding the sail.

"The wind. It's changing. That's a south wind."

I stood up in order to see if I could feel it. Sure enough, the wind was warmer, softer, like silk on my cheeks. It had a damp, flowery smell to it.

"There goes the ice," Old Van Slyke said. "The ice'll be slick and clean gone by tomorrow morning."

I dropped the sail and was off to deliver the news to Gussie. I stumbled over three sleeping sled dogs on the way and nearly lost a leg to one of them. Old Van Slyke wasn't the only person who had recognized what was happening. Men all over the place were jumping into action, starting to knock down tents, packing up, pushing boats into the water. When I got to the hardware store, Gussie was in her quarters packing her clothes into trunks and boxes. I gave her the news.

She had already heard.

"Now listen," she said. She went on folding a pair of dark brown silk stockings. They made me think of burnt honey. "I've got one last chore for you, Peek."

Just like that she sent me to spread the word to all her many customers.

There was to be a party. That very night. In her hardware store. She would hold a closing down party. And just to make sure everyone showed up, I was to say she had come into possession of some kegs of the best whiskey that money would buy.

I left the hardware store on the run. The narrow strip of open water along the shore was beginning to fill with boats. Tents were coming down as if the wind itself was the cause. Some of the men were wading knee-deep into the icy water to begin to load up. Others were refusing to lift a single box or bag, not yet believing the forecast, but watching for an arch of cloud with open sky beneath it.

In a matter of hours the town would begin to disappear. It would melt away, dissolve like the snow itself, like the ice itself, into the lake. People felt they had to get serious about having fun. There were going to be parties everywhere. There would be no end of celebrations. But ours, I had no doubt, would be the finest, and I told people so.

By the time I got back to the hardware store a fiddler had showed up. Gussie knew a group of stampeders who, until four months earlier, had been musicians. They had heard about the whiskey by the grapevine.

"For God's sake, Peek," Gussie said. "Get the whiskey."

I went back to our tent. Ben and Lou had agreed to part with some of their whiskey. But we hadn't settled on how much *some* might be.

Lou was doing her hair. "If I'm going to ride in that boat of ours for a week with Dan McGrew's who-er, I guess I might as well try to talk to her tonight."

"Lou," Ben said, "She's as eager to get to Dawson as we are. She'll pull her weight. Stop worrying."

I took a keg and was gone.

Four more musicians had arrived at the store, carrying with them two fiddles, a mouth organ, a banjo, an accordian, a uku-lele, a flute. Then there were five or six players, or maybe seven. It was hard to tell.

The tuning up began to draw a crowd. It was late in the afternoon. The days were so long that we couldn't wait for sun-down. It was breakup time, the ice, candled and rotten, was about to move.

When Ben and Lou showed up they started dancing before they said hello. I could hardly believe they were the same old Ben and Lou who ruled my life.

Actually, the orchestra was still tuning up, but quite a few people had begun to dance. Lou saw me serving drinks. She saw I was serving the whiskey straight. She stopped waltzing long enough to tell me to add some water. Then she let go of Ben and went and found a crock full of water and did the adding herself.

Quite a few of the men had actually bathed and changed clothes. They looked elegant. Or at least they did until they started dancing in the mud, in front of the orchestra, or behind it, or in it. There weren't enough women in camp to make for a regular dance. A lot of the men did jigs by themselves. Not to mention somersaults. Not to mention that some of them just fell down as a form of entertainment — they had drunk up their own caches of booze as a way to get ready for our party.

Gussie Meadows was the twirling, talking centre of attraction. She didn't have to bother giving orders. We just obeyed. All of us, I swear. Trying not to look at her was like trying not to look at a tornado. And once you looked you were done for. When she spoke, men turned into walking sets of ears. And walking pricks too, I might add. And when she started to dance they turned into galloping galoots who thought they knew how to dance. When she deigned to pour a man a drink, using the wooden ladle that Lou had put into a sauerkraut crock, along with too much water and too little whiskey, he felt he was receiving permission to shout, whistle, sing and fly.

I went and got the second keg from our tent, after consulting briefly with Ben. He was pretty well into the sauce himself, and hardly heard my question. He was talking Klondike with other stampeders, all of them shouting over the music about picking up nuggets in the creeks and gulches. They were getting rich, those men, just standing there wagging their tongues. They could taste the faraway promise of gold, along with the whiskey.

Gussie Meadows was dressed fit to kill and then some. Even the straw hat, set an angle over her left eye, was irresistible. She had on a yellow dancehall kind of dress that fit her behind to perfection and was flared around the ankles, showing off her red shoes. But the real clincher was the way her outfit looked when she danced. You didn't need a whole lot of imagination to figure out where she was located inside her clothes. The dancers filled the street in front of the hardware tent. More exactly, in front of Gussie. And behind her too. The orchestra moved this way and that, trying to keep from getting stomped into the mud.

I might as well confess, I felt lonely. Not all the time, but now and then. Sometimes I was dizzy with all the excitement. But sometimes I was lonely.

Gussie took one partner, then another, then another. Three or four times she just danced by herself. I was wishing she would ask me to join her, but I suppose she had her reasons. And there was the problem that I didn't know how to do the two-step or the polka or the schottische or anything else. I knew that if she so much as touched me I would know how to dance. Men were showing each other their knuckles, and all I wanted to do was bow and smile and then glide through that mud for two whole, uninterrupted minutes with Gussie Meadows in my arms.

Ben seemed to be drunk and sober at the same time. He pretended he was helping out by picking up empty cups out of the mud. Gussie had set out the last cups from her stock and didn't care what happened to them. Ben put them in stacks and then didn't know where to put the stacks. Now and then he checked the six tables made of sawhorses and planks, set up three on either side of the place where the musicians had started out. "Take care of the groaning boards," he said to me whenever I went by. He sliced up loaf after loaf of sourdough bread and filled up the platters when they needed more sausages or pickled eggs or smoked oysters or whatever. Someone had come up with five smoked salmon. Someone else had provided a haunch of smoked bear. There was also woodland caribou, grayling, lake trout, mountain sheep, mountain goat. There was something like thirty pounds of meatloaf made with horse that people thought was beef.

It was a feast. People were bringing out every delicacy they'd been hoarding for months.

That's why I went back to our tent on my own and got the third keg. As the drinkers were saying to each other, who's counting? Lou was making sure that I didn't drink, but she wasn't counting kegs. She was so busy dancing I don't think she ever had a better time in her life. She was swept along from partner to partner, dancing her legs off. Men were asking her to promise them the seventh or the tenth or the fourteenth dance. She was good at numbers. There was so much laughter in her voice it made me laugh too. Sometimes I had tears in my eyes, what with laughing and all.

Just at midnight Gussie Meadows made an announcement. She didn't mince words. A musician had showed up with a trumpet. Gussie asked him to blow a signal for attention. It took him four minutes, but when he finally ran out of breath Gussie had her chance.

She took off her straw hat and began to speak. "I want to thank you all, folks. Really thank you. I've made a tonne of money. A regular tonne of money. I don't mind saying so, right here and now. I've been minting money."

She'd had a drink or two herself.

The crowd gave her such a rousing bravo and storm of applause that she had to go on.

"Thanks to you, I've done it. I've got about as much money as three packhorses can carry. So I'm not going on to Dawson. I'm turning back. I'm heading for Skagway. And then for San Francisco. I'm too damned rich to do any more work. To hell with it."

The crowd gave a roar of approval that made me put my index fingers in my ears. She had done what the rest of us were going to do before the summer was out. She reassured us. She let us empty out the doubts we'd been holding back, concealing, living with, for days and for weeks.

"Just drink up," she said. "We'll stop drinking when the ice goes out."

She gave her straw hat a fling and it twirled out over that mob and landed in the mud, and a couple of drunks who were trying to dance together stomped all over it before I could get there. It was a party and a half. Drink up is what people did. It was a wingding. A smasheroo of an event. You could hardly hear yourself think. I don't know why I couldn't stay in the mood. A one-legged man asked me to dance but I said no. I had to shout in his ear. Lou was wearing her shortest skirt. You could see right up to the middle of her calf. Gussie's dancehall dress was mud all the way up to her knees. Nobody cared. She didn't, that's for sure. When one of her shoes came off in the mud she took the other one off and finished the dance and then her partner sat her on someone's lap and she lifted up her muddy, stockinged feet while something like ten stampeders put her red shoes back on. The orchestra played while that happened. They played a song I knew well, "Take Back Your Gold." The crowd thought that was hilarious. Gussie stood up again and asked for "Frankie and Johnny Were Lovers" and the orchestra complied and half the people in the crowd laboured under the impression that they were singers and they sang along in the chorus, "He was her man but he was doing her wrong," and then she sang the next verse by herself, "rooty-toot-toot, three times she did shoot." I was the only sober person in that whole tent city and the more people drank the more my vision cleared. I felt I could see right through that pale blue springtime sky to where the stars were trying, with no success, to shine. I could see all the way up to the blank god-damned silence.

23

The ice went out with a bang. Or with a crack. I thought I must be the only person who heard it, but something like twenty thousand people there on the shore of Lake Bennett heard it at exactly the same time that I did. It wasn't a cracking sound either. It was more like thunder. The sky was perfectly clear, a dawn sky, and then there was that sound that sounded like thunder.

There must have been three hundred parties going on,

there in Bennett City. They ended at 5:19 on the morning of May 29, 1898. Just like that. Boom.

We heard the sound, over the loud roar of voices and all the attempts at singing and the disagreements of fifty competing bands. We heard the ice crack. And then something like one thousand guns began their response. Men ran for their guns. It was as if we were being attacked by the moving ice. They fired rifles and shotguns and pistols into the air and it was as if all those discordant gunshots were signalling the beginning of a race.

And I guess it was a race after all. So many people went charging down to the lakeshore that some of those in the lead were pushed right into the icy water. The icy open water.

Three enterprising stampeders had lined up two poles on shore with a third pole out on the ice. It was agreed that when the pole on the ice move out of line, break-up had begun. They had a lottery running, the organizers, on when the ice would go. I never found out who won the pot. It was worth a small fortune. The south wind had turned into something close to a gale. The pole out on the ice was slick and clean gone.

People who hadn't been pushed into the water walked in on their own. As fast as you could count there were one thousand boats loaded and setting out, down to their gunwales with outfits and horses, and with stampeders waving their arms and trying to figure out how to move a sweep or raise a sail. There were people getting left behind by accident and rushing to catch the next boat and people rushing back to try to grab something left on shore. But they couldn't get to shore because another three thousand boats were being pulled and slid and wrestled and pushed over log rollers into the lake.

The first sinking took place one hundred yards from shore,

with three people yelling for help because they were drowning. Their entire outfit went to the bottom of the lake, but they were saved. On one boat two horses broke loose and leapt overboard. Two boats that had on them square sails simply collided a quarter mile from shore, and down came both sails.

We were sitting out in front of our tent at the table that Ben and Lou had put together with lumber left over from their boat-building. We were watching.

"Lucky thing," Ben said, "we didn't quite get our boat built."

"How long will we be sitting here?" Lou had her chin propped up on her hands. Her feet were killing her, she'd told us, but outside of that she felt fine.

"Three more days. Old Van Slyke says it will take him three more days to fix up that disaster I built."

I was glad to hear about the delay.

Ben thought for a while. "Not such a bad thing though. Clear the ice. Let the other guys hit the deadheads that might sink a boat." He had lived all his life by the Mississippi, and he knew about things like ice jams and submerged logs that you couldn't see that could punch a hole clean through a hull.

Gussie Meadows showed up at around 8:15 that morning, still wearing her party outfit, including her stained white gloves and her dress caked with mud. She had come to see me, it was obvious. But she didn't let on. She was always careful, in daylight, about our connection. She mentioned first that she had a couple of packers busy, loading her personal things onto their string of packhorses.

Ben said he was sorry she wasn't about to travel with us.

"I'm sorry too," Gussie said, whatever that meant.

Then Ben managed to ask, "Would you like us to say hello or anything? I mean to Dan McGrew."

She was still a little bit under the influence. "Dangerous Dan," she said, "would rather screw you out of a dollar than screw you. If you'll pardon my saying so. He would rather gamble than live. Well, tell him for me, he gambled."

"He's always been good to me," Ben said.

"Lucky you," Gussie said. She came over to where I was sitting on a block of wood next to Lou.

"You're a good man," she said. To me.

I wanted to reach out and touch her, but I couldn't. Not with Lou and Ben watching.

"You're a good man," she said again. To me. "Take good care of Ben and Lou."

I suppose that was the first time ever that Ben heard me referred to in quite that way. As usual, he looked puzzled.

"And as for McGrew," Gussie said, "I do have a message for him. I've taken the trouble of writing it down so you won't have to speak it to him in person."

She was slurring her speech a little. She held in her gloved left hand an envelope and a small piece of paper. She took the piece of paper in her gloved right hand and held it far away as if that was necessary so she could read.

"It says, 'I'm going back to Frisco, Dan. Just as well. I was coming there to kill you. Love. Gussie.'"

She gave us the strangest look. I couldn't tell if she was angry or sorry or what.

"There," she said. "Now you know what it says in the message that you're delivering. Would you like me to read it again?"

Ben and I shook our heads.

"We got it the first time," Lou said.

Gussie put the note into the envelope and licked the flap and sealed it.

Instead of giving the envelope to Ben, she handed it to me.

Then she turned away. Just like that. I could see she was taking off her gloves while she walked. Instead of carrying them she tossed them into the mud.

24

The Mounted Police reported that 7,124 vesels of one sort or another set out within one week to go downriver from the headwaters of the Yukon to Dawson City. We must have been number seven thousand and one.

Old Van Slyke took his time. Ours was his last boat. After it hit the water, he said, he was heading back to some little port on the Zuider Zee. Maybe he wasn't in a hurry. Maybe his bones ached. Maybe he wanted his last boat to be a good one. And if that was his intention, he succeeded. He'd made his fortune and a bit more. He had enough. I also think he had a soft spot for Lou. He shaped our boat into something that was an exact fit for Ben and Lou and me and our outfits. A doozer. He squared off the bow and stern a bit and shaped the boat into a kind of rapids boat, something that would carry a sail on a lake and still ride out white water. He rebuilt the stern so that one of us, seated there alone, could handle the long sweep. At the same time, when necessary, two of us could row, one on either side of the boat.

It wasn't until we were loading, three days after Gussie's departure, that Lou made another count of the whiskey kegs.

She wasn't too happy to find we were down to five. She repeated that number to herself, as if the very concept baffled her. "Five?" she said. She tried it two or three times, as if she was doing arithmetic in her mind again, and coming up with a bad tally. But outside of that she said not a word.

We hoisted our small sail, and the boat moved slowly into a sluggish current. That current, along with the wind, would carry us easily, we hoped, down the long trough that was Lake Bennett. Other boats went scudding past us. Late starters and late arrivals in a hurry to catch up. We took our time, admiring the mountains, getting used to being sailors. Ben knew something about rivers, but Lou and I had to concentrate on learning how not to fall overboard when the wind moved the sail. We'd had no idea that winds were so unruly. Men on the boats around us were rowing as if Dawson must be around the next bend instead of 560 miles downriver. We drifted out of the lake on a current that wasn't yet fed by heavy spring runoff. But even so, that first real current taught Lou and me how to grab for the gunwales. We camped near an Indian village called Caribou Crossing. It was a place where the caribou crossed the river, and just as we were pitching our tent an old Tagish man came by and offered us three freshly skinned caribou heads. He wanted to hitch a ride downriver to a place above Miles Canyon.

We took him and his canoe and his rifle and his three caribou heads aboard. Let's say he was travelling light. He guided us across Marsh Lake and into its narrow outlet. We had to stop while he shot four mallards and then insisted we land so he could prepare us a meal. He showed me how to skin and clean a duck and how to skewer it on a green stick and set it to roast. He did two and I did two. One for each person, he said.

Just above Miles Canyon he recognized his wife on shore and asked us to land and let him join his family in his trapping cabin.

We were on our own when we hit the top of the canyon.

A lot of outfits were pulled ashore. We got close enough so that we could catch hold of the stern of a big scow and hang on and ask for advice. No end of stampeders were debating what they should do. You could hire professional rivermen and walk to a place below the rapids and wait for the appearance of your boat and then pay cash for services rendered. Or you could set out.

But just as we were about to tie up a Mountie stepped into the scow we were tying up to. He gave his name as Sam Steele and then said, sternly, he had posted an order saying no women could travel down through the canyon, they must use the portage.

That was not the best suggestion to make to Lou.

Before Ben could figure out how to tie a double half-hitch she pulled at her oar. We were gone from the landing. I had no choice but to start rowing. We headed straight for the milky foam that roared and battered and echoed its way into between sheer sandstone cliffs. We were headed straight in, and dancing all the way.

There in the canyon the wreckage was something else. You could have had all the supplies you'd ever want, just for the trouble of picking them off the rocks. If you could stop. We went wooshing downstream and hardly had time to look up at the cliffs. Not that the cliffs were the real problem. We were riding a hump of water down the middle of the channel as if we were riding a bucking horse. We had to stay aboard it or join the debris. A barge one jump ahead of us was racing full tilt and turning around and falling apart, all at the same time. It was hardly twenty feet away and yet we couldn't do a thing as a stack of boxes tumbled overboard and the seven or eight men on board tried hanging onto their outfit and then onto their oars and then onto each other. They moved in absurd pantomime, shaping words with their large mouths. Their eyes were big too.

I glanced away. I looked away just in time to see a grown man sitting on a rock in the middle of the rapids, all by himself, looking bone dry, yelling something of which we couldn't hear the slightest sound. For some silly reason I waved.

The dead-still yellowish cliffs went straight up over our heads for one hundred feet and the cliff swallows darted within inches of our heads as if to the bathe in the spray, or maybe to taunt us.

We covered two miles in no time flat. We were out of the canyon. To our left was an eddy and in the eddy a raft turned circles, turned slowly around and around, making perfect circles. The men on the raft were trying to figure out what to do. They had a team of horses with them, standing dead still in the middle of the raft, swishing their tails at the horseflies.

Ben told us to row and Lou and I rowed for dear life. We were looking back, watching the men and horses on the raft in the eddy, when we hit the next stretch of rapids. That didn't seem fair. I just closed my eyes and put my head down and rowed. When I looked up again there was a rowboat beside us with two men in it, one seated behind the other, both rowing. They were both smoking pipes. They were travelling light. Which, it was turning out, was no better than travelling heavy.

We talked across the water with those two men. They asked us where we were from. It seemed an insane question. They were printers by trade. They had studied the route before attempting it. They assured us that the next set of rapids was only a quarter of a mile long.

I was pulling at my oar and didn't see the moment when we hit the Whitehorse Rapids. Out of one corner of my eye I could see our two new friends in their rowboat. Then we went into the first wave and I couldn't see the rowboat or anything else. I was getting drenched all over again. When we came up the rowboat was out of sight. We didn't see it for a long time. The waves were nearly as high as the mast on our boat. Ben shouted at me to start bailing instead of rowing.

That's when I noticed the rowboat again. When I started bailing. There was only one man in the rowboat. He was still rowing. He hadn't looked over his shoulder. He didn't know his partner was gone.

Ben saw the drowning man and pointed. He was in the rapids, hanging onto an oar, still holding his pipe in his teeth. Ben moved the long sweep mounted on our stern. Just as the drowning man seemed to be tossed within reach, he was tossed away again. His pipe was missing.

"Watch it," Lou shouted. I thought at first she was shouting at the drowning man about his pipe.

Ben had stepped up onto the gunwale so he could see more clearly what might be done. He lost his footing. More exactly, the long sweep at which he was pulling gave him a pull. Or it struck him a blow.

Very slowly, very gracefully, it lifted him over the side of our boat. Almost delicately, it dropped him down toward the racing water, allowing him, as he fell, to turn a somersault.

Ben disappeared.

We didn't have a life-buoy. I picked up a box and threw it. Then I threw another one.

Lou was shouting again, over the roar of the water. "You'll hit him." She untied and kicked off her shoes and dropped her duck skirt and her petticoat. There she stood in her blouse and her bloomers, swaying, grabbing now and then at her shipped oar.

She pointed, signalling me to hand her a line I'd been practising knots with. I had to unknot it first. The spray had soaked her. She was watching the water and waiting for me. I couldn't get the line untangled. Then I gave a pull and had it and I tossed it across the boat. I thought she was going to throw the line to Ben. Perhaps that was what she intended to do. But Ben hadn't surfaced. She took the line I had freed and wrapped it under her armpits and knotted it. She threw me the loose end of the line.

Lou jumped overboard.

I was alone in that boat. And that's putting it mildly. I was alone in the whole Yukon territory. I had to find Lou. I stood up in that crazy boat. And then I was dancing all right. After a fashion. The trouble was, I was trying to keep my body dead still. And maybe I was. Everything around me was swaying and dipping and leaping into the air and diving into the waves. They say a drowning man's life flashes before his eyes. The catch was that Ben was drowning and I was the one remembering a life. My own. And his. And Lou's. We were partners. It was as if it took the three of us to live one life. If you know what I mean.

Lou had Ben by the hair. I don't know when it was I first realized that. She'd been threatening for days to give him a haircut, but hadn't. We were into slacker water. We were through the rapids. Lou wasn't trying to swim or anything. I was holding the line taut. She was hanging onto Ben, trying to get some air herself, trying to keep his mouth out of the foam.

The water was half covered in dirty, gritty foam. There were sticks and branches and pieces of bark everywhere. I noticed a brown wooden hairbrush floating next to Ben's head.

There was no way we could stop. I was holding onto the line and trying to work an oar.

Purely by accident we were swept into a quiet back eddy.

Ben didn't have the strength to haul himself into the boat. First I helped Lou. I had to catch hold between her thighs. I had never really touched her bare skin that way. It was icy cold, and slick from the foam. She and I helped Ben. We didn't so much help him as yank at him. Hoist him. He fell slack beside the sweep, still trying to catch his breath. He went on spitting and gasping for breath and trying to speak, and after a while I realized he was trying to say he was sorry.

Lou crawled forward toward her clothing. When she could speak again she said she wouldn't go any further until she was properly dressed.

We stayed there in that eddy, turning slow circles, listening to the stillness. We didn't talk, Ben and Lou and I. Somehow we didn't quite look at each other. It was very quiet there, except that now and then someone out in the main current gave a shout or a scream.

After maybe ten minutes Ben said out loud, as if speaking to the sweep he was leaning against, "You didn't have to do that, Lou."

Lou was fidgeting around with her long hair, trying to get it to dry, and she went on fidgeting as if she hadn't heard him.

We pushed out into the current ourselves and floated a short distance, less than a mile, and then we pulled ashore where a lot of other outfits were tied up, all kinds of men, with hardly any women anywhere, spreading out rice and flour and bedding and clothing to dry in the sun. Some people had to empty their boats entirely and turn them over and make repairs. Green lumber is bad that way.

Our friend in the rowboat had landed there too. He was still in his boat, sitting there holding onto the stern of a scow, smoking his pipe, staring out at the water.

More boats came shooting through the rapids. Everyone on board looking dizzy and shocked and scared shitless and elated right out of their minds. We shouted encouragement. "You've made it," we shouted, and then the people on those boats began to shout and wave too, and some of them went right on down-river, without trying to land.

You could buy a whole Klondiker's outfit right there on the beach for something like ten dollars. I noticed there were no takers.

25

We crossed Lake Laberge with no delays except when we had to wait for some drift ice that hadn't cleared. Ben was feeling pretty weak. We camped more than we travelled. Six days after leaving the lake, just above Five Finger Rapids, we floated past a group of men on a barge who were tied up to shore and making a lot of noise, swearing and singing while one of their number thumped on a washtub. We pulled in to shore just below them. We wanted to get a good night's rest and then tackle Five Fingers first thing in the morning, when we were fresh. Once bitten twice shy. Or maybe I should say three times bitten, the fourth time shy. We were maybe a hundred yards below the men on the barge. They were pie-eyed right out of their skulls. You could tell by listening.

One of those stampeders came down to our camp to say they wanted to share their good fortune, so would we please join them.

"What good fortune was that?" Lou said. She had come to a rather skeptical view of the idea of fortune.

"Come and see," the stampeder said.

The mosquitoes were wicked and those men had their campfire lit and a smudge going as well. That's what made us accept the invitation. We walked up through the bush to say hello. I didn't want to go along but Lou insisted.

"A little company," she said, "might lift your spirits and cure your moping."

"What moping?" I said.

"Your godawful puppy-love moping."

"Is that so?" I said.

"That is so. Like a love-sick calf."

"Huh," I said.

"Don't 'Huh' me, young man. And you better learn to live with somebody walking away."

That was as close as Lou could ever get to showing sympathy. And it wasn't likely to last.

Those stampeders had snagged a box they saw floating in the river. It was so well made they couldn't wait to open it. One man had been willing to bet it was full of bullion. Another said it was more likely to be a coffin, given the winter they'd been through. Except that corpses didn't come packaged, another man said, not on that river. He'd seen four in one day, and not a one of them had been dressed up by an undertaker.

They went on like that, those drunks, each one of them telling the story in such a way as to make himself the hero. The box they'd snagged had turned out to have in it two kegs marked salt herring.

Back into deep-shit valley for me.

They were ready to throw those two kegs back into the river, two drunks tried to explain at once. They'd been right on the brink of doing it. Then one of them said he was so hungry for a change of diet he was even willing to try something called salt herring.

The kegs were full of the finest whiskey those men had ever tasted.

We hadn't thought of our missing boxes until then. To begin with, I might have killed Ben, instead of saving him. And now on top of everything else it turned out that one of the cases I'd chucked had been worth its weight in gold.

When the men offered Ben a drink he said he wouldn't touch the stuff if his life depended on it. I suggested we drink as much as we possibly could, to cut our losses.

Lou was waiting for an opening, and there it was. "That Gussie Meadows certainly turned you into a bold one." Then she added, "And a bad one."

I had, during the past week, written Gussie something like two hundred letters in my mind. She'd neglected to give me her San Francisco address, which was a disappointment to me.

Ben and Lou left the barge and went back to our boat to build a smudge of their own and to make some supper.

Lou hollered out of the bush that I was to be there in half an hour.

The man who claimed loudest that he'd been first to notice the floating box took charge. He knocked back his drink and offered me his empty tin cup.

"Thank you," I said, "I could stand a little of the milk of human kindness."

Three different men helped me fill my cup from their own. It was for that reason that I decided not to mention the source of their good fortune. On top of that, I wanted to leave Lou and Ben by themselves. They need time to think, I said to myself. And I needed some time to stop thinking.

Those men on the barge gossiped. We had visiting to do. I had to catch up on the river news. There was a lot of gossip, along the river. People stopped here and there to pan, hoping to strike it rich before they got to Dawson, and after they found nothing they told each other stories of finding traces of gold. Those stampeders told some gold stories, and then they talked a lot about food. They told each other what they would buy to eat, after they struck it rich. Everything from venison washed down with champagne to creamed garden peas and pan-fried spring chicken.

Talking led to singing. Those men on that barge drinking Ben's whiskey were great singers, and I sang with them. We sang "There Is a Tavern in the Town" about twenty-four times. Someone tried to sing "Sweet Rosy O'Grady" as a solo but we all joined in. Then it was time for "Oh, Dem Golden Slippers."

Somehow I had got the notion, maybe from the songs we were singing, that drinking would cure what was ailing me. So I drank some more.

I got drunk for the first time in my life. Snockered. Glassy-eyed, pissy-eyed drunk. Vomity drunk. I'm not bragging. I'm owning up.

They were great dancers, those stampeders, and I danced, doing a jig that one man said had to be the Klondike jig, because he'd never seen it performed anywhere else in all his travels, and he had seen much of the world.

Out there on the deck of that barge around a smudge and in a smudge, I pretended to myself that I was showing Gussie Meadows how well I could dance. I wanted her to regret not having asked me for one little dance, back there in Bennett City, while every clown and lout got his turn. I was dancing with about ten million mosquitoes. The men who were still on their feet clapped and sang while I leapt and plunged and pirouetted. "Better than the Whitehorse Rapids," one of the stampeders kept telling me. "You've got a gift, kid. I want to tell you, you're going to be a hit with the ladies in Dawson City."

That's the last clear statement I can recall, from that memorable evening. I have no recollection of how I got back to our tent. In fact I didn't quite get back to the tent, I got to within ten yards of it. Ben came out into the night and tried to drag me through the bush. He didn't succeed. Lou, apparently, said let him die. Ben covered me over with mosquito netting and set a pail of water within reach so that I might not perish of fluid loss and general dehydration. I was emptying my stomach at regular intervals.

Next morning my head was exactly the same size as our boat. That's why I couldn't lift it onto my shoulders and then stand up and then get aboard. It took Lou something like two hours to decide whether she should show a little pity or simply abandon camp and float away. While she was deciding she made beans and bacon and tea for her and Ben's breakfast.

The stink of frying salt bacon was especially cruel in its effect. But it forced me out from under the mosquito netting and onto the boat, where I could hang my head and half my body over the side and vomit in relative comfort.

"Nice singing," Lou said, when she brought the frying pan aboard to give it a rinse, right there beside me.

Five Finger Rapids was a breeze. The great hunks of rock that divide the channel into its renowned fingers were aglow with morning light and looked to Ben and Lou like the gateway to everlasting wealth. It was Lou who came up with that description. Ben was keeping an eye on me so that I didn't fall overboard while I tried to row. And I did row. Pride and honour demanded no less of me.

Ben was getting to be pretty handy with the big sweep on the stern of the *Trump*. He guided us along as if he was sketching pictures there in the river's gauzy covering of morning mist.

We were into a quiet stretch of river with gentle mountains off on either side. After a while we pulled ashore to make a billy of tea. That was Ben's idea. While we were resting there on shore the previous night's barge slid silently by before us, its appalling deck strewn with apparent corpses. There was no one at the sweep.

"A ghost ship," Ben ventured.

"Not last night it wasn't," Lou said. "That was real."

I tried my first little smile of the day.

Lou wasn't quite ready to start relenting. "We're down to three kegs," she said. But Ben's joke had worked its magic. She went back onto our boat and rustled up a few pieces of johnnycake.

26

That's how it was. At least for a spell.

Ben had his shoes and socks off and was lying in the bottom of the boat with his bare feet over the gunwale and his head on Lou's lap. I was sitting at the sweep.

They spent hours like that, Lou and Ben, doing nothing. There was no hurry left in us. I found a big stone and I took the line that Lou had used when she saved Ben and I made an anchor. Sometimes we stopped, right in the middle of the river, just to watch the people go by. Stampeders. Men mostly, with one or two women who wanted to chat with Lou, and now and then a child or a baby. They arrived or passed by in boats and scows, on rafts and barges. It was a pretty sight. We shouted back and forth to perfect strangers. We exchanged the names of places, trying to guess how close we were to Dawson, trying to let ourselves feel safe and arrived. I liked the geographical names. Rink Rapids, where a steamer had sunk the fall before. The Hootchikoo Bluff, looming over some dangerous gravel bars. Big Horn Crossing where we saw just what the name said we would, some mountain sheep watching from the top of rocks brought down by a rockslide. The Site of O'Brien's Murder. Devil's Crossing. Carpenter's Slough. Wolverine Creek. Pelly River.

We talked more than once of our first night on shore, back there in the Inside Passage, after our harrowing escape from the *Delta Queen*. We remembered how those two deckhands rowed us ashore in a pea-sized dinghy and we confessed, Lou and I, we'd thought we'd swamp and drown. And now, Ben said, we were old hands, all of us. And that was how it felt. We had been travelling so long that we were old.

We stopped more often than we had to. Lou would see a gravel bar and she'd say, "Maybe we should have a cup of tea." Sometimes other stampeders stopped as well, for a smoke and a cup of tea and some river gossip.

Maybe we were trying too hard, I don't know.

Sometimes while we floated along we'd see men in the mouth of a tributary creek or river, panning the gravel, just trying out their equipment, staring into a mining pan after they'd tried to wash out the gravel and sand.

I invented things to keep myself busy. For instance, I tried fishing. I tried to catch some fish off the stern of our boat while we were drifting. Once I caught a duck. Don't ask me how, but I caught a duck on my line. It may have been a mallard. I had one hell of a time getting it off the hook.

After I let it back into the water, its beak all bloody, Lou said, "Why did you do that?"

"Why did I do what?"

"Why did you catch that duck?"

"I wasn't trying to catch that duck."

"You certainly were. You saw that duck out there."

"It was an accident."

"That was no accident. You were being cruel," she said.

"I was not being cruel. I was trying to catch a fish. For our supper."

I became persuaded that I'd got fleas from the duck. Tiny little bugs were crawling all over my hands. Possibly all over my whole body.

"I got fleas," I said, "from that damn duck."

The duck had flown about fifty feet and then landed and

was now floating at exactly the rate at which we were floating. Every so often it stuck its head into the water and raised it and gave it a shake.

"Mites," Lou said. "Those are mites, not fleas. Just reach over the side of the boat and wash your hands."

I refused to move.

"You're moping around again."

I began to get a glimmer of understanding. Lou wasn't simply talking about me and Gussie Meadows. We were almost in Dawson City, and the partnership was scheduled to end right there on the bank of the river. That had been Lou's idea, right from the start.

"Maybe my hangover is back," I said.

"Hangovers don't come back."

"Is that so?" I said. "Since when are you an expert?"

Then, out of nowhere, Lou picked up our bailing can out of the bottom of the boat and threw it at the duck. The duck went stitching across the water, then slowly, finally, made it into the air.

"Good aim," I said.

"I know you miss Lake Bennett," Lou said. "So do I."

We had that moment right there and then. Lou and Ben and I. Ben didn't say much. I think he gave a little grunt of approval. Of agreement. It would have been better if we'd just kept quiet.

"Ben and I had a perfect time in Bennett City. We admit that, Peek. Now we're moving on." She lifted one of the shipped oars so she could fold her legs under herself, under her skirt. "That's one of the things you learn. How to move on."

"Is that so, Lou?"

"Love hurts people," she said.

"What would I know about love?" I said. "Who in the world would I be in love with?"

I desperately wanted her to say, Gussie Meadows, that's who. My whole aching body was begging her to speak that beautiful name.

"You're taking too big a risk, Peek."

"Good God, Lou. What in hell does that mean?"

"Don't you swear at me."

"I'm not swearing at you."

"Why do men swear when they're in love?" she said. "That's what I'd like to know."

"Shit," I said.

"Peek. I warned you."

Ben was pretending to steer when there was absolutely no steering to do.

"Taking a risk," I said, giving Lou another opening. "Who's taking a risk?"

"Want me to explain?" Lou said. "Want me to go on?"

I was afraid she was going to say something mean about Gussie Meadows. I wasn't about to give her the opportunity.

"Why not?" I said. "Tell me about going on."

I had to say that. I wanted to hurt her the way she was hurting me. And it worked. Her voice got very weak. Kind of wavery. "It's the beginning, Peek. Dawson City is the beginning."

I was sorry for what I'd said. I would have settled for more silence, but Lou went on, all the while trying to manage her voice. "It's where you and I are going so that we can do something with our lives. Remember that, Peek."

I said that I did remember. I said that I wouldn't forget.

"Remember the back rooms of that godawful pawnshop where I told you we had to get out of there, no matter what?"

I said I remembered. And I certainly did.

"You were playing one of those old pianos that someone had pawned. You stopped playing and said yes, and you put your head against me and I held you."

I said that yes, goddammit, I remembered.

Lou didn't reprimand me that time. Ben chimed in. "You mind your mother, Peek. We'll soon be there."

I didn't get the connection.

Lou pointed across a sandbar at the mouth of a creek. "I wonder, is that Lucky Joe Creek?"

"I don't think we're that far yet," Ben said.

27

A steamboat whistle just about made us jump out of our boat. It wasn't the loudness that made us start. It was the mournfulness. That steamboat gave a long, plaintive cry that was enough to break your heart. And then one thousand dogs set up a chorus in reply, barking and yelping and howling. We couldn't see the dogs, we couldn't see the steamboat.

We saw ahead of us a hugh gravel slope on a hillside. The Moosehide, we call it. If you pass The Moosehide you've missed your destination. We'd been watching for it ever since sun up, floating, drifting, trying to sail, even rowing at times. I sometimes wonder now, what was the hurry? We thought we knew what we'd see. But even so, it came as news when we saw it. Just like that, there it was. Up on the side of a mountain. A scar left by a rockslide maybe thousands of years before. A billboard with nothing on it. Not a word. At least it could have said WELCOME. Or something simple like BEWARE. But there it was, not staring at us, ignoring us rather.

"Look at that, would you?" Ben said. He'd let go of the sweep to clap his hands over his ears.

"Like a rug that a cat pissed on," Lou said. "I was expecting something else."

"Lou," I said. "Honestly." I was trying to mock her way of reprimanding me. With no luck. She didn't get it.

Ben let go of his ears and grabbed the sweep again.

I didn't have my pants on at the time. I was standing on Lou's side of the boat, the starboard side. The Dawson City side. We'd be there in something under twenty minutes. The thought of it took my breath away.

Lou had recovered her scientific composure. At least for the moment. She was pointing and offering her usual crisp commentary. "That must be the Klondike."

There it was before our eyes. The mouth of the Klondike River, where it flows into the Yukon. I guess she'd expected a golden colour, given that the Klondike was fed by more gold creeks that anyone had bothered to count. The water out of the Klondike was a swampish black.

We should have been jumping up and down, all three of us. I tried to show a little enthusiasm by giving a grunt and a wheeze or two.

On the upsteam side of the Klondike's mouth some rickety shacks were trying to hold each other up. A dozen tents were scattered in among some racks for drying fish. Not a fish to be seen. A dozen canoes lay bottom up among the drying racks and the tents. There wasn't a human being in sight.

That whistle lamented again.

It was then I noticed the steamboats. Not just one. Six of them. At least six. Below the Klondike's mouth, on the downstream side. We were drifting down on them fast. Six big white steamboats lay tied up to the shore. I counted, but it was hard to tell, with so many boats and scows and barges clustered around them.

"What do you think, Lou?" Ben said. He was ignoring me completely.

Lou didn't answer. She looked up from where she was biting off a thread. She was mending a tear in my only pair of pants. Maybe I didn't mention it, but I fell off the barge when I was on my little toot. My binge. She handed me the pants. "Here, put these back on." As if I had any choice.

I put them on and slipped my suspenders up over my shoulders and bent and dipped my left hand into the river and wet my hair and tried to brush it flat. All my life I've had unruly hair.

We could hear hammering. We could even see some of the dogs. The combination of hammering and howling was something else.

"I guess this is it," Ben said. He was using the sweep to ease us in toward shore. He was also trying to get Lou to speak to him.

"Don't miss it now," I said.

"Peek," Ben said, "you take your oar and see if you can pull a little on the port side there."

It was time for me to row. I hopped over some boxes and got hold of my oar. Lou did a little work with her oar too, slowing us down on the starboard side. Rowing that way, we were both looking back upriver instead of down. I couldn't stand it.

I had to twist my neck around while I was bracing my feet and pulling hard.

Two of the steamboats had two stacks each, towering behind their pilothouses. They were beauties. The other four had one stack each. The pilothouses were a dazzling white, up there ahead of us in the morning sun. One of the boats was puffing black smoke into the air while it landed in front of a crowd of hundreds of people. We could see hundreds and hundreds of men who seemed to have nothing to do but stand around with their hands in their pockets. Then we could read some of the steamboats' names, printed in bold gold lettering on the front of each wheelhouse. *May West. Victoria. Bella. Portus B. Weare.*

They were sitting low in the water, those steamboats, loaded to their gills with tonnes of freight. They had come up the Yukon, two thousand miles, all the way from the river's mouth. Gangs of stevedores were wheeling freight down gangplanks. Or carrying it on their backs.

I was pulling hard at my oar. I could handle it. I told Lou she could ship her oar while I brought us in.

She left her oar trailing in the water and stood up and turned around to have a look.

"You see that?" she said.

I tried to look while I rowed.

"You see those people?"

I saw she was looking at the grand steamboat that was trying to find a place to land. The *Susie.*

She was shaking her head as well as her finger. "No moose piss in their drinking water."

She was pointing up at the passenger deck. A number of men in suits and ties, along with two or three ladies, were watching the pandemonium below them. "High-muck-a-mucks," she said. "They've stepped out of their salon to have a quick look. Private cabins. Champagne for breakfast. China plates. Cut glass. Silver cutlery."

All that stuff made me think of the pawnshop where Lou had worked. But I tried to cheer her up. "Lucky for them," I said.

"Lucky," she said, "for the people who brought their money with them when they came."

She had to put a name to her hurting. She was in mortal pain. She had to talk to Ben and she couldn't, so she was taking it out on me. "Those muck-a-mucks aren't here to dig in the permafrost and mud. Not them. They're here to rob us."

"Of what?" I asked her.

Lou had got over some of her silence. I remembered how she was some nights when she came back from a twelve-hour shift in the pawnshop. She was that way now. "You just wait and see. Fancy clothing stores." She craned her neck to glance briefly at my pants. "Lawyers' offices. Doctors' offices. Beauty parlours and swanky hotels. They'll be *mining* alright."

She kept on glancing at me instead of at Ben. She couldn't bring herself to look in his direction. He was busy at the sweep as if he was trying to land a steamboat all by himself.

"If there's gold in people's pockets," I said, "there's got to be some place for them to spend it."

My observation didn't faze Lou. "Just you wait and see," she said. "See what happens. Just you wait and see what happens to people like us."

"Hang on," Ben shouted.

We hit shore.

We landed without being noticed because a big scow loaded with eight or ten stampeders and four horses had started the crossing too late and was being swept downriver, right past Dawson. No one noticed us. We sort of slammed into the muddy bank and Lou jumped ashore with a line and wrapped it around a stump as if the stump was a bollard. She held the line too tight and nearly swamped the *Trump* and Ben and me when we swung around sharply and slammed against the bank. Then she let some slack into the line and Ben was able to jump from the stern with a line in his hands.

"Perfect landing," I said, picking myself up out of the dirty water at the bottom of the boat. I checked for broken bones.

Ben and Lou leapt aboard again, each one trying to help the other.

The three of us just sat there. We could hardly hear ourselves think for the din, what with more boats landing from upriver and dogs greeting them and men cursing just to keep in practice and hammers doing their thing.

Lou was staring out at the river instead of looking toward the new streets. She pointed out another steamboat that hove into view. More high-muck-a-mucks and cheats and thieves, as far as she was concerned.

"Well," Ben said. "I guess this is it."

"You said that before," Lou said.

It was more than I could bear. I was rescued quite by accident. While I was trying to think of something positive to say, since both Ben and Lou had swallowed their tongues, I recognized an acquaintance. Whipsaw. I had worked with him briefly in Gussie Meadows' hardware store.

"Whipsaw!" I shouted, across another boat to where he was standing on a raft. He was hanging out his wash.

He gave me a big grin over the top of a wet shirt. "Hey, you rascal, Peek. I thought you'd be drownded by now."

We started shouting back and forth. Whipsaw was guarding the raft while his partners were ashore, scouting the territory. On impulse, I called and asked if he'd mind guarding our boat as well, while we went and did our own scouting.

"Happy to oblige," he said. "If you don't come back I'll assume you've picked up so many nuggets you can't walk."

Whipsaw liked to tease me. He had hurt his back while pulling a whipsaw, trying to saw lumber out of logs at Bennett. After that he worked for Gussie for about three days, but he soon discovered that lifting kegs of nails was no cure for a back problem.

"Just drop your boat down this way and tie up outside us."

We hopped to it, Ben and Lou doing most of the work while I made conversation. We tied up alongside the raft. Then Lou told Ben we should show a little interest in our new neighbour, just to be polite. They'd hardly paid him any attention at all.

Whipsaw and his five partners had built a shack in the middle their raft. They'd fixed it up really nice, with actual glass in the windows and a sandbox in front of the door where they could light a fire any time they wanted to. Whipsaw had done all the wash for his partners and for himself, now that they were tied up. He had on an apron. It was a minute or two before I noticed that he was wearing a kind of skirt under the apron. He saw me noticing.

"Easier to get into and out of," he said, indicating his skirt, "what with my back." It was ankle-length, the skirt, very plain, and his bare feet looked too large. Then he got a faraway look in his eyes. "You know," he said to me, "that woman Gussie Meadows was kind of an inspiration to me. When do you think she'll be getting here?"

"Gussie Meadows took her money and ran," Lou said.

I knew she was saying that to me rather than to Whipsaw, but he did the answering. "That doesn't sound like her, I swear."

"She decided to go back to Frisco," I said matter of factly. Then I added, "Any luck so far, Whipsaw?" That's what people said to each other.

"Hardly landed ourselves. Took a look at the prices in town and the whole bunch of us just about died of a unified heart attack."

It turned out that Whipsaw and his partners were planning to stay on the raft instead of tearing it up and selling the logs. That was the thing to do, there in Dawson. Dismantle your boat and sell the lumber. That way you had pocket money right away.

"Renting a space to pitch a tent in town costs a fortune." Whipsaw was hanging up a newly washed suit of long underwear that hadn't come that clean. "Me and my partners are going to stick together right here. We can live for next to nothing. I caught enough fish this morning for a free breakfast for six people, and with the heads and tails I can make fish soup for supper."

Lou asked if she could look inside the shack, there on the raft. When she came out she said a woman couldn't have made it look any homier. Whipsaw was pleased.

I guess we were stalling.

We had to talk for a while, chatting there with Whipsaw, comparing notes about our trips. The six men on the raft, he told us, had all got the runs and had spent most of thirteen days trying to shit over the side of a raft without falling into the river. That was their biggest adventure on the trip. A bear got all their bacon back at Five Finger Rapids. They thought they might pull the raft into the mouth of the Klondike, just above Dawson, and do some mining right off the raft. "You never know," Whipsaw said, "where you might strike gold."

Ben was hardly listening to all this. He went across the raft and stepped ashore maybe three times. Each time he got to the shore he hesitated. You'd have thought the mud burned his feet. Each time, instead of heading into town, he turned around and ran up the narrow gangplank and crossed the raft and returned to our boat.

It was Lou who got us on our way. She was talking to Whipsaw. Then, in the middle of telling him how best to run Miles Canyon, as if you had any choice once you started, she turned and looked across the raft at the tangle of humanity there on the muddy shore.

"We're going now," she said. Not to anyone in particular.

Ben and I followed her.

28

Hundreds of men were trying to figure out what they were supposed to do next.

They'd taken apart their boats and sold the lumber right there, spot cash, so in a way they were stuck. There were tents going up as fast as the boats came apart, and then the tents were coming down and buildings were going up. Not just shacks. Two-storey buildings, with regular false fronts. One of them was actually painted. A colour somewhere between orange and brown.

Ben and Lou and I were busy, saying hello. We knew quite a few people, it turned out, after our travels. At least we knew them to say hello.

We joined the crowd looking at the steamboats. Ben said they reminded him of home. We watched the freight coming off the freight decks. You name it, there it was. Not just the stuff that packers and their horses could carry. Those boats were carrying iron bathtubs and big oak tables and satin sofas half the size of the *Trump*. A four-horse team drove off one steamboat, pulling a wagon loaded with hay. Lou pointed out two crates of crystal chandeliers.

We were more or less propelled into town. Just swept along. I felt I was suffocating, with so many people around. Not just hundreds. Thousands. People we didn't know told us they were looking for hotels where they could rent a genuine spring bed for one night, before they headed out of town for the creeks. Others wanted to find restaurants where they could sit down in chairs and eat a meal off a table. They hadn't yet seen the prices.

I was just about the youngest person in the crowd. That made me feel strange. Lou felt strange too. She said hello every time she met a woman in that crowd.

The main street was mud and dust at the same time. We saw a team on dry footing trying to pull a wagon out of a mud-hole. You could get your legs splashed with mud while getting dust in your eyes, partly because there wasn't enough room on the wooden sidewalks for the people who were claiming to be in a hurry.

"We'd better find Dan just as soon as possible," Ben said.

That was the first actual mention, there in Dawson City, of Dangerous Dan McGrew.

I wanted to look at everything at once, at the brand-new store fronts and the signs saying things like FINE CIGARS AND TOBACCOS and GOLD BOUGHT HERE and VIENNA BAKERY WAFFLES AND COFFEE. I was all eyes, and Ben and Lou were willing to follow my lead. In no time Lou had a bad case of blind optimism. She started watching the mud for gold nuggets. To hear her, you'd have expected us to be rich and out of town on a steamboat by the end of the day. Ben was all for caution. I think he expected Soapy Smith to ride up and ask him whatever happened to Mr Plow's money belt.

There were so many buildings under construction the streets changed while you walked from one block to the next. At my suggestion, we stepped into a cigar store to ask about Dan McGrew. The cigar store, it turned out, was also a whorehouse. You could tell from the pretty pictures and the curtains on the doors to some back rooms. But it did sell cigars.

The man behind the counter simply said, "That son of a bitch. I wish he was as quick to pay for his stogies as he is to come in and take a boxful on credit."

Ben said he was a friend of Dan's.

The cigar man gave a grunt. "Too bad for you." Then he added, "You folks here to buy something or to take up my time?" But even while he said that he was offering me a cigar, holding an open box toward me over the counter.

Ben looked at the price while I stood there, inhaling and exhaling. "No thanks," he said. On my behalf apparently.

Lou hustled us out the door.

"Highway robbery," Ben said when we were back on the

sidewalk. "Fifty cents each. Those are nickel cigars at best, and even that is stretching it."

Lou was thinking again. "Funny," she said, "that your friend buys his cigars on tick. In a whorehouse."

"Whorehouse?" Ben said.

Lou and I tried to explain but he said we were seeing things.

The street had changed, I swear, while we were inside the cigar store. Someone was putting up a sign for a dentist's shop. There was a glass window where there'd been a hole in a wall across the street just five minutes before, and behind the window was a full display of fresh eggs complete with a live chicken.

"Wouldn't that be a treat," Lou said. She meant fresh eggs.

I elbowed my way across the street to have a look.

"What're they worth?" she called.

I read the sign. "One dollar."

"A dollar a dozen?" Lou just about exploded. "Thieves and scoundrels. What did I tell you?"

I looked again. "Whoops," I said. "These eggs are a dollar each."

"Your age and you can't read." Lou came tromping through the mud to have a look for herself.

She blinked in amazement. "That's a full day's wages, back in Seattle. One egg. And pretty good wages too." She pointed a finger in my face. "Think of the money these people are making, to pay that kind of a price."

The winds were shifting, I saw. It crossed my mind that I might be up for a new pair of pants. I knew I should look a little better than I did.

Ben stopped in front of a brand-new bank that had opened

a week before, according to the banner over the door. There were ten gold bricks stacked in the window, four, then three on top of those four, then two, then one.

"Those fakes are so good," Ben said, "they almost had me fooled." He said that as if he knew what real gold looked like.

I had to go into the bank and look for myself. Ben and Lou were all for going on, but they followed after me nevertheless.

I did the talking. I walked up to a clerk and asked him if the gold was real.

He gave me a sneering, condescending, pitying look. The little shit was about a year older than I was. "How long you been here?" he wanted to know.

"Long enough," I told him.

Lou came to my rescue. "We were wondering — is that real gold or what, there in the window?"

"Go give it a lift, ma'am," the kid said, politely.

Lou walked over to where the display was set in the window. Carefully, as if there had to be a catch somewhere, she reached down and lifted the top brick.

She tried to lift it.

The brick didn't budge.

"As I live and breathe," she said. "Ben. Come look at this."

"Go ahead," the clerk told her. "Give it a hoist."

On her second try she managed to lift one end. "It weighs a tonne. You try, Peek."

I gave a little shrug. Then I said, "Okay." I could be just as polite as any punk bank clerk.

I gave that top brick a little heft. "Gold is heavy," I said.

The clerk gave me a meagre little nod. He was just a shade bored with gold bricks and he wanted me to know it. "Fourteen times as heavy as water. That's why they use so much water, at wash-up time. The water takes off the gravel and sand and leaves nothing but gold." He pretended to stifle a yawn. "You see?" he added.

"Of course," I said.

Ben managed to lift the brick. But after he did it he scratched himself here and there, on top of one ear, inside his left thigh. "Must be worth a small fortune." He was flummoxed.

When we went back on the street we realized we'd forgotten to ask the kid about McGrew.

"Probably owns half that bank," Ben said.

"You go back in there and ask," Lou told me.

"We know our way," I told her in return. I pointed out a ginger beer shop.

"Time for a treat," Ben said. He was more or less out of focus. He needed to sit down. "We've earned one."

We sat down at a white iron table on white iron chairs and each of us had a glass of ginger beer. We made the mistake of drinking our glasses dry before Ben went to pay.

"That'll be one-fifty." The vendor looming over our table. People were waiting to sit down. He indicated the gold scales sitting on the counter. "Dust or cash?"

Ben was half ashamed to say he was paying with cash.

The vendor took the coins without bothering to count them. "I'm coining money," he said. "You wouldn't believe it."

Ben was still contemplating the high cost of ginger beer.

"That's good news," Lou said.

"Came in on the *Bella*. Just been here five days. I'm coining money. Can't avoid it. I just go on coining money."

Ben was going through his pockets as if he'd just noticed his wallet was missing.

"The boy there looking for work?" The vendor pointed at

me as if Lou might not know where I was. He was an oldish man and looked tired. I saw that a young live wire in that place could really make it hum.

Lou answered for me. "He's not interested. Are you, Peek?" She bent across the table and whispered in her usual loud voice to Ben and me and the whole place, "Ignore him. He's just apologizing to himself for not being out in the creeks where the real profit is."

Ben was on his feet again.

Wherever you looked, men were heading out. They had new maps in their hands and they were carrying huge packs on their backs, boxes and sacks and bedrolls, with picks and shovels and pans and axes tied on wherever there was room to do some tying. Some of those men could hardly walk. Their faces were clean-shaven. Their hands were smooth and clean. They seemed to know they should be embarrassed for themselves, instead of swaggering, but they tried to swagger anyway. One way to do that was to bump and bounce your way into a bar, implying that you'd like to have one last drink before you got on with the burdensome chore of striking it rich. The bars had special wide doors, so that stampeders, or cheechakos if you prefer, wouldn't have to unload.

We were walking. Ben and Lou and I walked up one street and down the next. Things were happening so fast you couldn't tell if you were on a new street or on one that had changed since you saw it twenty minutes before. After a while Lou said the ginger beer hadn't agreed with her stomach, she was feeling sickish.

"We could go back to our boat," Ben said.

That was about the last thing I wanted to do. I had a lot yet to see.

"Let's call it a day," Lou said. "We could go back to the boat," she said, as if Ben hadn't said it already. "Let's have one special day. Just for ourselves." She glanced around as if astounded at all the noise, the wagons and teams, the men jostling and pushing, the store windows full of mining gear, the packtrains with every horse or mule carrying mine props or grub or even a stove or a table. "We got here," she said, "didn't we?"

"I'll drink to that," Ben said. He was trying to sound cheerful.

That's when I pointed out the swinging doors we were walking past. On the left door it said SAL and on the right door it said OON.

Lou and Ben studied the doors as if they couldn't put the two halves of the word together. Finally Lou said, "Can we afford it, Ben?"

Ben didn't bother to reply. He was determined to be cheerful. He led us in through the swinging doors. He led us up to a long bar that seemed to trail off somewhere into the darkness at the back of the deep room. I could make out a couple of crap tables, in the light from the doorway. Then my eyes adjusted and I could see a blackjack table. I didn't let on that I was feeling pretty excited. I recognized two faro tables and, beyond them, a roulette wheel. I mean, I could actually hear the little ball going around inside the wheel that was going around. I liked the way the colours blurred, the red and the black, there on the turning wheel. I wasn't simply excited. I felt I was in a dangerous place. But I wasn't the least bit afraid.

The bar was polished oak, ornately carved on the sides, bunches of grapes and that kind of stuff, and shiny, wickedly smooth on top, there in the cozy light. I counted five kerosene lamps in a row on the bar, spaced out, far apart, burning right there in the middle of the day. A bartender set up three glasses before we could say hello and poured them full of whiskey without so much as asking what we'd like.

Ben raised his glass and studied the colour of the whiskey. He looked closely at me and then at Lou, and then at the whiskey again.

"Here's mud in your eye," he said. It was just a saying.

Lou raised her glass to Ben while pretending not to see that I was doing the same. I was amazed that Lou kept her mouth shut.

Ben knocked back his drink and grimaced.

"Too strong?" I asked.

"Too much water," he said. "This whiskey is watered."

The bartender ignored the comment. "Again?"

Ben nodded.

The bartender had set down the bottle beside a pair of gold scales. That is, those scales were for weighing gold. Nuggets or flakes or dust. They were made of solid brass. They looked to me like some kind of crazy huge golden butterfly. I was drinking on a stomach that was practically empty. Or some kind of insect. A huge fierce insect, all poised and polished, made of solid brass. They looked like they might at any second leap, or lunge, or take flight, or attack you head on, or even make some kind of awful mating sound. I shivered and felt a thrill at the same time, just thinking all those thoughts. I didn't knock my whiskey back, I sipped it.

The barkeep tiled the half empty whiskey bottle up and poured Ben another drink.

"What're you getting for this water?" Ben asked.

I sipped my whiskey again. It tasted okay to me.

"Four bits," the bartender said.

"That's about forty cents too much."

The bartender gave Ben a condescending look. "You should have been here a week ago. Before the steamboats arrived. We were trading gold and whiskey ounce for ounce. Flat even."

Ben and Lou gave each other a look that was full of arithmetic. Three kegs. Just last week, they would have had the grubstake. Gold at seventeen dollars an ounce. Whiskey at seventeen dollars an ounce. Fair trade, no questions ask, put down your bullion, drink up.

"We should have been here last week," Ben said.

"If pigs could fly," Lou said. She took a healthy sip.

I did likewise, again, trying to figure out how Ben knew the whiskey was watered. I thought of the two kegs I'd thrown overboard back there in the Whitehorse Rapids. Whiskey at seventeen dollars an ounce. Back in Seattle that would have been a month's wages.

We knew we were spending too much money too fast. But we were celebrating. Taking a day off. Announcing our arrival.

"We got here," Ben said.

Maybe he and Lou were getting ready to talk about their partnership deal. I don't know. But just about then a commotion started outside the swinging doors. We ignored it at first.

"What do you think those cigars would cost?" I asked, pointing at the rows of boxes on the high counter behind the bar.

"About the same as a new pair of pants," Lou said.

Ben stepped away from the bar to look through the swinging doors. I think maybe he was just signalling to Lou to lay off, give the kid a rest, we're taking a holiday from ourselves.

29

The piano came as a surprise.

There wasn't a piano in all of Dawson City until the steam-boat *May West* began to unload. McGrew had a talent for look-ing a long ways ahead. He had sent out his order to San Francisco six months earlier. The piano had travelled from San Francisco to western Alaska on a freighter and waited in St. Michael for a steamboat and then been brought up the Yukon to Dawson. All that in a mere six months.

It was the same piano the poet referred to as the music box. Music box indeed. I guess so. It was a grand.

Four men had driven up to the front door of the saloon in a wagon pulled by a team of underfed black Percherons.

I'll tell you what happened next. It was one of those moments when you know something before anyone has told you what you know.

The man reaching over the side of the wagon from inside — the man unbolting the rod across the back end of the wagon box — could only be Dan McGrew.

I had never seen him before, of course. But he had a look about him that told me who he was. He could only be the man I had heard about from Gussie Meadows. He was the man Gussie Meadows said she would have come to Dawson to kill, if she had come here at all.

He was handsome in a pale way, under his grey bowler. He looked as if he was startled to be out in daylight. It was a warm and sunny Yukon summer day. His face was unnaturally pale, behind his drooping moustache. He was wearing cowboy boots, which hardly went with his hat, but there you have it. They were reddish-brown boots, decorated with enough white stitching to hold together my jeans. There wasn't a trace of mud on those boots.

He managed to slide the rod out of the way. He jumped down from the back of the wagon.

When he stood on the wooden sidewalk he was taller than I'd expected him to be, maybe because of his boots. I'd say he was a good two inches taller than Ben. I was slightly taller than Ben myself, though he sometimes argued the point.

Dangerous Dan had a big-man way about him when he pretended he was going to lift one end of that piano all by himself, with the three men still in the wagon box trying to lift the other. The truth was, the four of them together couldn't have lifted it. There's enough steel in one of those things to sink a ship.

The piano wasn't crated. It turned out the captain had put it to good use in the salon on his steamboat. Hardly the way to treat a piano that's being transported at someone else's expense. It was resting on its side on two buffalo robes.

Lou and Ben and I were watching from just inside the swinging doors. The four men were having trouble deciding how to get the piano from the wagon onto the sidewalk. Lou led the way out of the saloon, through the swinging doors, indicating by her swiftness of motion that she intended to give some instructions. She had seen a few pianos delivered in her day, all of them to the back door of the pawnshop where she'd worked in Seattle.

Ben followed after her. So did I. So did five or six customers and a couple of bartenders. It was the middle of the day, so there weren't any dancehall women in for work.

Dan looked up sharply when Lou told him how to take hold of a piano. He looked up at Lou and noticed the man standing at her side.

Ben Redd and Dan McGrew had never laid eyes on each other. That's the funny part of it. They'd talked on and off for three days and well into three evenings, in a cooperage on the bank of the Mississippi River in Davenport, Iowa. They had whispered. They had let their silences do the talking, when they were in danger of being overheard. It had all been illicit. And irresistible too. Little could Dan have guessed that I knew the story. Gussie always trusted me.

Ben was used to Dan's voice having a kind of muted echo to it, that because Dan had been hiding in a huge oak tun while he did his begging and boasting.

As I said, Lou spoke up. "Take hold there," she said, pointing, "or you'll wreck that thing before you get it off the wagon."

Sometimes Lou had a way of giving advice that made it sound like she was giving an order.

"Thanks, lady."

Ben hadn't guessed up until then that he was looking at Dan McGrew. But he heard those two words and he knew.

Lou, with no success, was trying to say something more.

"Dan McGrew," Ben said.

"The same," Dan said. He wasn't looking when he spoke.

"Davenport, Iowa," Ben said. "Seven years back."

Dan McGrew would have dropped his end of the piano, if he'd been able to lift it. He stepped off the sidewalk and damned near got some dust on his boots. He stepped up onto the new wooden sidewalk again and turned around and stared at the man who had spoken.

"Ben Redd?" he asked.

"Likewise. The same."

"As I live and breathe," Dan said. "Good to see you. At long last. Where the hell you been?"

"Getting here," Ben said.

Dan took a step backward. While he was taking a look at Ben he polished the toe of his right boot on the back of his left pantleg. When he finished that he put out a hand.

Ben and Dan shook hands.

Ben looked sheepish. "We had some delays."

Dan slapped Ben on a shoulder. "You managed to miss one hell of a bad winter, I'll give you credit for that." He looked again at Ben. "So you're Ben Redd. After all these years. We never once laid eyes on each other, you know."

"I know," Ben said.

"You sure you're Ben Redd?"

"One and the same."

Dan turned to the men waiting in the wagon box and gestured back at Ben while he spoke. "This is Ben Redd of Davenport, Iowa. This man saved my hide. You better believe it. He's a gentleman of the first order."

Ben tried to introduce Lou and me. He was speaking to Dan's back while he did it. Dan turned around and tipped his bowler in Lou's direction. He hardly looked at me at all. He was trying to look past me, into the bar.

He was waiting to be surprised.

That was the trouble, you see. Dangerous Dan McGrew was waiting for Gussie Meadows to leap through the swinging doors and throw her arms around him and cry out his dangerous name and call him lovey-dovey things.

He waited all right. He stood there, just waiting. It wasn't like Dan McGrew to go charging in somewhere to find someone. He was the kind of man who stood there expecting to be greeted and embraced and coddled.

That's where the trouble began.

Dan kept on waiting and Ben just stood there. Ben was waiting too. He thought there ought to be something more to a meeting of two men who had, if I might say so, had a tangle with death and won.

Ben had risked his own life to save Dan. Or to put it another way, Dan had saved his own neck by risking Ben's. That's the way it was. Those two men, there in a cooperage on the Mississippi River, had whispered to each other without the reassurances of sight or touch. They had talked their connection. They had made promises. They had done all that. And then one day seven years later, now, out on a street and under a sun that wouldn't set, they were staring at each other. At last, they were meeting. They could talk straight out.

"Did you catch up with Gussie?" Dan said. To Ben. "Gussie Meadows."

I was tempted to answer. On Gussie Meadows' behalf. I wanted to say, Dan McGrew, you hid your ass in a big barrel while a couple of your card-partner friends were searching high and low because you cheated them in a card game and they wanted to string you up by your cheating thumbs from a riverboat loading boom. And now you're wondering why Gussie Meadows has disappeared.

"We did," Ben said. "We found her."

"I'll bet she's hiding out in the saloon. One of her tricks again."

It was then that Ben realized he had got himself a tough assignment.

"She isn't with us, Dan."

Dan's pale face turned dark. Not red. Dark. He used a thumb and a forefinger to separate the two halves of his mustache. "That so, Ben?"

"I'm afraid it is. I'm afraid it is, Dan. Yes."

Just like that, with no further ado, Dan turned back to helping get the piano off the wagon. There were six men working at it already.

"She was at Lake Bennett," Ben said. "Bennett City."

Dan was too busy to hear, apparently. He practically lifted one end of the piano by himself. I could see he actually was powerfully built, under his suit jacket and his double-breasted yellow silk vest and his boiled shirt and his red tie and his gold tiepin.

I had Gussie's message in the right front pocket of my tattered jeans. It didn't seem right to deliver the message right then. It would have been adding insult to injury.

Everything was going wrong. Dan didn't like the way the men on the wagon were pushing the piano around, and he said so in some pretty rough language. He told them to get it down onto the sidewalk in one goddamned hurry and stop pussyfooting around like a goddamned bunch of two-bit four-flushing virgins.

He turned to Ben. "This piano will make the Malamute Saloon unique in this town. You just wait and see."

I hadn't until then read the sign up on the false front of the building. It was a genuine clapboard building, not a tent, not logs. In big golden letters across the false front, above the swinging doors, was the single word MALAMUTE.

Dan didn't give Ben a chance to say anything. That is, he spoke, but he didn't wait for answers. "Gussie Meadows is quite a dancer," he said. "I've seen her dance."

Neither Ben nor Lou nor I said a word. Or at least we didn't speak until Ben couldn't keep his mouth shut.

"I've seen her dance myself, Dan. Get her in here dancing, you'll have half the miners in the territory lined up at the front door. She'll shut down the gold creeks."

I tried to kick Ben in the back of an ankle and missed.

Three men coming down the sidewalk stepped down into the street. Instead of going around the team and wagon they stopped to admire the piano.

"Now that's a piano," one of them said.

Dan saw and heard their admiration. He reached and touched the piano as if he was touching pure silk. Or pure gold. I couldn't tell which.

Pretty soon seven and then eight men were in the wagon box and that many again were working on the sidewalk. They got the piano off the wagon. But they wouldn't let it touch the wooden sidewalk. They held it suspended as if they were waiting for someone to sit down and play a tune right there. Ben rushed over to hold open one of the swinging doors. I held open the other one.

Deciding where to locate the piano in the saloon turned out to be a major undertaking. Dan kept telling the men to put it here and then to put it there. They'd put it down, then he'd say, "Step back for a moment please." They'd all step back and just plain oooh and aaah. While they did that Dan studied the whole room as if, once the piano was in place, it could never again be moved. He would study and think and then lift up his bowler briefly and put it back on his head. That meant we were going to move again. I was trying to lend a hand. "Let's try it over there for a minute," Dan would say, pointing, and we'd all go trooping after him again, maybe eight men carrying the piano, the rest of us following along, just touching it but not really lifting.

While all this was happening Ben was trying to apologize about Gussie Meadows as if everything that had happened was his fault. He was trying to explain about the hardware store and how she saw her chance and then made a fortune in no time flat and how she took her packtrain load of money and went back to Frisco. Lou saw that Ben was talking himself ever and ever into a tighter and tighter corner, so she put in her two cents' worth. She was all for pushing the piano up against the wall at the back of the saloon where the fiddlers stood when they played for dances.

"The dance floor is back there," she said.

"So is the door to the shithouse," Dan said.

Ben had a suggestion too. He wanted to place the piano inside the swinging doors where customers entering the saloon would see it right off the bat and be knocked over with, as he put it, astonishment and admiration.

"The customers," Dan said, "would be knocked over. And so would the piano. When these miners get drunk they get drunk."

Dan's special card table was in the back corner of the saloon on the side near the huge, long bar that ran the entire length of the room. From that table he could watch everything that happened at the bar and everything that was going on at the gambling tables and everything that was happening on the dance floor. He wondered out loud if the piano ought to be placed right there at his elbow.

That's when I finally spoke up. "That's not a bad idea. But people are going to crowd around the piano player. They'll block your view."

Dangerous Dan looked at me as if he hadn't until that minute noticed my presence. "Pretty smart, kid. You're right."

I could see that he made up his mind just then.

He gave me one more look. I could see him deciding I was a harmless and maybe even useless kid. It hurt me to think that such an insensitive man could have been Gussie Meadows' lover. Or perhaps he still was, in some way. Or would be again. Or at least he thought he would be again, since he didn't know me from Adam.

I had that message in my pocket, the message from Gussie that said, "I'm going back to Frisco, Dan. Just as well. I was coming there to kill you." I had memorized the message when she read it aloud. I had tried on each word the way you try each finger of a new glove. I had the envelope in the palm of my right hand in my pocket. I could feel the sweat from my palm making the envelope warm and sticky.

Dan turned away from me and signalled. "There," he said. He'd decided where the piano would go. He told a dealer and four players to move their blackjack table.

He was satisfied. He had the men place the piano in the middle of the room. The piano player, seated facing the gambling tables, would have the dance floor on his left, the bar on his right. His back would be to the card table at the back of the room where Dan did his card playing.

Dan walked in a circle around the piano. "Dead on," he said.

Lou went out onto the dance floor and studied the piano. She tilted her head this way and that, trying to imagine a piano player. Someone brought in the piano stool and put it down.

Dan pointed at the stool and then at the bar. The bartenders, he explained, could see the player in right profile. That was handy. All they had to do was give a little signal when the player was to stop and let the percentage girls get their dance partners to buy drinks. Dan was bald about his calculations.

He walked to the back of the saloon and sat down at his card table.

"How does it look from there?" Lou called.

"I'll be looking the piano player straight in the back." He laughed at his own joke. "And that's fine with me. So long as there's a beautiful singer at the other end of that damned piano, looking my way."

I realized he still believed that Gussie Meadows was going to jump out of nowhere and give him a big hug.

"What about the gamblers?" I said.

Ben came back to the piano. I thought he hadn't heard my question. He pointed around at the busy blackjack table, the faro tables, the crap tables, the roulette wheel. Then he said, "Gamblers don't listen to music. They gamble."

No one had touched a key on the piano. It was then that McGrew said, "Too bad we don't have someone here who can play this thing."

He was puffing a little, as if had done the lifting. He hadn't touched the piano since it was put in place. I'd noticed that.

Both Ben and I volunteered at the same time. I'd had no idea up until then that Ben knew the black keys from the white on a keyboard. He was just as surprised to hear me volunteer.

"You go ahead," he said.

"No, you, Ben."

"No, you," he said.

We said that back and forth a few times.

"Good Christ, Ben," McGrew said. "Stop talking. Sit down. Tickle the ivories a little."

Ben, reluctantly, sat down on the piano stool. He played

maybe twenty bars of something or other. He was muttering about Beethoven or one of those guys and apologizing at the same time. He jumped up as if the piano stool was on fire.

That's when Lou got into the act. "Go ahead, Peek. Show these folks how you can play."

I absolutely hated it when she did that. Sometimes when things were slow in the pawnshop she called a couple of listeners together and she'd say, "Play for us, Peek." And before I was allowed to start she'd say, "Taught himself, you know. Right here. Right here in this pawnshop. Plays anything by ear. Sing him a tune and he'll pick it up right now. Just try him."

Before I sat down to play I handed McGrew the message from Gussie Meadows. I put it into his right hand and said, "Gussie asked me to deliver this envelope to you."

Believe me, I played. I hadn't seen a piano in eight or nine months. My fingers were stiff. But I played. Having Dan McGrew stand directly behind me while he opened that envelope gave me marvellous powers of concentration. I played with such concern that the people in the saloon, even those at the gambling tables, or at least those at the bar, stopped whatever they were doing and listened.

"Hey, that kid's pretty good," somebody said.

"He's loud," somebody else said. "You've got to give him that."

You'd have thought Gussie's message was about twenty pages long, the time it took McGrew to read it. For a moment I wondered if maybe he couldn't read and was bluffing.

Then all of a sudden he spoke. I couldn't tell if he was speaking to Ben or to Lou.

"You got any place to stay?" he said.

It was Lou, standing behind me, who answered. "We can stay on our boat for a while. It's comfortable enough."

Dangerous Dan was silent. I thought maybe he was actually listening. Then he said, "I built a cabin for Gussie. It's been all ready for a few months now."

I made a mistake in my playing. I started to start over.

"That'll do," Lou said. "The piano is fine. You've done your duty, Peek. And no more drinks, understand?"

She was blaming my difficulty at the piano on my one little slug of whiskey.

"You might as well move into the cabin," Dan said. It was hard to tell if he was speaking to all of us or to no one in particular. It was as if the voice that spoke out of his mouth wasn't quite his to order around.

"No use having it stand empty," he said.

30

You talk about being shit-scared, well that's what I was. I thought the whole damned saloon might fall on my head. I waited for Dangerous Dan McGrew to be dangerous. You know. Kill the messenger. He couldn't get the piece of paper out of his hand.

He spoke so quietly that I could hardly hear what he was saying. He told us to take the team and wagon and go get our outfit from our boat. Lou and Ben and I jumped into the wagon along with the man who owned it. We drove through the streets of Dawson taking in the sights.

There were two-storey frame buildings along the street, log buildings, tents. Some of the buildings had fancy awnings. All of them had signs.

I read some of the signs aloud.

"KLONDIKE GUNS AND AMMO."

"I can read," Lou said.

"DOCTOR MERCHANT DENTIST."

"That's a good one," Ben said.

"GLOBE SALOON."

"Leave it to Peek to notice a saloon. What's becoming of that boy?"

"MRS McDONALD FANCY DRESS MAKING AND LADIES TAILORING. You ought to go there, Lou."

"Maybe I will." Then she read aloud a sign that said LAUNDRY. "You ought to go there, Peek."

Ben was getting into the act. "BURLINGTON LIQUORS AND CIGARS. That's for you, Peek."

I read another sign. "NUGGET WORK, POND AND CO."

"Company," Lou said. "The word is company. Co. is just short for company."

"I know that."

"Of course. You know everything. It must be wonderful to be your age."

We had to stop for two men who were trying to herd about forty hogs down the street. They were thin-looking hogs. Maybe a dozen men were following after the pig-herders, trying to buy fresh pork on the hoof.

We started out again. I was reading the signs, but just to myself. An old man had an anvil out in front of a tent and a sign leaning against the block of wood that held the anvil: **BLACK-SMITHING**. A huge tent had a banner on it: **OUTFITS BOUGHT AND SOLD**. Two men were putting up a sign over the front door of a new building: **TURNER AND CO. AUCTIONEERS**.

"What do you think?" Lou said.

She had changed the tone of her voice.

Ben and I pretended we didn't know what she was asking about.

"How's that?" Ben said. He was standing beside the teamster. Lou and I were standing on either side of the wagon box, holding on because of the ruts and all the jolts we were getting.

"What do you think, Ben? About your friend."

"You mean Dan?"

"Who else?"

"What do *you* think?" Ben said.

"He's sort of handsome," Lou said. "The tall, handsome type. I guess that's the first thing you have to give him."

"Handsome?" I had to disagree at once. "You call that handsome? I'd say he looks sickly and pale."

"About as sickly and pale as a healthy ox," Lou said. "And, if you ask me, just about as smart. That's what worries me."

It was Ben's turn to disagree. "He owns that saloon. More than you can say for us."

"Who wants to own a saloon?" Lou asked. "Did you see him trying to decide where to place a piano? A *piano,* for God's sake. You'd think he was erecting a statue."

"It's important," Ben said.

"That reminds me." Lou tapped Ben on the shoulder to make sure she had his attention. "You never told me you play the piano."

"We haven't seen a whole lot of pianos along the way."

"That's not the point, is it? How did you learn?"

"I took lessons. I had no choice."

Lou was, to use one of her own words, prying.

"Who was it gave you this no choice?"

"My mother. Who else? I had to take piano lessons. Everybody had to."

"Not *everybody,*" Lou said.

"Your mother pushed you around," I said. I wasn't sure if I meant that as an assertion or a question.

"Peek. That's a stupid thing to say." But no sooner had Lou said that than she added, "You've never mentioned your mother, Ben."

"You've never asked."

That was a pretty weak explanation. Ben knew it too. Something was in the air. The two of them were sparring and holding onto each other at the same time. I could hardly stand it. I let my body hang loose and jiggle in the bouncing wagon. I put my left hand into my jeans pocket and hung onto myself. Everything was jiggling.

"I shouldn't have to ask," Lou said.

"Well. Go ahead. Ask away."

"Did you care for your mother?"

Why do mothers like to ask that impossible question? I was ready to go to Ben's defence. But then he pretended he didn't quite understand what Lou was asking.

"I looked after her from the time I was thirteen years old."

"I don't mean look-after care. I mean, *care.*"

I recognized that I was being offered a little lesson in love and responsibility. Lou was feeling at loose ends and she was just about as scared as I was.

"She's sort of an invalid," Ben said. "My mother."

"That's a shame. What's wrong with her, Ben?"

"The doctors can't figure it out."

He was being quite direct. But sometimes Lou wouldn't settle for simple directness. "*Something* must be wrong."

"Well...my father died."

"What killed him?" I said.

"What makes you think something *killed* him, Peek?"

"The steam," Ben said. "It was a railroad accident."

"Like the opposite of an avalanche." Don't ask me why that came out of my mouth.

"Mind your own beeswax," Lou said to me.

"He was boiled alive," Ben said. He said that in a completely flat tone.

We had to stop while a packtrain crossed in front of us, heading for the gold creeks. There were a dozen packhorses in the train, most of them loaded with sacks and boxes of food. Two of them were loaded with lumber. One was carrying a stove.

"Do you miss your mother?" I said.

Ben nodded in that irritating way he had of nodding just a little bit too vigorously. "I'll be back there before too long, I hope."

That made us all quiet again. I had opened another can of worms. I pointed out a couple of dogsleds, sitting on their asses in the mud.

We stopped for an eight-mule team pulling a huge and heavily loaded wagon. That wagon was moving away from the waterfront while we moved toward it. When the way was clear we started out again, down streets that were busier and busier the closer we got to the river. Men came along the rutted and muddy streets carrying whole outfits on their backs.

One man was pulling a two-wheeled cart loaded with crates of live turkeys.

I wanted to hear more about Ben's and Lou's reactions to Dan McGrew, so I said, "He doesn't look the way I thought he'd look."

"Who's that, Peek?" Lou knew who I was talking about. She was forcing me to say the name.

"The handsome and irresistible Dangerous Dan McGrew."

"Oh, him." She pretended she was searching her memory.

Ben was giving the driver instructions so we could find our boat among the hundreds that lined the shore of the river. There must have been two thousand tents in the way, with more being unpacked and unfolded and set up. We had to get around three long stacks of firewood that stevedores were loading onto steamboats, for the boilers. Two more steamboats had arrived during the time we were in town, the *Alaska* and the *Bailey*.

"I was asking you a question," I reminded Lou.

"What did you expect, Peek? If Gussie Meadows loves a man, what do you think he's going to look like?"

I could hardly criticize myself. "Handsome," I said. "Smart. Generous. Kind. Loving."

"Wow." Lou threw up her hands in mock dismay and nearly lost her balance, because of the way the wagon was jolting us around. "Are we talking about a man or are we talking about God's gift to women?"

I wanted to say that I, so far at least, had not recognized my announced list of male qualities in the person of Dan McGrew. But I could hardly say that without inviting more questions.

"A pig's arse," I muttered, under my breath.

"What did I hear you say?"

"I forget," I said.

Ben was busy giving instructions to the teamster who needed no instructions at all but was busy trying to get his team and wagon in between staked tents and past dismantled boats and around heaps of freight. Not to mention about four hundred dogs that seemed to have been abandoned by their owners and were complaining aloud.

When we got to the shore we found Whipsaw sound asleep, in the midst of all the din, on the deck of the raft. His dress was up over his hairy knees. His washline was full of dry clothes.

"Peek," he said when I nudged him with my toe, "I thought you got lost. I thought you must be gone forever. I was just about ready to sell your outfit."

We told him we were taking the outfit, but the boat was his. Keep it, we told him.

Whipsaw wasn't totally delighted at receiving the gift, but he was gracious. "I could always just cut it loose," he said. "But thanks. Thanks anyway."

He helped us load the wagon, in spite of his back. We had to move our outfit across the raft and then up a gangplank onto the shore and then lift it onto the wagon. The teamster didn't raise a hand.

Ben and Lou were so busy piling our outfit onto the wagon they hardly said goodbye to Whipsaw. They were preoccupied. They were helping each other lift every little item, as if even a can of beans must weigh a tonne. But they weren't talking. I went back onto the raft and gave Whipsaw a hug. He gave me the sweetest kiss, on both cheeks, and told me to live long and to get filthy rich in a hurry, and then he'd ask me to marry him.

31

Which, by the way, I did. I don't mean I got married. I mean, I got rich. Not filthy rich. Not by a long shot. I got just rich enough so I could stay right here in Lou's cabin for another hundred years. And I'm still going strong. Except for my legs. And this damned constipation. You'd think the wonders of modern medicine could unplug an asshole. But no. The same miracle science that couldn't bung me up back there in Sheep Camp now can't figure out how to liquefy shit.

But I'm getting ahead of myself.

Dangerous Dan McGrew was waiting like a lost child in front of this cabin when Ben and Lou and I drove up with our wagonload of just about everything.

The place is shabby now. Back in 98 the logs were newly cut and peeled and shiny and fresh-smelling, the windows were new and their frames not yet painted. The shingle roof was new. The low picket fence around the yard was new and unpainted. I never did get around to slapping on a coat of paint. Nothing rots in this climate. Frozen all the goddamned time. The ground inside the fence was mostly stumps and fireweed, as it still is. When it isn't all snow. Dan McGrew had plans for the yard, back then. He just hadn't yet got around to executing them. He was waiting for Gussie Meadows' advice.

Actually, the fireweed is mostly gone. The berry bushes took over, mostly kinnickinnick.

Dan was sitting on the doorstep. It looked like he didn't have a key, or couldn't find it if he did. He jumped up as if he was going to help us unload. There was no path from the gate to the door, because no one had yet lived in the cabin. He came right at us, stepping over the fence instead of using the gate. He had long legs, for a man who wasn't all that tall.

Ben and I got down from the wagon. The teamster stayed on it holding the reins as if the horses might bolt if he so much as glanced in our direction.

Lou handed down a box. The light things were on top of the load, clothes and bedding and kitchen utensils. She tried to hand the box to Ben, but Dan took it. He pushed it at me.

"Here," he said. "You take this stuff in. I have to have a few words with Ben."

Lou wasn't about to leave the arranging of the cabin to me. She got down down off the wagon. "Ben," she said, "you take charge."

Ben went to the back of the wagon and took out a box and eased it into Lou's arms and she and I took in our first load.

The packers, on their way to deliver the piano to the saloon, had left in the hallway of the cabin a brass bed and an old Chippendale dresser and a solid oak commode with a porcelain chamber pot. Items intended for Gussie. Lou and I had to put down our boxes and clear a passage for ourselves.

We fell in love with the place right then. It was all furnished and everything was in place, except for the new things. It had the fresh, clean, woody smell of a new cabin. The smell of peeled logs and moss-chinked walls. The floors were unpainted pine. The glass in the windows had not yet been stained by any living.

Lou took the big bedroom, saying it was for herself and Ben. She seemed to have forgotten a few things. The room next door to the bedroom was small, almost tiny. Lou took one look at it, or into it, and said, "Well. Would you believe?

A dressing room for her majesty. This will do for your bed-room, Peek."

Only then did I realize the room had been designed as a special place for Gussie Meadows, a place where she could hang her clothes. And do her dressing. And her undressing too, for that matter. There was a full-length mirror on one wall. And facing it a space for her private commode.

Lou said it would be mine, that room, private and absolute. We could build a bunk in one corner. She pointed at something like thirty wooden clothes hangers all in a row. I thought of the trunks full of Gussie's skirts and blouses and dresses and stock-ings and garters. I guess I should add, so had McGrew.

"Try hanging up your clothes," Lou said. "See if you can master the art." Before I could remark that it wouldn't take me long, to hang up my clothes, she was pointing me out the front door and back to the wagon.

Ben, without saying as much to Dan, had located the three flour sacks that had in them lots of sawdust and three kegs of whiskey. I carried them in while Lou marvelled at having a whole room for a kitchen and another for a parlour. I put the whiskey in my room. I could use the kegs to make a table and a chair for myself, right next to Gussie's commode, which I then and there moved in to where it belonged.

When I went out to begin to bring in food and equip-ment, Dan McGrew told me, in a low voice, just to hang on for a minute.

I very soon caught the gist of the conversation, since Dan was doing all the talking. He was describing, or describing once again, the investment opportunities that abounded in Dawson City. He was talking in a tone that suggested he was trying to prime a pump rather than address a fellow human being.

Ben Redd, perhaps because my presence reassured him, finally got in a few words. He remarked that he was something like three thousand dollars short on the three thousand he had promised to pack in, like so much sow-belly bacon, from outside.

"Well now," Dan said.

I think he had guessed the situation when we pulled up in front of the cabin with a wagonload of mining gear. Not the stuff of investment.

"That's bad news, Ben. Bad news. Very bad news. As you may have noticed, I'm not in the charity business."

"I noticed that, Dan."

Dan could be a fast thinker in his own way.

"I wouldn't want to leave you stranded, Ben. You came here to be one of my partners." Dan checked the toes of his boots for dust. "You'll still be one of my partners. I stick by my friends."

"I'm glad to hear that," Ben said. "That's good news to my ears."

"I won't leave you stranded, Ben. You didn't leave me stranded, when push came to shove. I won't leave you stranded here in the middle of nowhere."

"I appreciate that."

"But you'll have to do some work, Ben. I'll have to put you to work."

It was obvious that to Dan McGrew the very thought of work seemed like pretty severe punishment. Something bordering on cruelty and torture.

"Like they say," Ben said. "Hard work never killed anybody."

Dan said something vague, like idle hands, the devil's playmate.

"You said it," Ben said. "I'm no stranger to work. You saw me, back there in Iowa." He corrected himself. "Or at least, you heard me." He tried to laugh.

"You guys pounding on those barrels, Ben. I'll never forget it. Damned near deafened me."

"We were driving down the hoops," Ben said, "not pounding the barrels. Two men swinging hammers. I loved that sound."

"The noise and the smoke," Dan said. "Terrible. Hellish. Wrecked my nerves."

Ben disagreed again. "Nothing like it. Nothing like it in the whole world. Firing an oak cask. The smell of it all. Got to keep the staves wet and warm at the same time. Fill a crosset with shavings. Burn them under the cask while you're driving down the hoops."

Ben didn't often talk about his work.

"Smoke nearly killed me," Dan said. "I didn't dare cough or I was a goner. Terrible. Think about it. One false move. You're dead."

Ben was into remembering the past. "Blister the staves inside. Blister the oak. That's what you need for a bourbon barrel. I could show you, Dan —"

"What kind of money did you make at that work?" Dan asked.

"Damned little," Ben said. "Goddamned little."

"See what I mean? See what I'm trying to tell you?"

Lou came out of the cabin and through the gate in the picket fence to see why I wasn't being my usual packhorse self.

"You men taking the day off?"

Dan gave her a curt nod and went on speaking to Ben. "There are miners going broke or getting sick every day of the week, out in the creeks." He let that sink in. "On one level, Ben, I need capital. We need capital."

Ben looked around as if he was trying to include Lou and me in the conversation. He wanted to go on telling us how to make a bourbon barrel.

"Men going broke," Dan said. "Men getting busted up. Accidents. Or just getting plain fed up, what with the loneliness and the permafrost and the muck and the fourteen-hour days."

"I can see that," Ben said.

"All they want is out. Just plain out. What I'm saying is, we could snap up some very good claims for a fraction of their potential."

Ben was a wet cooper by trade. That was his business.

"Big Alex McDonald," Dan said, "the King of the Klondike they call him. I know him personally. I've met him. He's worth millions. He never lifts a hand. Just puts up the money. Makes the arrangements."

"They mentioned him there in the saloon," Ben said. "One of those miners said he thought you'll be the next Big Alex."

Dan tried to look modest but didn't succeed. "I wouldn't say that," he said. "I'm just saying I've got some pretty good leads. Some pretty good connections. Being in a saloon, you make connections."

Ben nodded, indicating that he understood perfectly well.

Dan went back to his attempt at a lucid argument. "If you don't have any capital, then you and I can't snap up any bargains, can we, Ben? Certainly not the way Big Alex does."

Ben gave a sympathetic nod.

"However," Dan went on. He paused to let that word sink

into Ben's head. "However. I did get hold of a small claim up on Eldorado Creek. A fellow owed me a little money. Gambling debt. Card game. I settled for the claim."

Ben cleared his throat but didn't speak.

McGrew lowered his voice. "Let's say we're partners. Let's say the two of us, we go shares."

"Sounds like a possibility," Ben said.

"It's my claim," Dan said. "You do the mining. We share the gold, half and half. Fifty-fifty."

Ben was thinking.

"I'm saying, Ben, you'll have to look after the mining end of things. I'm a busy man. Half of what you find is yours."

"That sounds fair enough to me. More than fair."

"You have food in the wagon?"

"A pretty good supply."

If you like beans, I was tempted to say. And Lou's version of sourdough pancakes. And bacon that's gone just a little bit green.

Dan McGrew turned to me, as if I hadn't been standing there all the while

"Young fella." He waggled a finger in my direction. "You just leave a grubstake there on the wagon for Ben. We don't want him starving to death, do we?"

Dangerous Dan was almost ready to pitch in and help separate whatever had to stay in the cabin from whatever had to go to the claim. But then he decided against it.

"Come to think of it, Ben, there's no time like now. You ready to go?"

Ben seemed to be baffled by the question.

"Good enough, Ben. Good enough. We'll be at the creeks by late tonight. There's a sort of a cabin out there. You and me can stay the night. We can get the lay of the land. We can get you set up."

Lou was beside me, listening.

Ben and Lou were confused. I could see that. Lou saved the day by saying it would be good to have Ben out of her hair for one night, that would give her a chance to unpack in the new cabin and to get organized. She was always a great believer in getting organized.

"Time to get settled in," she said. "Enough of this travelling."

She didn't try to elaborate. She left everything hanging. And Ben didn't do any better. He was heavily into scratching the top of his right ear.

32

That's how it came about that Ben and Dan set out for Eldorado Creek on the day of our arrival in Dawson. Dan McGrew was putting Ben to work as a partner.

They didn't come back into town that night.

Lou and I waited up for a while, just in case they had a change in plans. Lou didn't make it to her bedroom at all, she fell asleep on the couch in the lovely room that was the parlour.

"At last in our long lives," she said, "we have a parlour." She was taking her blankets off the couch. "We've never had a parlour, Peek."

She said that as if I didn't know.

When the knock came at the door around noon, I hoped it was Ben.

McGrew was at the door. When I looked past him I saw that the teamster on the wagon was alone.

"Where's Ben?" Lou said. That was her greeting to McGrew.

He was standing there in his cowboy boots and his bowler, admiring the doorstep.

I had slept for the first night ever in the room that would have been Gussie's. The first perfect night of the many to follow in the next hundred years. I had used her commode in the middle of the night. I had sat there in the dark and alone on her commode, listening, watching. And waiting. The dark of the night is about fourteen minutes long, here in the summer. I could just vaguely make out a shadow in the mirror. I sat there thinking of love. And of stockings too, if the truth be told. Stockings emerald and rose. And of garters. I thought about Lou saying, None of that love shit. I jacked off. You better believe I jacked off. Wacked off. I pulled my wire. I flogged my duff. And along with the pleasure I punished myself. It was flogging all right. Kill the messenger indeed. Like some kind of relief from an ache that haunted my mouth. I thought of cinnamon and honey. I thought about cloves.

Dangerous Dan was speaking to Lou.

"I thought Ben should get right to work. The men on the claim below ours are doing their clean-up. They're washing out their piles of gravel. They're sweeping up nuggets faster than they can weigh them."

"What a pity," Lou said.

"Ben has staying power, Lou. As you well know, from what he tells me. Going up over the Chilkoot. Coming down the Yukon. He says you were the leader every time. He gives you full credit. But he has a way of just plain sticking to the job. You know that as well as I do."

"We're here," Lou said.

"That's what I'm trying to say. Staying power. That's what does it. If there's gold in that gravel and muck, Ben will find it. You mark my words."

Lou wasn't quite ready to buy the argument. "Why did you have to start looking for gold on the night of our arrival?"

"Why did you come here, Lou? Ask yourself. Why did I come here? To make hay while the sun shines, that's why. Why did you come here? Make your pot. Get out."

Lou was mad at both men. She was mad at Dan, but she was mad at Ben too. And perhaps she was angry with herself as well. McGrew was breathing easier. "Ben jumped when I sent him that letter. Get here fast, I told him. Real fast. But you know, Lou. Fast is not the same thing for Ben as it is for you and me.

She backed off a little. She knew that if Ben hadn't come to our rescue there on the *Delta Queen* he'd have been in Dawson City with time to spare. He'd have been grubstaking others instead of working a claim himself. He hadn't planned to bring along so much as an axe or a hammer.

It was as if Dan read her mind. "The claims on Eldorado Creek," he explained, "they've all been staked. Some of them twice over. Some of them three times over." He was pretending to let us in on a secret. "People jumping claims. You've got to be right there, all the time, watching." He looked Lou straight in the face with his squinting blue eyes. "You know what I mean?"

But then the fakery went out of his voice.

"My partner didn't get here, Lou."

Just like that, he said it.

For a whole second there, I almost felt sorry for him. He was talking about Gussie Meadows. I was right at Lou's elbow, listening. I came close to knowing how he felt. For a moment it crossed my mind that Gussie had abandoned both of us.

Dan was looking Lou straight in the eyes again. He had recovered himself. "Ben tells me you have a lot of experience with money. And with meeting the public."

What could Lou say to that? Her experience in a pawnshop was a way of meeting a portion of the public that wasn't in the highest of spirits. But it was a meeting. She knew more than she wanted to about the pain a face can wear.

Maybe Dan McGrew was wearing his own kind of pain. I have to give him that. But he was hiding it behind his fast talking.

"He says you know something about gold."

"Not really, Dan. I know something about engagement rings and wedding rings and gold watches, and how much they're worth in a pawnshop." She grimaced. "Or how little."

That didn't faze Dan for a minute.

"I thought maybe you might be interested in a first-rate job."

Lou spoke her mind then. "I've been thinking, Dan. We moved in here yesterday, without so much as time to say hello. I guess I was at my wit's end, in a way. What with —" She trailed off into a mumble. Then she caught herself. "Everything. I thought about it half the night. Everything. I hope you know that if Gussie Meadows shows up —"

Dan didn't let her go on. "Gussie Meadows isn't going to arrive. She said in her note she isn't going to arrive. That means she isn't going to arrive."

That hurt me, I'll admit. That hurt bad. Dangerous Dan

was speaking to me instead of to Lou, but he didn't know it. I was tempted to remind him of what else she'd said in her note. I guess I had sort of been clinging to one small hope.

"I need a weigher," Dan said. "An honest weigher. One I can trust with sacks of gold."

I hardly listened while Dan talked. He was offering Lou a job in the Malamute Saloon.

He needed someone he could trust to look after the gold scales. It would be a demanding job, he explained, but she had the advantage of not knowing anyone in town and not being under pressure from anyone to ignore a few ounces of sand or a scoop of brass filings in the gold. She could be dead honest.

He went on explaining what the job would involve and I could see that Lou was thinking about all kinds of things that Dan wasn't saying. She was thinking about Ben and her partnership with him and how they had shaken hands and agreed that it would end when they set foot in Dawson City. She was thinking about how she planned to come up with a scheme for getting rich, and how she kept drawing a blank.

"Twenty bucks a day," Dan said. "For starters."

For one day. That was four times the money she'd made in a week, back in Seattle. She turned and gave me a questioning look. "What do you think, Peek?"

It was my turn to speak my mind. Usually it was Lou who was asking what the price was. The real price. She didn't often ask me. But now it was my turn.

I guess the honest truth is, I wanted to be connected with the Malamute Saloon. I wanted to be there, where Gussie Meadows would have been, if she hadn't gone back to San Francisco. I guess that's the truth of the matter. It hurts me to say so. It kills me.

"Well," I said. "Mr McGrew is in a kind of partnership with Ben. If you work for him then in a way you'll be working with Ben."

Gussie Meadows would have filled the Malamute Saloon with bars of solid gold. I knew that. Dan knew it. Lou knew it, even if she would never let herself say so. But she would do an A-1 job.

"On top of that," I said to Lou, "you have a head for figures."

Dan lifted up his bowler for a moment, as if to let in some air. Or maybe he was trying to say thank you. To Lou. Or to me.

"When can you start work?"

Lou was still trying to catch up with what was happening. "Give me a couple of days."

"Make it twenty-two. Cash or dust, you choose. Mind you, our days aren't short. I'll need you by tomorrow noon."

Dan was turning away when Lou spoke. But he was still within earshot when she said to me, "Peek, this could be my chance to learn the gold business. It might be a good thing."

33

She went to the Malamute next morning, to learn what she was supposed to start doing at noon. She told me to get the cabin straightened up and to split some wood.

The cabin was perfectly clean to begin with, except for our few breakfast dishes. Lou made us still another batch of sourdough pancakes before she set out, all dressed up in her only surviving clothes. I found an axe out back of the cabin. I split up enough wood to provide us with further pancakes for a month. I went out into the bush and cut some spruce branches to put under my bedroll and my bearskin.

By the time all that was done it was still just four o'clock in the afternoon on a day when the sun was going to blink out of sight around midnight and then come up again. The Arctic Circle is so close you can almost see it from here. I was totally alone.

By next morning I had a plan. I suppose I should have called it a scheme, to impress Lou. While she was getting ready to leave the cabin for her second day of work, I told her I was heading out to check on Ben. She said that might be a good idea. She told me to take along some of the biscuits she'd made for our second breakfast in our new home.

I set out walking. The gold creeks were only twelve to fifteen miles out of Dawson, depending on which trail you followed. The weather was sunny and clear.

People offered me rides on wagons. Someone offered to let me sit on a packhorse along with something like forty brand-new pick handles. But I preferred to be alone that day, so I stayed off the main trails. And the trails at best were trails, believe me.

I found my own path, in the acres of stumps that had, before the past winter, been trees. There were still a few men hacking around at what was left. The winter had been a bad one, at least for the forest. The miners used wood to melt the permafrost when they dug down through the muck toward the gravel that might or might not have sprinkled through it some placer gold. They used logs to shore up their diggings. They used logs to build their cabins. They used every scrap of wood they could find to keep themselves from freezing to death. And now they still needed more wood. For their cooking. For the flumes they built to carry water down to their sluice boxes and their rockers.

The men around me, working in what had been forest, were covered in mud and in the soot from old fires. They moved around me like scorched old trees that had learned to walk.

I came to the first diggings. It was as if something like four thousand men had all together and at once lost their minds. There were eighty-five miles of diggings, along the gold creeks. The valley of Bonanza Creek was one of the busiest creeks of all. It was full of men who were digging at great huge mounds of gravel and muck as if there'd been a mudslide and someone was buried. All winter long those men had worked in holes in the ground, thawing the permafrost with banked fires, loading the muck and gravel and then the pay dirt into buckets, winching the buckets by hand up to the surface, heaping up the possible pay dirt for the coming of spring. And a water supply.

It was clean-up time in the creeks. The miners were washing the gold out of their heaps of pay dirt. And dirt it was. Muck and gravel and sand. And maybe a trace of gold. If you were lucky. June had come, and with it runoff water and full streams and creeks and springs. No running water, no gold. No hope of gold. At last the miners had running water. The flumes snaked out of the stripped hills and clung to bare slopes and reached their long, loud troughs down to the heaps of what might be pay dirt muck.

Now and then I saw a head pop out of the ground. A human head. Then it would duck back in again, as if I'd scared it. But most of the men I saw were shovelling pay dirt into rockers and pouring in water and rocking like they were having seizures.

Then they shovelled some more and rocked some more. Or they opened the flume gates, onto their sluice-box riffles. And then they were peeking and hungering, under the riffle bars.

Every so often someone gave a cry that was either joy or agony, I couldn't tell which. Other men rushed to join him and they all paused for a moment, like they were offering up two minutes of silence. Maybe less. And then they'd go whooping back to their wheelbarrows and their shovels and their rockers and their sluice boxes and their flumes, and they'd all be into seizures again.

I was at the site of Discovery Claim.

Right there, on August 16, 1896, George Washington Carmack walked down to a creek where he and his Tagish wife and two of her relatives were camped out on a moose hunt. He went there to get a bucket of water and to take a piss. While he was pissing away he noticed in the gravel bank a gold nugget the size of his thumb.

At least that's one version of the story. Another has it that George was taking a nap when his Tagish brother-in-law, Skookum Jim, took a mining pan down to the creek because he'd become enough of a white man to hunger for gold. And found it.

Lou had her own version of the story, as you might expect. She believed with a kind of fervour that George's wife Kate made the discovery while she was doing the dishes in a mining pan. All three men, George and Jim and Tagish Charlie, were napping. She glanced down into the pan and saw a nugget staring at her like a golden eye.

There was no Dawson City at the time. The site was muskeg. That's all it was. The three men left Kate with the dishes and paddled downriver to the trading post at Fortymile. They registered claims for themselves. While Kate broke camp. At least according to Lou. She developed her version while she was weighing gold for drunk miners, and listening to their lies, in the Malamute Saloon.

Carmack changed the name of Rabbit Creek to Bonanza while he was filing his claim.

I walked on up Bonanza as far as the group of cabins that called themselves Grand Forks. I stopped for a drink of whiskey. And then I branched off from Bonanza and went up into the gulch that was Eldorado Creek.

Ben's cabin was quite a hike up Eldorado. The fireweed was thick all round the cabin, mostly because the claim hadn't been worked for a month. When I first saw Ben he was sitting dead still. He was the only man in the whole place who wasn't frantic. It was like he was waiting for someone.

He didn't look at me. "Hello, Peek," he said.

I said hello.

"Lou with you?"

It was pretty obvious that she wasn't. I was standing alone in front of the log cabin where he was sitting and there wasn't another person around for two hundred and fifty feet in any direction. A claim was five hundred feet in length along the bed of the creek.

"Nope. She isn't with me."

"What brings you out here?

"I dunno."

Ben nodded as if he understood my answer. He was always trying to agree with people and getting things wrong.

I looked around. "Where's the mine?"

Ben shrugged. This from a man who had risked life and limb to get to the Klondike to find gold. Then he pointed at a windlass set over a hole in the ground.

I walked over and took a look. The hole was about four feet by six. At the top. And too dark for measuring at the bottom.

"Too wide for a grave," I called, to where Ben was sitting. I was trying to make him smile.

There was a small heap of dirt beside the windlass. Nothing like the dozens of heaps I'd come by on my way.

Ben pointed downstream.

"You see those men down there?" He was pointing at four or five men who were running and shovelling and waving at each other and slapping their knees. "Six hundred dollars a day. In their clean-up. Four hundred and twenty-two dollars in one pan. And then, twenty minutes later, a nugget that weighed one pound and three ounces. They keep charging up here to tell me."

"Sounds easy. Sounds like a cinch. What're we waiting for?"

He turned awkwardly and pointed upstream. "You see those guys?"

There were six men, two of them shovelling gravel, two pouring water, two madly pulling a handle back and forth, rocking the rocker back and forth, back and forth. It made me dizzy just to look. Those big wooden boxes were like hand-run washing machines. Even from that distance you could hear the swish, swish, swish, swish, swish of water and gravel. And desperation.

"I hear them," I said.

"So far they've made seventeen dollars each. They paid sixty thousand for the claim."

I saw that Ben needed help. I noticed that the mining pan by the door was the cleanest item around.

"You done any panning?" I said.

"I took a quick look."

"Any luck?"

"We're not down deep enough. Apparently. That's what they tell me." He pointed downstream again, toward the men who were finding a fortune.

"How do we get down deeper?"

Ben didn't move. "McGrew's cheechako couldn't find the pay streak. That's why he went into Dawson for a drink. That's where he ran into McGrew. The Malamute Saloon."

"I guess the first thing we'll have to do," I said, "is crawl down into that hole and build a fire."

I had learned that much, on my walk along the creeks. You had to crawl down to where the gold might be and thaw more permafrost and dig your hole deeper. The walking corpses and hollering ghosts were one season ahead of us. They'd mined all winter. Now they were washing up and filling sacks with gold dust and nuggets.

"Admit it, Ben. It's just sheer good luck that you're getting into the gold creeks at all. Every square inch of this territory has been staked, claimed, traded."

"Dan told me that," Ben said.

I went right on. Call a spade a spade. "Every inch of it," I said. "It's been remeasured, lied about, sold, stolen and resold. And the stampeders are still pouring in."

Ben wouldn't budge. "And killed for. You missed that one."

"Look," I said. "Here. Now. Someone free of charge hands us a share in a claim on the richest creek in the Klondike territory."

Ben wasn't often into self-pity. But he was into it that time. Luck wasn't doing much for his face. I wanted to make him feel better. That's why I said, "You and Lou and I can make it here, Ben."

I guess I shouldn't have said that. I didn't make it clear. I meant that with her working in the Malamute Saloon and Ben working the claim, they might, if they kept in contact, really do well.

I couldn't bring myself to say that Lou had taken a job in the Malamute. I went on ranting and raving about good fortune and making hay while the sun shines and things like that. Things that Dan might have said. After a while Ben had to do something just to shut me up.

He stood up from the little work bench he was sitting on and went to the wall of the cabin and took hold of the pick that was leaning against the cabin wall beside the mining pan and walked over to the windlass. I went with him. We looked down into the hole. It was dark down there, believe me. The ladder seemed to disappear into darkness. Maybe that's what happened to the cheechako whose name Ben didn't know. Maybe he just couldn't crawl down there one more time.

Ben hesitated for a moment, testing the ladder by putting both feet on it. Then he took one step down. Then he took another. Then he said to me, "You stay up here, partner."

34

It's best to have a partner when you're working a claim. Ben wouldn't let me go down into the shaft. He said I'd have to turn the windlass and heap up the muck he sent up in the windlass bucket.

To get to the gold-bearing gravel there on Eldorado Creek,

we'd have to dig down through muck at least twenty feet, maybe more. Maybe forty feet. Maybe fifty. That doesn't sound too bad. Except that the muck wasn't just muck. It was frozen muck. It was so-called muck the consistency of pig-iron, from two inches under the moss to the frozen gravel that we were looking for, the layer next to the bedrock. Down there we might possibly hit a pay streak.

Our cheechako had got through the muck and down to the gravel. He had even got to bedrock. The trouble was, he hadn't found the pay streak he was looking for. That meant he had to tunnel. Drifting, they called it. Or, worse yet, he had to start all over and dig another hole. And then another. And then another. Until he did find the pay streak. Assuming it was there to be found.

Ben started drifting away from the hole, staying on bedrock, looking for a stream bed that disappeared about fifteen thousand years before we arrived. That's where the flakes and nuggets and grains and tiny specks of gold might be found.

Poor Mr Plow. We had his equipment. You might say we had delivered it for him, all of it, all the way from Skagway. The trouble was, we didn't need it. The cheechako who lost the claim to McGrew, in a card game, after a few drinks, had left all his gear, all his outfit, all his grubstake right down to the cans of beans on a shelf and six sacks of flour in a locked wooden box. A bear could have had the whole shebang in about thirty seconds.

Ben and I put in four hours before our aching muscles told us to call it a day. He did the digging and I did the hoisting and dumping. I was beginning to think the sun was stuck in the sky. We didn't bother to wash our hands, after all that dirty work, which would have upset Lou. We ate some beans and drank some tea.

Ben looked just a shade old for a man who was supposed to dig a cavern in permafrost. He was only forty-two, forty-three now I guess. He didn't tell me the date of his birth. Maybe I forgot to ask. He said he was five years older than Dan McGrew.

We fell asleep with our clothes on. At least when I was sleeping I couldn't see the cabin. It had a damp dirt floor. The roof was made of poles with moss spread over the poles and dirt spread over the moss. The roof and its crop of grass and weeds was a happy home to spiders and mice. The entire cabin was the size of the parlour I'd left behind in Dawson. It had in it a Klondike stove, a table and a chair made of lengths of birch, a wooden box, a set of shelves nailed to the wall over the stove. The bunk wasn't a bunk, it was a heap of dried out spruce boughs under a pile of woolen blankets that had somehow got mouldy damp, much to the delight of a variety of insects and bugs and worms.

In the morning we walked downstream and talked to the miners who were striking it rich. They turned out to be a former tram driver from San Francisco, an escaped convict from a New York pen, two ex-lawyers and a minister who had given up the cloth. They helped Ben refine his plan of attack.

In addition to looking after the windlass, I sawed logs into short chunks and split them and sent the split wood down the shaft in the square wooden bucket that the cheechako had hammered together. He had not been, Ben remarked, a cooper by trade.

Permafrost means permanent frost. It means that the earth and all the water in it froze solid fifteen thousand years back, that is, during the last Ice Age, and so far hasn't thawed out.

After each day's digging Ben built a fire that would thaw enough gravel for the next day's digging. While that fire was doing its thing he and I headed out into the distant bush to cut down more trees and haul in more wood.

The system worked. Each morning, after the fire had burned itself out, Ben was able to go down our shaft, smoke allowing, and dig out a few more inches or even a couple of feet of gravel with a pick and shovel and fill the bucket. I winched the heavy, dripping bucket to the surface on the windlass and dumped it onto our growing heap and sent it back down empty.

Ben and I kept at it for fourteen days running. In addition to all that, we filled our gold pan at least twice a day with gravel and walked down the few yards to the creek and did some panning. You had to keep testing. One time we thought we saw some colour.

Ben said it was fourteen days. I had lost track. On what he said was the evening of the fourteenth day a miner on his way into Dawson stopped by our claim. He was leading two packhorses. They were loaded with gold. They weren't too heavily loaded, he assured us. They were carrying two hundred pounds of coarse gold each. He stopped to bum some tea.

I asked him to deliver a message to Lou. In the Malamute Saloon.

"Why in the Malamute?" Ben said.

I'd let the cat out of the bag.

I told him the simple truth. "Lou has a job there in the Malamute. She's the weigher. She weighs gold for the miners and holds it for them while they drink and dance and gamble. Then she gives them back what they haven't spent." I tried to make it sound pretty awful.

"In other words," Ben said, "she's working for McGrew."

"That's about what it amounts to."

We were sitting on the ground in front of the cabin, having a cup of tea with our rich visitor. Or, more exactly, Ben was having a cup of tea. I was picking at my calluses.

The miner's name was Charlie Anderson. He liked the idea of going to the Malamute, to deliver a message or not.

"Who should I say the message is from?"

"Just say it's from a rascally young man who is working with Ben Redd and no doubt making a fortune."

Anderson stood up to leave. Then he paused and turned back just long enough to give me a close look. "I started prospecting when I was your age. I struck it rich three times."

It wasn't until after he left that I said to Ben, "Why did Anderson have to strike it rich three times?"

Ben knew the story. "Because he got drunk the first two times, before the steamboat sailed that would take him out."

Then it was Ben's turn to ask a question. "What was the message you were going to send to Lou?"

I had forgotten to give Anderson the message to deliver.

"I was going to ask him to tell Lou that we are planning to pay her a visit."

"That's a good message," Ben said. "Maybe we should go deliver it ourselves."

35

Lou was at work behind the gold scales. The pair of scales stood over two feet tall in the middle of that long bar in the

Malamute Saloon. Along with the piano, they were McGrew's pride and joy. The wide, stiff arm could balance a poke or a dish of heaped coarse gold on one side, a dish of shaped brass weights on the other.

I don't think Ben recognized Lou at first glance. He was staring as if he didn't see her. She was wearing a high-necked yellow blouse and her dark hair was coiled under a spray of feathers. I mean, luminous feathers. Ostrich or something. You couldn't really tell, they'd been dyed all sorts of colours. They moved when she moved. Or, when she moved in one direction, they seemed to move in the opposite direction. That's what we could see, mostly, over the crowd of men in front of the scales. The feathers in Lou's new hairdo.

She was talking. She was weighing gold while she talked. We couldn't hear what she was saying, but we could hear her laughter. It was different from the talk and laughter of the miners, there at the bar. It had a golden ring to it.

Ben and I got into line in front of the scales. Not that we had any gold on us. We couldn't bring ourselves to try and elbow our way through the crowd. We heard Lou tell a miner what his poke was worth. An astronomical sum. We thought she must be mistaken. Just as casually, she set the poke on the shelf behind her and turned to the next miner.

She saw us over his shoulders. She cried out in sheer pleasure.

"Ben. Peek."

We both said hello.

"I thought you two would never show up."

I wanted to reach across the counter and touch her. Under those dancing feathers, green and red and blue and orange, she was Lou. I wanted to say I loved her.

241

"A sight for sore eyes," she said.

Ben and I had made an effort to wash our hair and to have a sponge bath in the mining pan before we came into town. Our clothes, however, weren't the cleanest. I could smell my own stale sweat, and Ben's, along with the whiskey and cigar and pipe tobacco smell of the saloon.

She called to a bartender to give her a hand and stepped away from the scales. She couldn't leave entirely, she had to keep an eye on things.

"Peek," she said. "Ben. I've been asking everyone. A man came in from Eldorado who said you two are digging your way down to China."

"We're trying," Ben said. He finally managed to grin a little.

I wanted to inquire about the man, who must have been Charlie Anderson, but Lou didn't give me a chance. She looked closely at the shirt I was wearing. "Good God, Peek. I bought you and Ben some new clothes. Go up to the cabin right this minute and change."

She was better than ever at giving orders. She gave Ben a closer look. "You could have sent word, Ben."

"I know, I know." He was trying to apologize. "We just thought that any day we might — we might at least find an ounce or two of the yellow stuff. You know what I mean."

"We were hoping to show off," I said. "We haven't been too lucky."

"It doesn't matter," Lou said.

"Of course it matters," I said.

Lou had to turn and help the bartender with a poke. "That's Cariboo Billy's," she said to the bartender. "It'll be pure. Just weigh it."

She knew everyone, it seemed. She turned back to us, at the

same time indicating the miner whose gold was on the scales. "He found gold up on a bench, where there isn't supposed to be any gold. A cheechako who didn't know any better. He's making millions."

Ben and I wanted a drink. We weren't quite sure we had enough ready cash.

Lou spoke to Ben again. "I thought maybe you fell into a hole. Disappeared."

"I didn't want to bother you," he said.

"Bother me! How would you be bothering me?"

Lou was busy. She didn't hear Ben's attempt at a reply so I repeated it for him. "We thought you'd be settling in."

"A fine excuse. You mean," she said, "you two were too busy finding gold to think about me. That's what the trouble was."

Ben pretended to go along with her argument. "Nothing ventured, nothing gained."

The truth was we had hatched a plot, Ben and I, while walking into town from Eldorado Creek. We thought we might ask Lou if she'd care to join us out on the claim.

Lou kept an eye on the bartender who was weighing gold for her and somehow, at the same time, managed to go on talking to three or four miners who were waiting to have their pokes set on the scales. She was a miracle of organization. She spoke to Ben and me without glancing in our direction.

"Dan says you're surrounded by producing mines."

Ben noticed his sleeves were leaving bits of dried muck on the bar and tried to brush it away. That only made matters worse. "If you can be surrounded on one side. The men above us haven't found anything so far but a mastodon tusk."

"A what?" Lou said. She had a contagious way of showing excitement.

Ben told her again.

"Tell them to bring it in." She indicated a blank space on the behind her. "We could use it as decoration. We'll pay good money."

There it was. The old pronoun trouble again. Her use of "we" left Ben and me on the wrong side of the bar. Lou, watching out of the corner of her eye as the bartender tried to weigh a fistful of nuggets that was more than he could handle, motioned him to move aside. She took over the weighing again.

"He's a good worker," Ben said. He was talking about me but didn't say so.

Lou understood. "Dan has a job for him." She was shifting nuggets from one hand to the other. She could pretty much state their weight just by lifting them. "For Peek," she added.

Watching while she hefted gold nuggets, looking at the glitter of the mahogany bar and all the glasses and bottles, Ben and I couldn't concentrate. It was hard to figure out how to say we had a job for her.

We weren't going to offer her wages or anything like that. It would be straight shares. Lou and I would get equal shares in Ben's half of the claim and the gold we found. No more of this working for wages. That was our scheme. Lou could handle the finances and maybe keep things in order around the claim.

She was pointing between Ben and me.

"We've got that beautiful piano sitting right there, and we can't find any players who'll stay on the job more than two nights. They get talking to drunk miners and they believe what they hear and next night they don't show up for work. They're off to the creeks."

Ben and I turned to look at the piano. It was directly in front of the scales, but quite a distance away, leaving lots of room for men to belly up to the bar on busy nights. Or up to the scales with their pokes. It sat in the middle of that huge room, all by itself, as if there was an invisible fence around it.

That's when I noticed Dangerous Dan. He was playing cards at his special table down at the far end of the bar and not paying attention to much else. While I was looking at him he glanced up. But he didn't look at me. He looked at the piano.

Lou was trying to get my attention. "Dan wants you to play the piano for a few nights. Until he finds somebody permanent."

"I'm helping Ben," I said.

Ben was forever taking Lou's side. "Lou might have a good idea, Peek. We aren't exactly striking it rich, are we?" He seemed to have forgotten our scheme. "I'm saying, this is a chance for you. I could get a man to help out until I get a new shaft down to bedrock. Then you could come out and help me reap the harvest."

Lou was listening after all. "How are you going to pay a man?"

"Pay, nothing. I'll give him a percentage. Men don't want wages on Eldorado. With that kind of pay dirt, they want percentages."

I felt left out. Ben and I had never talked about practical matters.

Lou was lining up her brass weights, small to big. "Peek, you heard what Ben said."

They were ganging up on me, the two of them. Lou had a way of swinging Ben to her side of any argument.

A miner came to the scales to pay his bill. Lou picked up his poke from the counter behind her and turned to the scales there on the bar and began to measure out ten ounces of coarse gold. What he owed. I want to tell you, she poured a little river of gold into the brass dish. Heavy. That dish plummeted. You could *see* it was heavy, the gold. Yet each little flake and speck and nugget flashed light along the bar. The mahogany glowed. The glasses of whiskey looked as if they were singing.

The trouble was, watching Lou weigh that gold made Ben realize he didn't have a penny to his name. That's when he turned to me and said, "Okay, partner. I want you to stay here and work for a few days. I'll go back out to the claim. I'll come get you when I hit pay dirt. That's the deal."

He turned away. But not toward the swinging doors. We saw he was going to head for Dan's table.

Lou called after him. "Ben, maybe you shouldn't. He's cross as a bear these days." She lowered her voice, then spoke for my benefit. "If you ask me, it's that stupid Gussie Meadows. That's the trouble. You know what men are like. Damn, when they get women on the brain."

Ben kept on going. I left Lou and went hurrying to catch up. I walked down along the bar with Ben. We were still partners, in a way. We stepped up to Dan's card table.

Dan was playing a game called solo with two other players. The other players looked up at us and nodded. Dan didn't so much as glance away from his cards. He pushed a stack of blue chips into the middle of the table. The blue chips were five bucks each. Then he turned toward Ben. He barely acknowledged him.

"You aren't going to strike gold in here, are you, Ben?" Dan said. Then he turned to me. "Listen, kid, I want to make you an offer you can't refuse."

He could never remember my name.

36

He said that if I played the piano until he managed to hire a regular player he'd pay me enough money so that I could go out and grubstake a couple of miners on my own. He explained that I could do my mining from the piano stool.

Ben and I needed a little more capital than we actually had, if we were going to fix up the cabin on the claim and persuade Lou to join us there. I told Dan I'd consider his offer and let him know in the morning. Meanwhile Ben and I went on up to Lou's cabin to try on our new clothes and to wait for Lou to get off work. I went into my little bedroom, or Gussie's little dressing room I should say, and I tried on my new jeans in front of her full-length mirror.

When I went out to show Ben, he was nowhere to be found.

I'd heard him in the parlour, changing into his new shirt and pants. I looked in Lou's bedroom, thinking maybe he was taking a nap. But he wasn't there either. Then it struck me that maybe he hadn't been able to stay away from Lou and had gone back to the Malamute.

I had time to think. I hadn't spent much time alone in a while. I thought that if I worked in the Malamute, even for a few days, I could please both Ben and Lou. Dan hadn't actually mentioned the kind of money I'd be making, but I knew I could walk away from the job on a moment's notice if I didn't like what I got. Everybody else seemed to do that.

When Lou finally showed up she was dead tired. "Where's Ben?" I asked her, when I saw she was alone. "He's not here."

"I know," she said.

"He's in the Malamute?"

"He came by." Lou collapsed onto the parlour sofa. Her new shoes were killing her. She kicked them off. "He came by to tell me he'll be back."

I didn't quite follow. "Later?"

"Later. That's right. Later. That's what he said."

Talk about being cross as a bear. You'd think I was the one who had gone hiking back to the claim. She told me what the routine was to be. It wasn't as if she was waiting to hear if I'd take the job that McGrew was offering. I'd play evenings. Just up until midnight. After that, home to bed.

"It'll hardly be worth going out," I said.

But the bald truth was, I have to admit, inside of two days I was half liking the routine. There was no school here for people my age, which was a blessing. I got up while Lou was sleeping and did my chores. I read books. Stampeders carried books with them here into the Yukon and then swapped them around. Books and newspapers. A newspaper a month old was hot news to us. There were two newspapers here in Dawson, both of them one-man shows, each of them stealing stories from the other and improving on them in the process. Sometimes when I read stories in the *Dawson City News* or *The Klondike Nugget* I said to myself, somebody ought to be setting the record straight. That's why I started making notes to myself. Even back then, I wasn't afraid to face the facts.

After Lou had gone to work I made myself a sandwich. Canned ham or sardines. Some days I heated up a few beans from the bean pot. Then I moseyed on down to the Malamute.

A lot of the miners didn't show up until shortly after supper. They expected music with their drinks. They left their moosehide pokes with Lou while they gambled and drank and jabbered and danced. She would never cheat them when weigh-ing their gold, whether they were sober or drunk. She stacked the counter high behind her with their pokes. That was her department. The music-making was mine.

I thought I was doing okay. Then, on my tenth night or so, there in the Malamute, I got myself booed and threatened. I was down in the dumps for some reason. I happened to play a tune the percentage girls and their partners claimed they couldn't dance to. Somebody threw an empty poke in my direc-tion and hit the back of my head.

Dan McGrew got up from his card table and came down along the bar to the piano. I thought he was going to reassure me.

"Either you start playing what people want in here," he said, "or you try on those swinging doors for size."

That brought me up short. "Fine with me," I said. "Fine. It's your saloon. You decide."

But I was pissed off. I started to play as if to tell everybody in that place to go straight to hell in a handcart, and please take along dry matches. And a bundle of kindling. And a few seasoned logs.

The percentage girls, up until then, had hardly noticed that I existed. Their job was working the miners. If you wanted to dance you bought ivory chips at the bar and each chip entitled you to one dance. A chip cost one dollar. Each dancehall girl kept the chips she collected in the course of the night and then turned them in at the bar and got a quarter for each. She could make thirty dollars in one night. On top of that she got a cut on any drinks she persuaded a partner to buy.

There were maybe a dozen girls working that particular night. I was playing to say to all those people, stop pretending you know what love is. I played that way. And I meant it. I wasn't playing for the mighty Dangerous Dan. Or for anyone else in that saloon. I was hammering those keys for one reason, and for one reason alone. I was sending a message to Gussie Meadows.

One of the percentage girls came off the dance floor. Bonanza Jill. Before I knew what was happening, three miners had hoisted her up onto the piano. She looked down at me and winked. Then she tried to kick a hole in the ceiling.

Right in the middle of what I was playing I switched to "She's Such a Nice Girl Too." The crowd cheered. Even Bonanza Jill liked it. She wasn't that easy to impress. She kicked higher. She kicked her stockinged legs right over my head. The miners thought that was so great they didn't know whether to laugh or holler. Bonanza Jill spilled her drink while she was trying to do what looked like to me like the splits.

Two miners down on their luck were panning the sawdust on the floor under the piano. The spilled drink wet the sawdust they were panning. They thought it was wash-up time, in the creeks. They dumped some of their findings into an ashtray there on my piano. They said the dust was for me.

Next night the girls wanted me to play their favourite songs, or the songs of their favourite customers. I almost had to fight them off. They came over to where I was playing and they stroked the back of my neck and ruffled my hair. Dangerous Dan left his card game long enough to tell me to go ahead if I wanted to help myself to the pickled eggs and the smoked oysters sitting on the bar. He offered me a cigar, but I could just feel that Lou was watching.

She and Dan had a little war going on between them. Lou couldn't stand the way he squandered money. The worst thing was, he liked to jump up every so often and make the announcement that the next drink was on the house. That just about drove Lou out of her wits. She'd stand there behind her scales, helpless, watching while Dan strutted around slapping men on the back, getting himself slapped on the back, clinking glasses with every stranger in the place, adding free cigars to the free booze.

One time he told me to go out into the street to call in all the passersby. Lou heard what he said and then told him she would do it herself. She went out onto the crowded sidewalk and shouted at the top of her lungs, "This way, folks. Come on in and say hello to the living end. We'll even stand you a drink."

Her fourteen-hour shifts were killing her.

You wouldn't believe it. About two hundred people took her up on the invitation. Dan welcomed the crowd, telling people that Lou had more gumption than half a dozen gumboot miners put together. He said that straight to all those miners. They applauded.

Lou was pissed right off. "Gumption, your ass. What's going to happen next in this loony bin?"

"What's going to happen next," Dan said, ignoring her evaluation, "is that I'm going to offer your a fifty-fifty deal. Right here in the Malamute."

Lou ignored him.

"Did you hear what I said?" Dan said.

"I heard you."

"You don't have to put up a nickel. I want you to be my partner."

Lou gave him a look that would have withered the Sphinx. "That will be one goddamned frosty Friday in hell."

I mean, that's how it was, that summer. The whole town was nuts. Out of it. The miners were washing out the gold from the dumps they'd spent the whole winter heaping up. Their own bragging couldn't keep up with what was actually happening.

There was a miner on upper Bonanza who washed out six hundred and forty dollars worth of gold from one pan of gravel. That's a fact. A miner from Number 3 Eldorado brought in a nugget that Lou told him was worth four hundred dollars flat. Six men sluicing just a mile above where Ben was working used dogs to take out their gold, because they couldn't wait for a packtrain. They came into town with a string of eighteen malamutes, all of them loaded with bags of gold.

Dogs were too small for Mike Bartlett. He brought in his clean- up gold on twelve mules, a man with a Winchester riding at either end of the train. A sack of gold is so heavy it bores a hole in your back while you walk. One man threw half his load back into a creek so he could get to see Diamond-Tooth Gertie before her last show of the night was over. Big Alex McDonald had a share in forty different claims. He brought out his gold on the backs of twenty-nine horses, each horse carrying two sacks of gold, each sack weighing one hundred and twenty pounds.

People wanted extravagant meals and they wanted to dance and they wanted to gamble. Champagne was forty dollars a bottle. One miner treated all his horses to a bottle each when he rode into town with his gold. That's how it was. There were maybe four thousand miners out there in the creeks who were actually digging gravel out of the permafrost and sluicing and rocking and cleaning up and finding gold. They were finding tons of the stuff. And bringing it into Dawson. There were thirty thousand people in town, trying to figure out how to get gold without digging for it. It was a circus and a sideshow and a calamity all in one. A waiter named Alex Pantages, on a bet, put up an opera house. And filled it with customers. One man wagered five thousand dollars on the turn of a roulette wheel, and then went on doubling his bets until he was broke, and then walked back to the creeks to dig himself another fortune. One man put gold dust on his eggs each morning, instead of salt and pepper.

I worked later and later at night. McGrew said that men at night, sun or no sun, were quicker to spend money than they were during the day. He liked to think he had people figured out.

He had a soft spot for that piano, even if he couldn't tell the black keys from the white. He would look up from a hand of cards and actually listen for a moment or two, as if his thoughts were a million miles away. Or he would stop by the piano and rest his hands on the lid while I played, as if he was feeling the songs rather than hearing them.

I sort of liked the man. It hurt me to recognize that. I couldn't resist playing tunes that would help him remember Gussie Meadows. "Absence Makes the Heart Grow Fonder." "I'll Marry the Man I Love." But there was more to it. I wanted Dan McGrew to realize I had a secret that he would never know. I'd bend over the keys and pretend I too was lost in recollection. I mean, I was just as faithful as he was to Gussie Meadows. And why not? We were two men in love with two different women, even though Gussie Meadows was both of them.

One time he said to Lou in a voice that I was meant to overhear, "Sometimes I think that kid is one brick short of a load. The way he gets that moony look when those women hang around the back of his neck."

He was referring to all the beautiful dancehall girls who ignored him and clustered around my piano when they didn't have partners.

"Still water runs deep," Lou said.

I went right on playing.

Dan was shaking his head. "He comes close to scaring me at times."

"Dan, I'm surprised. I can't imagine anything scaring you."

That's how Lou talked to him, at times. Sort of sarcastic and intimate at the same time. They could talk with each other because they'd both been in hiding. That was my theory. Dan in his tun in a cooperage by the Mississippi, Lou with me in a lifeboat. That sort of hooked them together. Being in hiding, let me say, marks you for the rest of your life. It fills you up with secrets. I wonder sometimes, how much gold it would take, to throw light on that.

"Did you think about it some more?" Dan was saying.

"The answer is no," Lou said. "I like wages. It makes the counting easier."

37

In September in the Malamute Saloon we took off the swinging doors and put in a door that was supposed to keep out the cold. Good luck, I thought to myself. The fall colours were mostly yellow and brown, and if you found time to walk up onto a slope above the town you could try to count all the flocks of geese that were heading south. You could see a new kind of mauve in the sky. A mauve that gave you a little shiver.

October came, and the first snow as well. It wasn't a heavy snowfall. I went for a walk. I hiked on down to the Yukon shore. There were maybe twenty steamboats tied up, or puffing around in the snowflakes, with twenty crews and dozens of wagons and a couple of hundred stevedores all at work, and more crews loading cordwood as if they were in a race. And they were. Freeze-up and greed were head to head. That's what Lou would have said. But she was at work. There were floes, running in the main channel. There was ice along the shore where the eddies had stopped their twisting and turning.

The miners were beginning their winter work. The winter wasn't yet fierce enough to drive them into town for a drink and the roar of a woodstove. Some afternoons when the saloon was almost deserted, Dan McGrew asked Lou and me to his special table, away from the piano and the scales, down at the far end of the mahogany bar. He needed someone to play with. "We'll play for fun," he'd say.

His idea of fun was beating the ass off me and Lou in a solo game. He'd give us each two hundred dollars worth of chips. The white and the red, not the blue. The white were worth two bits a chip. The red were worth a dollar. He never said we'd have to give back the chips if we won. He simply assumed he'd be the winner.

I have to admit it felt sort of good, stacking those chips on the green felt covering of the table, then picking up a hand of cards. You play solo with a short pack. With thirty-six cards, that is. You take everything from the deuce to the five-spot out of a poker deck. You deal eleven cards to each player, leaving three cards down as the blind. The skat. The player who gets the bid tries to beat the other two, who then play together against the bidder. The bidder plays without a partner.

In some awful way, that's what Dan liked about the game. It let him prove something to himself. And maybe that was why I outbid him, about the fortieth hand, one lazy afternoon in late October. I was being plain obstreperous. I got the bid.

The catch was, my winning bid was spread misère. I was saying I could play out my hand without taking a point. It also meant I was going to play with my hand laid out face up on the table.

I was laying it out when I saw Dan glance away from his hand and look at the piano. He did that every so often, even in the middle of a hand. But this time he didn't look back at his cards.

I looked away myself, from the table and my cards and my stack of chips.

Ben Redd had come into the Malamute. He was standing at the bar beside the gold scales. More exactly, he was standing halfway between the scales and the piano. It looked like he couldn't decide which way to turn. We hadn't noticed his arrival at all. He'd unbuttoned his parka. Or maybe he'd been walking with it open. He must have been there for a while. He saw that we had seen him and he waved. It was a futile kind of wave, as if he assumed we were so far away we wouldn't see him.

But then he came down through the room, past three or four miners who were having a drink with a bartender. It was so quiet you could hear all of them munching their free pretzels.

We were playing our last hand. I had just said to Dan and Lou, "Let's make it all or nothing. If I win, all the chips on the table are mine. If I lose, you and Lou divide them." I was up maybe one hundred dollars on top of the two that Dan had given me. I knew he hated to lose.

Ben stopped behind my chair. I could feel him looking over my shoulder. He hadn't spoken to us. We hadn't spoken to him. We were all acting as if we'd seen each other just an hour before, and greetings weren't necessary. Trust Ben to mess things up. "Good grief, Peek," he said. "What did you bid?"

My hand wasn't that bad. It was an odd one, but then isn't every hand of cards an odd one? I had laid out a string of spades, except for the jack. I had the six of diamonds. I had the six and seven and jack of clubs. I had no hearts.

Spread misère is a no-trump bid. I had dealt. Lou was sitting to my left. It was her lead. She led with the eight of clubs. The truth is, I think she was trying to help me out. Or maybe she had already looked at her own hand, and mine, there on the table, and was feeling sorry for me.

Dan didn't follow suit. He sloughed a small heart. I saw I was in trouble. Dan didn't have any clubs. The missing clubs were in the blind. I played my seven on Lou's eight.

She was keeping an eye on the bar and the scales, instead of concentrating. Dan gave her a look that told her to concentrate on the game. His buried blue eyes again. And that moustache of his, like a tombstone over his mouth. She played the nine of clubs. Dan sloughed another heart. I played my six.

It was Lou's third lead. The trouble was, with Dan watching so closely, she had no choice. She played the ten. The ten-spot counts for ten points in solo.

What could I do? I played my jack and took the trick. The jack is two points. That on top of ten for the ten. I was set.

"We did it," Dan said. He reached across the table to shake Lou's hand. "Put her there, partner."

You see, I think that's what did it. Lou's reaching across the table and shaking Dan's hand. While Ben stood speechless behind my chair.

Ben didn't know we were playing for fun. It wasn't for keeps. I could hear his silence, behind me. He had stopped breathing. All that mining of his wasn't doing his lungs any good. Just a minute before, I'd noticed his breathing.

Dan pointed at my stacks of chips and signalled with a forefinger, as if coaxing. Deliver the goods. Pay up or else. That was your Dan McGrew. I folded my cards and threw them into the centre of the table. I deliberately didn't touch or move my chips. "Lucky in cards," I said, "unlucky in love. Right, Dan?"

He reached across the table and pulled away all my chips, toward himself. Half of them belonged to Lou. "If that's how you see it —" He tried once again to remember my name and didn't succeed.

That's when Ben got back into the business of breathing and gave out a huge sigh. He spoke up. He leaned over my shoulder and said in my left ear, "I brought you a little gift for your birthday."

"Peek!" Lou said. "What day is it today? I thought your birthday was next week."

I hadn't even thought of it myself. I'd lost track of time.

"Whose birthday is it?" Dan said. The idiot. He was stacking chips in front of himself as if he was building a fort.

"Peek's," Ben said. "It's the twenty-fourth today. He's an old man of fifteen."

"Happy birthday," Lou said. She was a shade flustered, I'll have to give her that. But she managed.

Ben fished a small bottle out of one of his parka pockets. He set it on the table in front of me.

The plain glass bottle with a cork stopper was full of gold dust.

You want to see beauty itself? That was it.

"Hey," Dan said. "I'll be go to hell. Would you look at that? Would you look at that now?" I thought he was speaking to me but it turned out he was speaking to Ben. "Would you take a gander at that there bottle?" He was trying to sound restrained and not quite succeeding. "We're finding gold out there, are we, Ben?"

"Things are looking up," Ben said, "looking up. I think we're close to the pay streak."

My birthday sort of got forgotten. Dan and Lou had to look at the gold. Dan reached for the bottle and held it up toward the fancy kerosene lamp with the naked lady on the globe that stood on the bar to his right. "It's the real thing."

"One pan," Ben said. "That was one pan. Not a picked pan. Just two shovelfuls that I scooped up at random and put in a bucket and took up to the daylight and into the cabin to wash." He was pleased and proud. "Our first big pan. I thought to myself when I saw it, this is for Peek's birthday."

"It's goddamned completely beautiful," Dan said. He handed the bottle to Lou. "Here, Lou. You're the expert. What do you say?"

Lou opened the bottle and tilted some of the dust onto the queen of clubs. She looked closely at the gold. She nodded, whatever that meant.

"There's more where that came from," Ben told her. "You bet your sweet life there is. And I'm going to find it."

She bent the card just slightly so she could raise the dust close to her eyes. I thought she was going to taste it. "That's as good as it gets," she said. "That's from Eldorado Creek. Look at the brassy colour. It's the silver alloy that does it. That's Eldorado gold. That's the best there is."

I might have been one of your Spaniards then, looking at Inca gold. So what if I arrived five hundred years too late? It was iridescent, that gold. What did Lou mean, brassy? Gold shines without light. That's why it's gold.

Dan, carefully, took the card and the gold dust from her and studied it as if he was short-sighted. He returned the card to Lou and she poured the dust back into the bottle. She corked the bottle and handed it to Ben.

"How much more?" Dan said. "You got more with you?"

This time Ben stuck the bottle into my left hand, none of that setting it on the table. I sat there holding it.

"That's the sum total for the moment," Ben said. "But I've got two men helping. We're coming right along."

I guess I had thought he was going to say it was time for me to go out to the claim and help him. Dan signalled a bartender to bring us a round. Ben went on explaining that he had two men working for him, and with their help he was making up for lost time. He kept repeating that they were making up for lost time. It sounded as if he had the two mixed up in his mind. Gold and time. He could no longer tell the difference. And yet he was the one who remembered my birthday.

When the three drinks arrived at the table, Lou picked up her glass. "To Ben," she said, "who is just about to strike it rich."

They drank a toast, Lou and Ben and Dan. Then Lou turned to me.

"And to Peek. Happy birthday."

The three of them drank a toast while I sat there. I wanted to study the little bottle and its gold but instead I slipped it into a pocket of my jeans. Thieves and scoundrels, as Lou would have said. Ben tilted his head and emptied his glass. He was shaking his head and coughing the way he was supposed to.

That's when he noticed his keg of whiskey.

It wasn't marked as whiskey of course, it was still marked as BENJAMIN REDD SALT HERRING.

There it sat, on top of the grand piano, before his watering eyes. One of the perfect oak kegs that he'd made, back in Davenport, Iowa. It looked like a sculpture. Or a bouquet. It was my idea, putting that keg on top of the piano. The dancehall girls like to sit on it. What they lacked in talent they made up in effort. They'd kick their legs right straight out over my head while I played. That always brought the house down.

"What in the world," Ben said, "is that thing doing there?"

Lou sipped her drink before she spoke. "Peek put it there. It was his idea. But now I like it, sitting across from the scales. It reminds me of you, Ben."

"Herring?" Dan McGrew said. He was losing patience with the three of us. He kept moving chips from one stack to another, as if his hands were not his to control. "Herring reminds you of Ben?"

Lou didn't answer. She watched Ben take a sip out of his empty glass. "You like Dan's whiskey, Ben?"

"It's pretty good stuff. If you like moonshine and water."

Lou spoke more softly, which was quite an accomplishment for her. "The river froze early this year. The last riverboats didn't make it." Ben could be slow at times. He wasn't getting the message. Lou was telling him that whiskey was scarce. And expensive. "There must be ten boats in the ice. Downriver. Ten boats and all their cargo that didn't get here."

Even Dan had the decency to be embarrassed at the excuse for whiskey that he was selling. "We're running out fast. But what can we do?"

I could hear Ben wheezing in another deep breath. He was uneasy. Restless. He was catching on. Maybe he was trying to do arithmetic in his head again. Miners were like that.

"Lou will come up with something," Dan said, answering his own question.

It was then that Hegg showed up at the table. He loved to play cards with Dan. But he didn't pull up a chair or point at the deck of cards in the middle of the table. He pointed at the grand piano and spoke to Lou. "Did I hear you say those herring are yours?"

Lou shook her head. "They belong to Ben here."

Eric A. Hegg was a spender. Sometimes he paid me good money to play a polka. He was a photographer all the way from Sweden who had struck it lucky by taking photos and selling them and using the proceeds to grubstake miners. He owned shares in four claims that were producing gold faster than the packtrains could bring it into town.

"How much you want for that keg?" Hegg asked. "I haven't had a decent feed of herring for so long, I'll pay any price. Your price. You just name it."

"That keg isn't for sale," Ben said.

Hegg turned to Lou. "How much gold have I got back there?" He was talking about the counter behind the bar where she kept the miners' gold while they were in the saloon.

"Today?" she said. She reckoned. "Something like two hundred ounces."

An ounce of coarse gold was selling for seventeen dollars even.

Hegg turned to Ben again. "How much do you want? Name your price."

Ben shook his head.

"One hundred ounces?"

Ben shook his head again.

"Two hundred ounces?"

"I couldn't part with that keg for the world. I'm saving it for the party I'm going to throw when I strike it rich."

Hegg thought Ben was being a dunce and said so, but politely. "A bird in the hand," he said.

That's when Dan McGrew got into it again. "You're thick between the ears, Ben. I swear." He had the floor and went on. "I mean it, Ben. This Hegg here has more gold than he knows what to do with. Sell him the fish. Invest your money right here, right now."

"No way," Ben said. Then he also got carried away. He hadn't done a lot of talking in a long time. "That claim of ours is going to be a big one, Dan. You just wait." He buttoned up his parka. "Happy birthday, Peek. I've got to be going."

"At least stay for supper." Lou, in a way, was pleading. But she made the invitation sound like an afterthought. Like an exercise in politeness.

"I'd love to, Lou. Love to. But you mark my words. We are just this far from hitting it big." He held up his left hand with his thumb and his first finger hardly an inch apart. "We are just about there. Get yourself bigger scales, Lou. Get braced and ready."

Ben could fire you up when he talked that way. I could see that Lou and Dan were persuaded.

"Time," Ben said. "I'm wasting time." He tried to button up his parka and found he'd already buttoned it. "Got to pick up something for my two helpers."

38

I jumped up from the card table and grabbed my new parka and fur cap and went with Ben. I guess I was hoping he might ask me to go with him out to the claim. I said I'd help with his shopping. He didn't need much, but his two assistants wanted a few pounds of tobacco. He was in such a hurry I could hardly keep up.

"You still dining off Mr Plow's grubstake, Ben?"

"About all that's left of Mr Plow's grubstake," Ben said, "is the old Peacemaker." He patted his right parka pocket.

The trading post was so crowded we could hardly get in. Some of the customers there at the counter by the door were waiting to pay with gold. Some were using cash. Some of the Indian people were using marten and fox pelts, and bargaining in the process.

And who was there milling around inside the store with us but Whipsaw. He saw me first.

"Imagine," he said when he saw me. "Peek. You're still alive. I thought you be killed off by now. Some bear ate you, or a mine caved in on your head." He didn't let me speak but went right on. "I heard just last night about two miners. Got themselves smothered right to death. Down there in one of those mines. Must be frightful."

He liked his calamities. But even so, it was like meeting an old friend, running into Whipsaw. He always had a store of bad news to share. He was wearing a new beaver coat with a matching hat. The outfit must have set him back two thousand dollars.

"You still on the raft?" I asked.

"The boys are. They hauled it up onto shore. It just kept growing, that raft. More rooms. More people." Then he remembered. "Hey. They made a shithouse out of that boat of yours. Sawed it in half. Set the two halves up on end. Perfect. A three-holer."

That was hardly what Ben needed to hear. I could see his affection for so-called civilization going into further wane.

Whipsaw was carrying two blouses on wooden hangers, both of them with leg-of-mutton sleeves, one of them a shade of pink, the other one chartreuse. He bent closer to Ben and me so he could whisper. "As for myself, I moved out. Crossed over the Klondike River. Moved into Lousetown."

"Cribs there, they tell me," Ben said, "got more miners in them than we've got out in the creeks."

I think Ben meant his remark as a criticism. But Whipsaw heard it otherwise. "Dead on, dead on, Ben. You've got it. We're flourishing." I noticed he was wearing rouge. "You wouldn't believe it," he went on. What some of these gentlemen request." He waved the two blouses at the crowd of shoppers. It was an all-male crowd. He rolled his eyes up at the ceiling. "And what they'll pay for it."

Ben was trying to calculate the cost of what he was purchasing. He'd picked up two cans of evaporated milk and some sugar. It was then he found out prices were going through the roof, what with the steamboats frozen downriver.

Moccasins like those I bought for fifty cents were up to eight dollars a pair. Flour was sixty dollars for a fifty-pound sack. Trousers, thirty-two dollars a pair. Nails were an even dollar a pound. I knew I should have brought along all those kegs of nails that Gussie Meadows left on the beach at Lake

Bennett. Kerosene was forty dollars a gallon, so I began to guess what whiskey was going to be worth. It went on and on like that. A pound of smoking tobacco was an ounce of gold flat.

Whipsaw was trying to decide which of the two blouses to buy. He asked my opinion.

"Why not both of them?" I said.

"Peek, you're a genius, a genius. Of course. Why didn't I think of that?" He reached over and gave me two of the biggest, sweetest kisses, one on each cheek.

Then he got tears in his eyes. "It was too sad," he said. "Soapy Smith getting shot that way. There in Skagway. Did you hear?"

I'd heard about the death of Soapy Smith and had thought of it as a good riddance. I hadn't until then realized that even the death of a thug and a bully might bring sorrow to someone. Once again, I was hauled up short.

Whipsaw was dabbing carefully at his tears with a hand-kerchief that must have been worth twenty dollars. I saw that he'd drawn some pretty heavy lines around his eyes, top and bottom. His tears were making the paint run. "The day I heard the news, I moved off the raft. That very hour. Right bang off. And into Lousetown. Life is short, Peek. Remember that. Do what you want to do, no apologies, no regrets. Let the devil take the hindmost."

He was turning away, hurrying off to pay for his blouses. I couldn't resist watching. He paid in gold dust. Out of a white deerskin pouch decorated with dyed porcupine quills. It was a work of art.

Ben was in a hurry too. And so was I; I had to get back to the saloon. People would be arriving to hear me play. Ben didn't quite have the gold to cover what he was buying. I reached into my pocket and took out the bottle and gave it to him. He said he would pay me back next time he saw me.

39

The winter, as Dan McGrew kept on saying to anyone who would listen, was getting a good start. I'd show up for work and he'd say, "Freeze the balls off a brass monkey." Then he'd add, for good measure, "Freeze the nuts off an iron bridge." He never said those things to anyone else. But he said them to me. All through November. Then into December. And he was right. The snow just kept falling. And so did the thermometer.

One evening in the middle of December Lou told me that Dan was giving her a day off, what with a busy time ahead. I guess he meant the Christmas season. Not that giving was his thing. Lou said we should do up a roast and take it out to Eldorado Creek. We went right out and did some shopping, and that night Lou prepared a full meal and wrapped it up and put it in a basket. Early next morning she and I went to the office of Orr and Tukey Stage Lines. We had the money. We rode in a covered sled pulled by a four-horse team. Inside the sled we were buried so deep under buffalo robes we hardly knew it was cold outside.

It was pitch dark in the late morning when we set out. Half an hour later the sun was trying to come up. Our driver turned away from the Klondike and followed the Bonanza. In that first red light all the cabins and dumps, scattered everywhere, looked like they'd fallen off the back of a wagon and no one had noticed. The cabins had a doghouse look, dwarfed beside the gravel dumps. The dumps were maybe thirty feet high and crowded close together. We drove until we were dizzy, and still nothing changed. The long flumes were covered in snow, waiting for spring and water. Each tiny cabin sent up a smoke signal that everyone ignored. Some of the holes in the ground sent up columns of smoke of their own, like new volcanoes getting ready to erupt. In that thin light we only caught glimpses of the men who were at work. They were the same grey colour as the dumps, and hard to see, like tired ghosts.

When we got off the stage, the sun, low on the southern horizon, was as high as it was going to get. We were in Grand Forks, at Belinda Mulroney's roadhouse, and the end of the line. She had brought with her into the Klondike five thousand dollars worth of hot-water bottles and cotton underwear. Would you believe? People laughed. And then in seven days flat she had sold her goods for thirty thousand dollars. She used that money to build a roadhouse where Eldorado Creek flowed into Bonanza and, as Lou liked to remind me, again people laughed. And three months later she built the fanciest hotel in Dawson.

Her roadhouse was so crowded with miners and packers we didn't bother trying to get so much as a cup of coffee or a doughnut. I didn't mention whiskey. We struck out walking. We walked on the ice and snow, following a trail through the stumps that the packtrains used.

We weren't simply under a blanket of smoke. We were in it. I wondered if we'd be able to breathe. Smoke filled the valley from ridge to ridge, the feeble sunlight filtering down orange and mauve and blood-red onto the tree stumps and the snow. The air had a smoky, ashy taste and was gritty on my tongue. We climbed upstream. Upstream was hardly the word. Up ice. Lou and I crossed claim after claim. Now and then someone we couldn't see said hello. The dumps around us were red and purple and black. We saw ghosts working windlasses. We saw more ghosts pushing wheelbarrows, moving out along planks or pathways, emptying more muck and gravel onto more dumps. I'm talking about ghosts that were darker than black.

Ben's cabin was almost out of sight, surrounded as it was by four dumps of its own. The muck and gravel from shafts that hadn't panned out. Let's try over here. Let's try over there.

I found the doorway and led Lou into the cabin. It stank inside. It stank of filthy clothes and of damp, filthy blankets. It stank because of a frying pan on the sheet-iron stove, a pan that was full of cold bacon grease. Three bunks filled half the cabin. In the middle of the dirt floor stood a round wooden panning tub, maybe two feet high, four feet across. A skim of ice covered the grey water. Beside it was was a pile of gravel and a miner's pan.

Lou touched the wooden panning tub. "Ben made it. You can tell."

She was pretty close to tongue-tied. I could tell she had a temptation to hold her nose. She set the moose roast and the roasted potatoes and the jar of gravy and the mince pie in the mining pan. "The only place he's likely to look," she said.

We went outside. There was no one in sight. Only one of the dumps had at its top a windlass. The windlass was set on cribbing that someone had built up higher and higher, as the dump grew. The frozen muck and gravel slope was hard to climb. Lou and I got our clothes dirty. We couldn't hear a thing from the bottom of the shaft. That scared us. We could smell wisps of smoke from a fire used to melt the permafrost somewhere below us.

Without hesitation, Lou climbed down the wooden ladder. Then I could hear her calling me to follow. What had seemed to be darkness wasn't quite that. My eyes adjusted as I descended. I stumbled over a wooden bucket. Tunnels went off in three directions from the base of the shaft. We couldn't walk. We had to slouch. Sometimes we were almost on our knees. Lou, I have to say, was fearless. She groped her way straight ahead. If you can call a bunch of crooked tunnels straight ahead. I hung onto her coat-tails.

Three candles burned in a low space that was more a cave than a room. The candles were in holders mounted on spikes that had been slammed into the frozen gravel walls. Three men were at work. Two of them were on their bellies. All I could see was their boots and pant legs. They were digging into a space that was hardly two feet high, working like badgers or moles. They pushed their diggings back past the soles of their boots. Ben, on his knees behind them, swept the sand and fine gravel with a bare hand onto a shovel. He didn't appear to have seen us.

They were drifting, those three men, digging horizontally across bedrock, determined to find the pay streak. They had to find the course of the old stream, the stream that wore the mother-lode itself into flakes and nuggets, and then hid them in gravel and sand. Those three men had to find that dead stream. If it was there. And then they would have to follow it the length of the claim.

Ben straightened his back so he could pitch his shovelful of sand into a wooden wheelbarrow. He was the colour of the gravel cave and smoke. He turned away from his shovel and the wheelbarrow to spit. That's when he acknowledged us. He spat out phlegm that was the same colour as the cave and his clothes and his face.

It was as if he remembered, vaguely, something about his manners. In a way he had good manners. He always did. He tapped his two helpers on the soles of their boots.

They wriggled backwards, the two men, out from under the frozen gravel directly over their heads. They didn't bother to get up off their bellies.

Ben introduced us. His two assistants were Chinese. Railroad workers. Or they had been railroad workers. They spoke no English. Ben said the only thing they could say in English was gold mountain. He said that proudly. They were the same age, the two men, very young. But older than I was. At least by a couple of years. They were impatient at the interruption and turned away to get back to work. The man on the left, as I had heard it, was called One Luck. I was left with the impression that the other man had the same name.

"Just let us finish this," Ben said. He still hadn't got up off his knees.

I had no idea what they thought they were finishing. Lou and I stood and waited. We began to hear the steady drip of water, along with the sounds of digging. The fires that melted the permafrost turned the mine into a wet, smoking cave. Bat shit, I thought to myself for some reason. I had never seen bat shit, but I thought of bat shit. Tonnes and tonnes of it, whole rooms, caves and caverns, full of bat shit.

I desperately wanted those three men to find gold. I began to feel they weren't crazy mad at all. They were the sanest men I had ever seen. I was one of them. I wanted to be. I wanted to kneel down and help. One more shovelful of sand. One more foot of permafrost. One more yard of gravel and muck. And then the dark would glow yellow.

Ben swept up a handful of the sand that spurted out behind One Luck. He held it to a candle.

"Ben," Lou said.

He studied the sand. He threw it into the bucket and went back to loading his shovel with his bare hand.

"Ben. We don't need this gold." Lou was talking as if he'd actually found some. "We don't need this gold at all."

Ben tried to reach in between the two men who were digging. He couldn't wait. But he couldn't find a space for as much as one hand and straightened onto his knees again.

"Ben. Peek and I have saved up a lot of money. We don't have anything to spend it on."

I gave a shiver, from the cold and the damp.

"What we could do, Ben, is this. We could go to Iowa."

Ben glanced up as if someone had unexpectedly kicked him in the face. The flickering glow of the candles made his features shift and move. His nose threatened his right eye. One of his ears vanished. I noticed his hair was full of gravel.

"We could go there. To your home." Lou bent forward, as if she was trying to make herself visible to Ben. I think she was half tempted to kneel down herself. "I never had a home, Ben. We were moving all the time. Vancouver. Portland. Bellingham. Spokane. And Peek had even less than that. He didn't even have a father. Not one that he ever saw alive."

Lou had to remind me of that.

"You see, Ben," she said, "I was thinking. We could go there. To Davenport. You could work in the cooperage. We could move in with your mother. Until we find a place of our own. We could look after her. Peek could go to school."

She was getting to sound philosophical. That business about school, I mean. I was a grown man very early.

Ben burst into speech. It was almost speech. At first it sounded mostly like babble, but then I realized he was telling us about the four men on Claim 14 Above Discovery. He probably hadn't spoken in a long time. The candles guttered. "Those four men. They found nothing. Eight months. Nothing." He gave a crazy chortle. "And for the last eighteen days they've washed out one thousand ounces a day." He waited. "They melt snow and ice to get water."

He was waiting for Lou to be impressed. He looked remarkably calm. But he did sort of look like a lunatic too, dressed in nothing but rags, and those rags caked in mud and gravel and the snot from his nose. Phlegm clung in gobs in the whiskers on his chin. He had wrapped older rags around the rags on his knees. He was kneeling there, being lucid one moment, chattering the next.

I think Lou wanted to cry.

"Did you hear me, Ben?"

He stopped the noises he was making. He reached up delicately and scratched the top of his left ear.

"I said — we could go back. To your home."

Maybe Ben realized that Lou had finally hit on her scheme. She had got hold of it at last.

Lou heard her own voice echoing there in that hole in the ground. It sounded as if she said everything about six times.

"I'm doing well, Ben. I'm making all we'll need."

Ben was staring into the candle flame instead of looking at Lou. Maybe he thought he was seeing gold.

"I'm saying, Ben, we can go to Iowa. We can go out on the first steamboat in the spring."

Let me tell you, I didn't want to go anywhere. I didn't want to leave. Not ever. I hadn't been consulted. I wanted to pitch in and help. But down there in that hole under thirty feet of frozen gravel was no place to start an argument with Lou. I was willing, right there and then, to kneel down and help out. Or I could have gone up top and run the windlass.

Lou put out her right hand. Toward Ben. She wanted to shake on the deal she was offering him.

He had hold of his shovel. Just then the two One Lucks send out a torrent of sand and gravel. A torrent and a storm.

Ben was shovelling again. He was pitching sand and gravel at the wheelbarrow as if had got himself into some kind of wild game at a carnival and knew in his bones he was on the cusp and verge of a big win.

Lou let her hand go limp. Or rather, all of a sudden her hand was too heavy for her arm. It fell down. She turned away and went toward the place where she could get to the bottom of the wooden ladder.

I waited for a minute, to see if Ben was going to call her back. I thought he might. I hoped he would. Then I followed after her. What could I do? I followed her up the ladder, huffing and puffing, bracing myself for the cold air at the head of the shaft. It was hard going, leaving Ben behind that way.

1899

40

When out of the night, which was fifty below, and into
  the din and the glare,
There stumbled a miner fresh from the creeks,
  dog-dirty and loaded for bear.

The poet was only off by four degrees. It was a hard winter, the winter of 99. A tough one. Steamboat Sal, after, liked to say the thermometers froze stiff seven nights in a row. I can't vouch for that. But there on the first Saturday in February the temperature dropped to fifty-four degrees below zero Fahrenheit. I know, because I stepped outside to take a reading. And a leak.

Saturday had just begun, you might say. It was two a.m. Even the Northern Lights were crazy with cold. They were red and green and yellow, trying to get warm. They lit the whole winter night with the stabs and swirls of their darting leaps and their sudden retreats and their violent swerves and turns. Dancing, people call it. It looked more like fighting to me. And they weren't making the noise people say you can hear. Not that

I listened for very long. Frostbite in the lungs, if you took a deep breath. Talk about risking your dong.

The Malamute was jumping, partly because the outside air was so cold the customers claimed they'd freeze in their tracks if they tried to walk home. Miners crowded three deep at the gambling tables. The bar was doing a fine trade too, even if the whiskey was watered.

The two fiddlers at the back of the dance floor, taking their turns while I rested, played waltzes and jigs. They called it playing. Sometimes they were joined by a one-armed drunk who claimed he could play anything you named on his mouth organ. The percentage girls who were waiting for partners left my piano and gathered around him to marvel. That pissed me off in a way. It made me crank up the tempo.

I was at my piano, calling on the miners to get their partners for a schottische, when a gust of the cold night air caused me to turn my head.

I wouldn't say that someone or anything stumbled into the Malamute Saloon. And no one else could say that either. A cloud of fog formed around whatever it was that came in through the door. The cold air from outside hit the warm, damp air inside and, just like that, no question, ice fog was all you could possibly see.

"A miner fresh from the creeks," the poet says. He wasn't there at the time and didn't show up in the Yukon as a bank clerk for another six years. No, indeed, the poet wasn't there. He, not the miner, was the stranger of whom he goes on to speak. Why are poets such bluffers and prevaricators, such dotards in the face of the bald truth? Why do poets fail, ever, to look at the facts themselves?

I was there. I was playing the piano. From where I sat on the piano stool I could see the front door. My back was to the rear of the room, where Dan McGrew, as usual, was playing cards.

Granted, yes, the figure that emerged from the cloud of ice fog was no doubt a miner. That was obvious from his dirty old clothes. His clothing was more rags than clothing, from his ragged and dirty drill parka to his blackened mittens to his filthy woolen trousers to his long woolen socks and laced-up high boots. But he was only a stranger to me for, at most, ten seconds.

He may have been a stranger for a longer time to Lou or to Dan. He looked like he was dressed in the winter night itself. What looked like a fur cap turned out to be his hair. He had pushed back his parka hood. His unshaven face and his eyebrows were caked with frost.

The poet says he was carrying a poke of gold. In fact Ben Redd was carrying two heavy leather bags. They were joined by a leather thong that was hooked over his right shoulder. Ben looked more like a packhorse than a miner, one leather bag on his chest, a second bag, I saw when he turned to check to see if the door was closed, on his back. The two bags and their gold were so heavy they might indeed have caused Ben to stumble. Or fall flat on his face.

Dangerous Dan McGrew was sitting in on a solo game. Sometimes he was a bigger danger to himself than to anyone else. He was playing cards, gambling, and once again losing pretty heavily. A lot of people knew he was losing, even though he tried to keep it a secret.

Lou was indeed, as the poet suggested, watching him. She was watching him, not from behind his chair, but from behind her gold scales that were set dead centre in the middle of the long bar. Only she knew how seriously Dan was losing. She got to look at the books. In fact she kept them, since Dan never found time. While she was heaping up bullion for the Malamute, Dangerous Dan was, as he liked to say, on a little losing streak.

Ben put down his pokes on the floor. He pulled off his mitts. He patted both pockets of his parka.

It was then he rubbed both hands together. They were so dirty I thought at first he was still wearing gloves. Then I realized he was warming his bare fingers.

He waited his turn in front of the scales. After what seemed a long time he reached both hands into his pockets. He stepped up to the bar where Lou was trying to do her job and keep an eye on the whole saloon.

Ben Redd lifted something from his left pocket. He placed it on the counter in front of Lou.

It wasn't too difficult to see what the object was. Ben had placed in front of Lou a gold nugget about the size of a fist.

Lou never got over her notion that the world is a pawnshop. She stood there looking at that outrageous, gleaming nugget of Klondike gold, and I could tell she was trying to decide how much credit to allow this unfortunate man.

The nugget was the size of a very small brain. A golden brain. It was oblong and smooth and dented at the same time. It glowed iridescent and alive, there in the light from the lamps. Eldorado Creek gold is different from Hunker Creek gold, and Hunker is different from Bonanza. Lou could recognize a dozen different creeks or gulches or benches by a flake or nugget of gold. She had a judgemental eye. Just a glance and she knew. Nuggets from Gay Gulch, where Emil Gay was taking out three thousand dollars worth of gold from every foot of his five-hundred-foot claim. Dust and flakes from Homestake

Gulch. A homestake, I should add, will take you home the way a grubstake will send you out. There at Homestake Gulch a claim jumper got himself chased naked into the bush and the mosquitoes and was never heard from again. Dominion Creek. Sulphur Creek. Cheechako Hill, where Oliver Millett guessed that an ancient stream had taken a different course. He filed a bench claim. Sick with scurvy and out of cash, he dug for gold on a bench claim above Bonanza Creek. And got himself laughed at. And found gold. French Hill. Gold Hill. And then there were showings from Gold Bottom Creek, where Robert Henderson thought he saw a stream's bedrock paved with nuggets of glistening gold, and then told Siwash George Carmack and Skookum Jim and Tagish Charlie to go look at Rabbit Creek. And didn't bother to go look himself.

Lou failed to recognize Ben. She didn't touch the nugget.

Ben untied the thong and lifted a poke from the floor onto the bar. Lou helped him place it on the scales. Ben reached down and lifted the second poke and placed it on the bar beside the scales.

He tried to unbend his body and couldn't quite do it. I expected Lou to tell him to straighten up. I think she was about to when her mouth, surprising the rest of her, said, "Ben Redd. What on earth?"

He had walked and stumbled fifteen miles through the winter night with nothing but the Northern Lights to show him the way. Lou tried to reach out. But the sacks of gold were in between her and Ben. The sacks of gold and the nugget. He reached with his stained hands and broken fingernails and pushed the nugget past the sacks.

"It's yours. It's for you. I just found it." He pointed back over his shoulder as if to show her where. "Six hours ago."

It was as if for all those weeks and months he had been looking for that one astounding nugget to present to Lou as a gift.

"For God's sake, Ben."

Lou couldn't touch it. Don't ask me why. For a moment she hid her hands behind the bar.

"It's yours," Ben said. "It's for you."

"Then keep it until we get to the cabin."

That's what she said. I don't know if Ben heard her. She was talking about home. A homestake. She said cabin but she meant home. She was telling him to go up to the cabin and just be there.

"Put it away," she said. She pointed, but not at the nugget. She indicated all the men at the gambling tables, the couples waiting, talking, on the dance floor.

Ben took the nugget off the bar and dropped it back into the left pocket of his twill parka. He stood there, puzzled, rubbing the fingers of one hand with the fingers of the other. He'd been out in the night a long time.

Lou knew that Dan McGrew was watching. He was losing his shirt in a card game with Hegg and a young cheechako who had a way of looking as if he was about to faint. Speelman. That was his name. He had come in from his claim the day before with one small poke of gold and was mightily pleased with himself. He kept his poke on the floor by his chair.

Lou lifted the first of Ben's two sacks onto the pair of scales. They were big scales, but she was going to have trouble finding enough weights to balance out the sack. She started to load the brass dish while Ben stood watching in front of the tilting arms of the scales.

Lou managed to balance the arm. Absolutely dead even. She stood still, marvelling at the weight.

"Well, Ben. You can stop worrying."

I couldn't see Ben's face from where I was seated on the piano stool. He was hanging onto the bar. He was dazed by the heat and the lamps and the smoke. If he wasn't filthy rich, at least he was filthy, believe me. Even in that saloon, with its cheap perfumes and cheaper cigars, I could smell the sweat and the muck.

He tried to talk. It was hard to understand what he was saying. It sounded as if, at last, he had learned Chinese from his two assistants.

Lou pointed at the keg of whiskey sitting in front of me on the grand piano as if it was a bouquet of roses.

"You're rich twice over, Ben. Your whiskey is better than bullion."

Lou hadn't even bothered to weigh the second sack of gold. Maybe she thought she couldn't lift it. She went on pointing. Ben turned around.

His face had frozen in spots. I could see the dead whiteness at the tip of his nose, on his cheeks above his whiskers. His eyes had gone back deep inside his skull. He was looking at the keg. Or at me. Or at the piano.

Lou was trying to reassure him. She wanted him to feel safe.

"You're not just rich. You're doubly rich."

Half the gold that Ben had brought in from the claim belonged to him, that was true. But the other half belonged to Dangerous Dan. Maybe Lou didn't bother to weigh the second sack because she knew it was Dan's.

Dangerous Dan McGrew, all of a sudden, was out of debt. I realized he could walk away. That struck me. He could, so to speak, load his packhorse and vanish. He could wait for the first steamboat out, after breakup, and head on back to San

Francisco. He could go looking for his, as the poet might have put it, light-o'-love.

Lou was watching both Ben and Dan. She didn't move the gold. She left the two sacks of gold sitting right there on the bar, one on the scales, one beside it. She was so honest she was a legend. Men trusted her with their fortunes. And with their lives as well, if it came down to that.

41

As I say, half the gold there on the counter was McGrew's. But maybe he wanted all of it. If your partner died, you got his share. That was one of the unwritten rules.

My playing, soft as it was, made Ben and Lou speak to each other more loudly. I could see them talking. One time Lou reached and touched a frozen spot on Ben's left cheek. I saw that. So did Dan.

Lou was facing toward me.

"You really must go up to the cabin," she said. "You should go get some rest. I'll be there in a couple of hours."

Dan was too far away to hear the conversation. He was, you might say, watching it.

There was never any sexual connection between Lou and Dan. I'll swear to that on a stack of bibles. Lou was here in Dawson to make her fortune by hard work. Dan was here to make his by gambling. That brought them together. Fortune. And the business of hiding. They had both hid out, with all hell after them. It was another kind of caring altogether, and didn't require words.

Ben ordered drinks for the house. That's what a miner did when he came in from the creeks and entered a saloon carrying a fortune in gold. Many a time I saw it. And I liked the custom. It was about the only time I could get a drink without having Lou breathing down my neck.

Ben didn't speak to the bartender. He turned away from Lou and from the bar and he spoke aloud. Talking with Lou had given him back his voice.

"Okay, folks. This one's on me."

That's all you had to say on such an occasion. Everyone knew what it meant.

The trouble was, on this occasion, the drinks weren't exactly drinks. Every saloon in Dawson was just about out of booze, not just the Malamute.

Somebody shouted from a faro table, "Tell them to put some whiskey in the water this time."

A lot of the customers there in the saloon guffawed and snorted. They laughed when they should have been shouting and congratulating Ben and slapping him on the back. I was getting nervous. I thought he should open the keg that was sitting in front of me on my piano. It was time.

I got up from the piano stool to go tell Lou that maybe Ben should open his keg and give everyone a taste of real whiskey. I had things to tell her. I was going around the end of the bar nearest the door, heading for Lou, when I noticed Ben leave the bar.

He sat down in my place in front of the piano.

At first people thought he was clowning around. As part of his celebration, you might say. You had to put on something of a show when you struck it rich. People thought Ben was doing that. Some of the gamblers beyond the piano pretended they were going to listen. They stood stock-still.

Then Ben began to play.

Robert Service says he was wearing a buckskin shirt that was glazed with dirt. Ben was wearing a parka. But then the poet says that he clutched the keys with his talon hands. And I want to tell you, that's how it looked. The poet hit it smack on. Ben was playing something we had never heard before. None of us. And he wasn't just clutching at the piano keys. He got hold of all of us, and each of us, our skin and our bones. He got all the way in. And he started to claw and rip. From where I was standing behind the bar, I could hardly bear to watch. I glanced away a couple of times. I noticed the nail heads around the front door, each of them white with frost. They looked like teeth.

The poet talks about hunger. He talks about some kind of gnawing hunger that bacon and beans won't satisfy, and, believe you me, every man and woman in that saloon had tried enough bacon and beans to know what that was. A hunger not of the belly kind. Another kind entirely. Something about love. That's what Ben's playing was all about.

I was standing beside Lou, who was standing behind her scales. I put my back to the shelf that held the pokes of some of the customers and a few bottles of watered whiskey. I was careful not to bump the bottles and make a sound. They were mostly empty, those whiskey bottles. Customers who were irked at getting watered whiskey would soon be irked at getting no whiskey at all.

The bartenders were serving up the round that Ben had ordered. They did it quietly. Ben went on playing while that happened. He was being slow, careful, as if he was trying to eat ice with a knife and fork. Just for a moment it sounded as if a splinter of that ice had hit a hot stove, a red lid. But then he backed off.

Ben was in his cooperage on the banks of the Mississippi, giving shape to an oak stave. It felt that way, listening to him. You could hear him pull a hollowing knife up the inside of a stave. You could smell the shavings. You could smell the cask being steamed. He had often told me how it was. Back home. The smell of steamed oak. Then the small fire under the cask, keeping the steamed wood warm while he hammered down the hoops. He played that on the piano. Two coopers with their drivers and hammers, driving down the chime hoops, the quarter hoops, the booge hoops. It was echo and din. And then the gentlest smell of paint. He was quietly dabbing the head of a barrel, with a small brush, with paint that was malachite green.

Dan and Hegg and the cheechako went on with their game. I heard the click of the ivory chips. I heard Dan say, "I guess I'll make it a spread misère."

That takes gumption. Ironclad balls. To make that bid. I tried it once. Spread misère, as I said before, means the other two players become partners. You propose to beat them while your own hand lies there face up, exposed for them to peruse and estimate, on the flat green top of the table.

Winner take all. That's the name of the game.

Ben's music wasn't the dancing kind. Three dancehall girls tiptoed over and stood in front of the bar where Lou and I were listening. They weren't about to get up onto the grand piano and dance, the way they liked to, showing me their garters. Not for Ben's playing. They did that for me. They were special to me. They always were. Sometimes I told them I loved them and they laughed, but then they gave me hugs and kisses. I think they were lonely too.

Somehow those three women connected Ben's playing with Lou. They stood in front of the bar, looking serious and sad. They were all on the plump side. Maybe you've seen some of Hegg's photographs. Not his photos of the variety girls like Snake Hips Lulu and the Belgian Queen. I'm talking about the percentage girls. I'm talking about the women who danced with the miners for a net profit of two bits a dance, plus a percentage on any drinks their partners bought after the dancing stopped. They were losing money while Ben played.

I had to stretch my neck to see over them. I gave a little hop and sat on the counter.

Dangerous Dan didn't like to do the managing in the Malamute Saloon. He saw that the dancers weren't working, but he didn't budge. He must have been irritated. He was leaving all the managing to Lou, but Lou, obviously, was just as entranced as everyone else.

Dan was continuing with the card game. He called to some roulette players who were standing as still as statues, "You boys want someone to get you a drink?"

The miner who replied spoke so softly you could tell he didn't trust his own voice. "Why bother, Dan?"

Ben's playing drowned out whatever Dan said next. Nothing, I expect. What could he say? Or do? I saw him play a card and I saw the cheechako play a card.

We listened as Ben moved close to a crescendo. He prowled around its edges. Its jagged lips. You could hear riverboats in his playing. Steamboat whistles. Arrivals. Departures. Departures from home and then the returns. Not just the Mississippi boats. Ours too. The Yukon steamboats. The *Victoria*.

The *Healy*. The *Australian*. Coming through ice and run-off floods. Coming to get him.

Then he let the music fall off again, toward something resembling silence. It sound like candled ice tinkling down into water on a warm spring day.

Ben could make up music right there on the spot. I could hear a tune and sit down and play it, but Ben could make up his own. That's what he was good at. And he was doing it all the way.

I thought of how I had buried my head in Gussie's lap, there on the shore of frozen Lake Bennett. Her tangle of skirts. I could hardly breathe. I remembered whole gardens, in my mind. Basil and thyme. And a hardware store too. Oakum. And white satin gloves. And canvas. And the rub of silk. And roses. And nice clean sweat and the taste of acid. It was like that, listening to Ben play.

I saw a miner over by the far wall trying to wipe his eyes with his red bandanna. The guy right next to him looked like he was heavily into goose bumps. He was scared.

Just as Ben was persuading us to let ourselves dream a little he nearly knocked our socks off with a chord that came like a hammer through the smoke.

My God, he could play. It was like looking at the Northern Lights. He could turn you upside down and then he'd turn you inside out, just for good measure. I imagined Gussie Meadows standing there beside him, belting out some kind of a song. My joints were confused. And not just mine. Everybody's. You could feel it, we were all jangly and nervous. We were squirmy and riveted and sweating and cold at the same time.

It was as if we were all unhinged, I swear. The dance-hall girls held onto each other, there at the bar, the way they sometimes held me. The way they would hold me again. The three of them. And others too. They held each other close. The dealers at the tables unfolded their cards, then folded them and stopped watching their stacks and rows of ivory chips and sometimes closed their eyes.

Dangerous Dan got up from his card table. He walked in behind the far end of the bar, the end near his table, and he walked along behind the bar, behind the motionless bartenders. He walked softly, as if he didn't want to keep anyone from listening to Ben's playing. But no one could ignore him. He had on his bowler and his favourite yellow vest.

All the men in the place were wearing hats. They drank with their hats on. They danced with their hats on. Maybe they slept with their hats on, I wasn't sure. But even in a crowd like that, Dan's bowler was special. It made him look like a stranger in the place.

He stepped close to Lou and I heard what he said.

"I've just lost a big one," he said.

I knew he was talking about his card game and his spread misère bid.

"I couldn't concentrate," he said. "That damned music."

That's when Lou spoke. "What did you lose this time, Dan?"

She was tired of his losing. He had been losing before Ben showed up and started playing the piano. She had seen all that.

"Just about everything," he said.

Lou was listening to Ben's music. It took her a long time to turn her head. But even then she didn't speak.

"I paid off that damned cheechako," Dan said.

"Is he a cheechako?" Lou asked him. "Or is he just pretending?" She was always suspicious like that. "About the only calluses he has are between his thumbs and his index fingers."

Dan didn't let himself hear her. "It's Hegg that's the trouble."

Lou was trying to listen to Ben.

"Hegg," Dan said. "He wants to play me for that keg of fish."

Ben glanced over just then. He saw Lou and Dan whispering together. I could tell that he saw them because I could hear the change in his playing. For just a moment or two, he played one note with the ring finger of his right hand.

Dan pointed at the keg on top of the piano. "Hegg keeps saying, 'What's your saloon to me?' And what can I tell him?"

Hegg was that sort of person. He was philosophical.

Dan whispered again. "He says I can bet that keg of fish up against everything he's won tonight."

"You can't have it, Dan."

"Who says so?"

"Ben won't part with it. Believe me."

They were whispering like that.

"One damned card," Dan said. "The queen of spades. The Old Lady. She beat me."

Then Lou relented a little. She indicated the sack that wasn't on the scales. "This one sack of gold. It's yours, Dan. Ben told me it's for you. The partnership. Your half."

That's when Dan said something that made me wonder if maybe I should have listened more closely when Gussie Meadows defended the man. And there were times, when she wasn't criticizing, that she did just that. She said he could surprise you. Those pleasant surprises, she told me, were the most dangerous thing of all about her Dangerous Dan McGrew.

He was half talking, half whispering. He was speaking to Lou. He said, "You tell Ben that if he gives me that keg of fish he can have his sack of gold."

"You can't have it, Dan."

"How can you say that? You haven't even asked him."

"I don't have to ask him."

Dan was quiet then. I thought he was listening to Ben's playing. But it turned out he was thinking.

Things happened pretty fast. I didn't have time to interfere.

Dan McGrew indicated with a gentle shove that I should move my legs to one side. I was still sitting on the counter behind the bar and the pair of scales and Lou.

There was a drawer under my knees. The counter was fancy, expensive, with curlicues and knobs. And deep drawers that moved easily on their slides. Dan opened the drawer that was directly under the counter where Lou stacked the miners' pokes. I knew there were two six-shooters in the drawer. The guns were there in case there was ever any need to protect the customers' gold. I had more than once been tempted to take one of those revolvers out of the drawer and up to our cabin and try some target practice on the slope out back. Those revolvers made me think of Gussie and how she would hold my hands when I was trying to steady my aim.

Dan took out one of the six-shooters. He stuck it into the band of his trousers, just below his vest, with the handle hooked onto his belt. I knew he wanted to tell Lou to get the women back to work, but he saw they were totally captivated by Ben's playing. He didn't bother to close the drawer when he turned away. He pretended he didn't notice me. Or his sack of gold, sitting on the bar. A ticket, you might say, to a long life in San Francisco.

Lou reached and caught him by a sleeve. "Dan," she said.

Dan hesitated. Lou had that kind of power over him.

"It's yours," she said.

I nearly died right then.

"Dan, the keg is yours. If it means that much to you, it's yours. Take it."

"Thank you," Dan said. He had a smile that knocked people over, and he gave Lou one of those smiles. "I knew you'd understand. We're in this together, Lou. You're going to come round. We're going to partner up and make a fortune here."

Lou saw his confidence come back. Just like that, it was back.

"There's just one thing, Dan."

He nodded.

"Your keg is full of the best whiskey that money can buy. Hegg might be pleased. Or he might not be pleased."

"You're lying," Dan said.

He turned away from Lou and left.

I suppose Lou could have tried to stop him. But he had hurt her pride. She was listening to Ben's playing again. Just that quickly. She had to. Dan went back to his card game and sat down in his chair. He picked up the deck of cards as if he was going to deal a new hand.

Hegg signalled him to put down the cards and listen.

I picked up the six-shooter that remained in the drawer. It was a beautiful machine. A Colt .45. A Peacemaker. Just like the one Ben was carrying. I sat there holding it between my knees. Using my right thumb, I eased back the hammer, just the way Gussie had taught me to do.

In a way I wanted to be like Ben. He trusted everyone, but he wasn't fool enough to walk around in the middle of the night with two bags of gold with no protection. I could see he had Mr Plow's revolver in the right pocket of his dirty old twill parka.

The lighting in the saloon wasn't all that good. Dan liked to say that the less the customers saw the better. The place was lit with coal oil lamps. Kerosene lamps. They were fancy things mounted on brass stands. The tall globes set over the wicks, to protect the flame and to magnify the light, were etched and painted with pictures of naked women.

If you put your hand on top of the globe of a kerosene lamp it quickly snuffs out the flame. I wanted to do that right then. To all the lamps. I wanted to be in the dark. I wanted to cover my head.

The only motion in that whole saloon, I swear, was that of Ben's fingers. And maybe Steamboat Sal was moving her hips just barely, trying to figure out how on earth you would dance to such music.

Dan, I could see, could hardly bear the stillness. He was trying to get his card game going again, but neither Hegg nor Speelman would so much as glance in his direction. Dan was seated between them.

Ben began to play so softly that we could hear his laboured breathing, over the sound of the piano. His face was wet, partly from the melted frost, but from sweat too. It was hot in that saloon. Desperately hot. My whole face was wet. I could see small beads of sweat on Sal's bare neck.

Ben Redd, I suppose you could say, was making love. It was the only way he really knew or had ever learned, back home in Iowa. He was a bachelor virgin all the way. In spite of everything. I understood how he felt. I wanted him to announce his love, the way I wanted to announce my own, to every damned person in that saloon.

We all heard Ben when he spoke. We hadn't expected him to utter a word.

"One of you here is a hound of hell."

We hadn't expected the strength that was in his voice. And yet it seemed that the speaking out had exhausted him again. Maybe we all felt, each of us listening, that we'd been singled out. Accused. What had I done? And then I thought, maybe he's talking about himself, about his life down there in that hole in the frozen gravel.

He stopped his playing. He stopped and we heard nothing but the absolute silence. You talk about your Northern Lights. I guess that each of us, for that long moment, was absolutely alone. We wanted him to go on. We wanted him to go on and on.

He touched a couple of keys. It sounded as if he was trying to come back from the dead.

Or maybe he was simply asking if he could have our attention one last time. He was playing, ever so softly, when he spoke the second time. He spoke softly, but out loud too, so that every person in the saloon had no choice but to hear what he was saying.

"And that one is Dan McGrew."

42

It was a lovers' quarrel after all. Ben Redd believed that it was Dan McGrew who kept him apart from Lou. Ben was jealous. Dangerous Dan believed that gold kept him apart from Gussie Meadows, and gold would take him to where she was. He was badly in need of a winning streak. He saw what he had to do.

It was I who fired the first shot.

I did it the way Gussie Meadows had taught me to, using the two-hand hold. I concentrated on the sights. That revolver was equipped with what is called the standard partridge sight. Rear sight a square notch. Front sight a square post. Align the post in the notch.

I squeezed the trigger just as Ben was about to repeat what he had already said, and what we had all already heard.

I wanted to keep the peace. I didn't want anyone to get hurt. I wanted Dan McGrew to know and believe that the keg on the piano was full of whiskey. Then he would stop wanting it. I wanted him to stop all his wanting.

I had to bend forward to aim past the scales and past those three women standing on the other side of the bar. Steamboat Sal and Sissy Jean and Bonanza Jill. They liked giving themselves special names. They must have been deafened by the report.

I hit the keg that was sitting on the grand piano.

I wanted to show people there was whiskey to be had for the asking. Good whiskey. Topnotch whiskey. Give those men a decent drink and they'd all relax, including Dan and Ben. I imagined a crowd of people rushing to pick up the keg and keep it from losing any more of its contents. People filling their glasses. Filling their hats. I remembered those men on the *Delta Queen* and how two kegs of Ben's whiskey had made them forget death itself.

It was not the sound of the shot from my revolver but rather the sound of whiskey squirting out of that keg that made Ben hesitate while twisting the revolver out of his coat pocket. It was the sound of the whiskey that made him lose the rhythm of his hands. He glanced down to where his keg of whiskey was pissing a neat, bright stream into the sawdust beside my grand piano.

If Ben hadn't hesitated it would have been no contest. He was a dead shot. McGrew had to struggle to draw his revolver out of the space between his heavy wool trousers and his vest. I wish he'd pulled the trigger right then. But no, he was fairly sober, thanks to his own watered whiskey.

Lou saw the disaster that was about to befall all our lives. She understood it better than I. I had not intended what was to follow. She had been standing to my right, almost directly behind her scales. She must have seen my hands and the gun before I fired. She was already moving when I squeezed the trigger.

It was not Lou who screamed, though God knows there was screaming and cursing to be heard. She was around the end of the bar before the lights went out. She had time to start toward Ben.

I believe it was Dangerous Dan who fired the second shot. I say I believe he fired the second shot, because I cannot quite be certain. The direction of the sound gave me some evidence, but sounds roared in that saloon. They roared and echoed. The trouble was that a number of people had reached and put their hands on top of the globes of the few kerosene lamps that were expected to light the place.

Not all of the lights were extinguished at the same time. The poet, in his poem, fails to make that clear. It was difficult to see in that room, but not entirely impossible. Granted, the clouds of cigar smoke did not help to clarify matters.

By the time Ben fired his own first shot Lou was reaching to take him into her arms. His first shot went slightly wide of its mark.

It is difficult to explain exactly what happened next. There was an exchange of gunfire. I could feel the open drawer cutting into my left leg. I put down the six-shooter. I had fired it once, and once only. I placed it in the drawer and in the dark closed the drawer.

Each of the two men fired three shots. We had only to dump out the spent cartridges from each revolver to establish that.

It's a miracle we didn't all get killed. I could hear people hitting the floor everywhere in the room. I thought that some of them had been shot. The three women who had been standing in front of me, constituting a kind of barrier or shield, absolutely vanished.

Lou had surely been trying to make it impossible for McGrew to aim at Ben. She believed he wouldn't risk hitting her.

All the shooting had stopped for a good while before anyone dared stand up and relight a lamp. The shouting had turned to whispering.

"Pitched on his head, and pumped full of lead," the poet says, "was Dangerous Dan McGrew." And after a fashion he got it right, the poet, though pitched on his head was something of an inaccuracy.

It was Hegg who lit the lamp that was sitting on the bar next to McGrew's card table. He had obviously not bothered to duck under the table, since his broad-brimmed white felt hat was rigorously in place on his head. And sporting in its crown a new hole.

When he moved the lamp onto the table we saw McGrew still seated in his chair, his head tilted slightly forward as if, while the lights were out, he had hoped to catch a few winks. His bowler was slightly askew.

He held the deck of cards in his left hand. That deck, a short pack, for solo, for a moment obscured the fact that he held in his right hand a revolver. He had knocked over someone's stack of blue chips, which he sometimes did while drinking, and I expected him, in his usual manner, to begin to stack them again.

It was not until we saw the blood seeping through his yellow silk vest, just above the chain of his gold watch, that we realized Ben had plugged him clean through the heart. He had hit Dangerous Dan McGrew twice. The two holes were not an inch apart.

43

"The man from the creeks," the poem says, "lay clutched to the breast of the lady that's known as Lou."

Did the poet cry when he wrote that line? I want to tell you, I cannot keep from shedding a few tears when I read it. We are told that pain fades. I'd like to know when. I cannot begin to read the first, immortal stanza of that poem without beginning to anticipate that fatal line. We suffer and die, we are told. But we also suffer and live.

The poet cannot be faulted for his details. He got them right again. Exact. Lou was bent forward, slumped, on the sawdust-covered floor, facing the piano, holding Ben in her arms. He had slid from the piano stool. He was almost invisible, both because of Lou's bent form and his own ragged parka.

Two of Dangerous Dan McGrew's three shots had missed by a mile. Two bullet holes in the front door, as we shortly discovered, were letting in blasts of icy air.

At first we saw no mark at all on the back of Lou's yellow blouse, and for an instant I hoped that she was only bent there on the floor to hold Ben. She had stepped in front of him.

It was I who first noticed that Lou held in her right hand the nugget Ben had given her. She and Ben were face to face. She was at once protecting him and holding him close. He must have, in that embrace, in one final gesture, insisted again that she accept the nugget that was the token of his love.

What the poet and his poem do not tell you is that Ben and Lou had in fact been struck by one and the same bullet. It had entered into Lou's neck through her long, dark hair and her feathery crown and then into Ben's left ear. They had both been shot dead by Dangerous Dan McGrew.

44

I alone had survived unscathed, if you don't count Hegg. He had won the whole saloon, we discovered, on the turn of a card. He so much hated owning a saloon he became a tee-totaler. He hired me to run the show and asked me to forward any profits that might accrue and headed for Seattle where, I was to learn subsequently, he opened a successful portrait studio.

Managing a saloon turned out to be an easy enough chore, mostly because we had hardly any customers. Thank heavens I was rich, I could afford to run a saloon. Most of the miners ran off in 99 to fight in the Spanish-American War, which was over by the time they heard about it. Trust stampeders.

The tourists show up in the summertime. No February nights for them.

I hibernate in the winter. Come spring I roll my wheelchair from room to room, here in this cabin, following the drift of Yukon light. I need it. So I can find the page and follow my notes. I want to make a few things clear. I want to set the record straight, especially about Lou.

As for the cheechako who was Hegg's partner at the card table, there in the Malamute that night, it seems that he shit his pants when he heard Ben's bullets hit McGrew. Just as the first lamp was relit he leapt out from under the card table and went hightailing out the back door toward the bog, gripping in one hand his little poke, in the other the fulsome seat of his new jeans. Hegg kept saying, over and over, how unbearable was the stench.

The two moosehide bags of gold fell to me. I keep them right here in the cabin, on the kitchen table. They made great paperweights, at least until I could no longer lift the damned things. They contain the results of Ben's prospect pannings, the gold he came up with panning gravel for colour, checking to see if he'd found the pay streak. And he had. The smaller bag weighed in at four hundred and eleven ounces. Its partner came in at thirteen ounces more.

The claim was mine as well. I paid two lawyers a small fortune to prove as much. Those guys would steal the hairs right out of the crack of your ass. Ben had, with a vengeance, found the pay streak. A lot of miners never did. It was a pity and a shame. They broke their bodies and their spirits, thawing permafrost and shovelling gravel. And all they got was some exercise.

I paid those two Chinese assistants of Ben's their weight in gold to keep on digging and shoveling and sluicing. Then they waltzed off one night with half the clean-up. The police couldn't trace them.

45

The wake for Lou was held right here in this cabin. Word spread through town. The crowd began to arrive with the first red blotch of mid-morning light. People truly worshipped Lou, and they came to the wake as a column of mourners, in spite of the bitter cold. There were, strangely, by noon, three sundogs visible in the sky. People lined up all the way to that log shack where Robert Service would hole up, as a bank teller, six years after the event. Shopkeepers came from all over town, the owners of boot shops and clothing stores and pawnshops and trading posts. Dentists and lawyers. Six outfitters and two auctioneers. The captains of two steamboats that were frozen in a dozen miles downriver. Three women who ran what they called cigar stores. A couple of doctors, arriving, as usual, late. Drifters who thought there might be food. Dancehall girls and dancehall performers, including Diamond-Tooth Gertie herself, and the famous Cad Wilson. Bartenders and croupiers and dealers from fifty other bars and saloons. Four high-muck-a-muck government officials from the claims registration office. Cooks and waiters and dishwashers. A troupe of vaudeville actors from the opera house. Even Whipsaw was there, with seven whores from Lousetown, all of them, and Whipsaw as well, dressed like millionaire widows.

Word spread to the creeks. Men who wouldn't step outside in that temperature if it was snowing flakes of gold got all cleaned up. They walked toward town, in spite of the iron cold, in ones and twos, then in groups, then in columns of their own. Miners from Eldorado Creek and Bonanza, from Gold Hill and Magnet Hill, from Grand Forks and Dominion and Hunker.

The wake, modest and teetotal, continued all through the day and into the evening. It was only interrupted then, or superseded, by the more rambunctious wake being held in the Malamute Saloon.

Dangerous Dan and Ben Redd were well enough known. Or at least Dan was. Ben was too, but in a different way. Word soon spread that he'd taken a whole cupful of gold out of a single pan.

The undertaker, a local hardware man, set up four saw-horses and the two coffins, side by side in the Malamute. In between my piano and Lou's famous scales. Except that the scales went missing before the wake was decently underway. Lou had no end of admirers.

The wake at the Malamute was a three-day affair.

I think it was the whiskey that brought some of the crowd. Someone had managed to plug the hole in the keg before a whole lot was lost. But that one keg by itself would never have been enough. We still had two kegs under my bunk in the cabin. Or, I should say, I had them. I sent those two kegs down to the Malamute with Whipsaw and Steamboat Sal and Sissy Jean and Bonanza Jill. I was praised for my generosity.

The naked truth was, I needed some time. I had to keep that other wake going.

Digging graves in that kind of weather was a bit like mining for gold. The Dawson graveyard was in a swamp, the only place where gravediggers could dig a decent grave without hitting solid rock. The trouble was, in February, the swamp was frozen solid. The miners who volunteered to dig the three graves had to build fires first, then dig out the muck that thawed in a few hours, then build more fires.

We placed the three coffins side by side, with Lou's in the middle grave. A missionary who worked with the Han Indians in Lousetown came across the Klondike and read the service. It was cold out there in the wind by the frozen river. We didn't waste a whole lot of time, covering over the coffins in their shallow holes.

But we had made a miscalculation. The Klondike, tributary to the Yukon, come spring turned into a raging torrent. It washed the whole, entire graveyard into the Yukon River. The Yukon itself was in full flood, sweeping floes and uprooted trees and no end of badly moored boats and even a few tents clean out of sight and, I would suppose, all the way down to the Bering Sea. I mean, everything went. The coffins. The frozen bodies of Dangerous Dan McGrew and Benjamin Redd. The wooden crosses that bore their names.

It took away Lou's cross too. And the coffin that was supposed to be hers. And the gravel that was in the coffin.

As for Lou's body, well, in those terrible February hours while the wake in the Malamute went on and on, I too was busy. While the crowd in the Malamute drank toasts to the corpses and to Ben's perfect wooden kegs, I was working up a sweat of my own. I had to work like a madman, I want to tell you. The heat wasn't doing Lou any good, for all the cold outside.

Here, under this cabin, after lifting a section of the parlour floor, I did some excavating of my own. Permafrost makes for exacting labour. I built a fire of split and dried wood. Every tent and every building in town was heated by a wood fire. There wasn't a breath of wind. The little bit of smoke I produced was nothing, not in a town that was muffled and smothered and cloaked in smoke in that spell of bitter cold.

The frozen soil melted too slowly for my intention. I went at it with a pickaxe and a shovel, blisters or no.

I made a bed of spruce boughs and roses. I shaped the roses out of red crêpe paper. Dozens and dozens of roses. More than I could count. That was the rule I made for myself. There had to be more roses than I could possibly count. I placed Lou's body on that soft bed. I placed in her cupped hands the gold nugget given to her by Ben. It filled both her hands.

There in the permafrost she will endure long after I have played my last tune. The tourists come crowding into the Malamute Saloon on a Saturday night. They trail their fingers along the mahogany bar, kicking their way through fresh sawdust. They look for empty tables, making a great racket about which was Dan McGrew's. They drag chairs around. They order drinks as if they were buying the place. Then two dance-hall women roll in a wheelchair. The funny old man in the chair sets his nitroglyercin tube where his music sheets should be, there on that banged-up wreck of a grand piano. For the old ticker, he says. That gets a laugh.

There's always a giggler in the crowd. And a couple of people who talk too loud. I hear them, with my good ear. I hear them talking, while I'm trying to clear my throat and make my speech.

"He claims to be one hundred and fourteen years old."

"That's surprising. He looks older."

The sonsabitches. Maybe it's because I hate to comb my hair. It comes out when I comb it.

Some nut taps his bald head and says, "Wonder if he's all there?"

And then, before I hit the keys, I tell them the fib they're dying to hear. I tell them I play all my sad songs in memory of Dan McGrew. That's what they came for. Then they feel they're getting their money's worth. It cost a pile of dough to take a cruise ship up the Inside Passage from Seattle, a bus from Skagway into this famous little tourist town of twelve hundred souls. It costs those tourists quite a bundle to come and take a look and sample a drink or two and have a listen. But they're more than willing to pay. And there's always one in the bunch who starts to bellow before I can start to play. He gives me the opening lines from the old poem. As if I might not remember.

> "A bunch of the boys were whooping it up
> in the Malamute Saloon;
> The kid that handles the music-box
> was hitting a jag-time tune..."

I give an approving nod. Then I start, as McGrew liked to say, to tickle the ivories a little. I wish I could say the tourists fall silent. That isn't quite the case. They get to be rowdy. Rowdy and raunchy. You can feel it in the air. You can smell it. Like oakum mixed with cinnamon and honey. They're far from home. Nobody's going to snitch or squeal if they stray a bit. And the bartenders and the waitresses, in their old-time outfits, are happy to provide them with all the watered drinks they wish to buy.

They never know the truth, those latter-day stampeders. I never tell them who I really am, funny old geezer that I might seem, or that it was Ben Redd and not a stranger at all who sat down on the piano stool when I got up to go to the bar. And I did not go, as the poet would have it, for a drink. I went to stand beside my mother. I went to give her my assurance. There in the Malamute, that February night way back, she was about to declare her love.

I never tell those randy tourists who it was that fired the first shot. I simply go on playing. Even a long life is short. We must learn to hold each other. I play to join two partners who, once they were together, were never really apart again.

A Note About the Author

Robert Kroetsch is the author of numerous works of poetry and fiction, including *The Studhorse Man*, winner of the Governor General's Award, *The Puppeteer* and *Badlands*. He recently retired from teaching at the University of Manitoba and now lives in Victoria, B.C.